Acclaim for Stephen Greenleaf's latest
John Marshall Tanner mystery

PAST TENSE

"The twelfth John Marshall Tanner novel lives up to the tradition of excellence found in Greenleaf's recent *Flesh Wounds*. . . . Moving and full of valuable insights."

—*Library Journal*

"The plot is bold, the storytelling well-paced, and Greenleaf doesn't shy away from the ending, which is a shocker."

—Susan Cohen, *San Jose Mercury News*

Praise for previous John Marshall Tanner mysteries

"A fascinating journey down a dark and twisty lane, deep into shadowy cold family secrets."

—Minneapolis *Star Tribune*

"The Tanner series continues to be among the most emotionally and intellectually challenging in the genre. Outstanding."

—*Booklist*

"A logical and suspenseful tale that makes for an engrossing read. Mr. Greenleaf always gives his reader a full-blown and well-realized story."

—*Mystery News*

"John Marshall Tanner is the long-sought heir of Sam Spade, Marlowe, and Archer."

—San Francisco Examiner

"An excellent mix of technical detail and low-life grunge."

—Booklist

"Greenleaf is a pro, so the rapidly unfolding events make for an engrossing read, but more importantly, the book is as fine an exploration of the perils of genetic narcissism as you're going to find."

—Boston Globe

"Tough, meaty prose, sly twists in plot, and immediacy of action."

—Library Journal

"Greenleaf's portrayal of the wealthy Colbert family's misguided efforts to insulate itself from the consequences of prior mistakes is unerring. He is a master of the succinct but revealing descriptive phrase."

—San Francisco Chronicle

Books by Stephen Greenleaf

Past Tense*
Flesh Wounds*
False Conception*
Southern Cross
Blood Type
Book Case
Impact
Toll Call
Beyond Blame
The Ditto List
Fatal Obsession
State's Evidence
Death Bed
Grave Error

*Published by POCKET BOOKS

STEPHEN GREENLEAF

PAST TENSE

POCKET BOOKS
New York   London   Toronto   Sydney   Tokyo   Singapore

This book is a work of fiction. Names, characters, places and
incidents are products of the author's imagination or are used
fictitiously. Any resemblance to actual events or locales or persons,
living or dead, is entirely coincidental.

POCKET BOOKS, a division of Simon & Schuster Inc.
1230 Avenue of the Americas, New York, NY 10020

Copyright © 1997 by Stephen Greenleaf

Originally published in hardcover in 1997 by Scribner

ISBN: 0-671-01947-3

First Pocket Books printing February 1998

10 9 8 7 6 5 4 3 2 1

POCKET and colophon are registered trademarks of
Simon & Schuster Inc.

Cover design by Tom McKeveny

Printed in the U.S.A.

For Jim Harris

PAST
TENSE

PAST
TENSE

CHAPTER

1

IT WAS MIDMORNING OF A CHILLY WINTER WEEKDAY. TIME was glutinous and so was I—there were things I should have been doing but I wasn't doing them; there were places I should have been going but I was too soporific to move. Instead, I was drinking coffee and wondering if my net worth could finance a trip to somewhere sunny, somewhere like Mexico. I like Mexico, Mexico is cheap, if I were any kind of a success at all I could kiss San Francisco good-bye and spend March in Guadalajara or Guanajuato without even blinking an eye.

I opened my checkbook. Cash on hand: $973.28; rent past due: $500.00; reliable receivables: zip. Bottom line: I make do with remembering the last trip and pray that baseball solves its labor dispute so I can abandon my boycott. I was so despondent I almost didn't pick up the phone when it yelled at me.

But I did, because answering phones is something I do: I don't cheat on my taxes, I don't sleep with other men's wives, and I don't hide behind technology. I'm not sure I'm the better for any of those vows, incidentally; some of the happiest people I know violate all three and then some.

"Marsh?" The voice was raspy and unnerved: a fighter after a knockout; a drunk after a night in the tank.

"Yeah?"

"What the hell."

"What the hell what?"

"Charley."

"Sleet?"

"Yeah."

"What about him?"

"You ain't heard?"

"I guess not."

"He's been busted."

"Charley?"

"Yeah."

I laughed because it was time for the exchange to turn funny. "Busted for what? Cornering the market on doughnuts?"

The offer wasn't accepted. "Murder, most likely."

"Murder? Charley? You're kidding."

"I wish to hell I was."

And suddenly everything in my life wasn't mundane and dull and unexceptional, everything was odd and electric and awful. "This is bullshit. Right? Who is this, anyway?"

"Glen Bittles, clerk for Judge Newell. Used to be the admin officer down at Vallejo Street back in '78, '79. I'd see you once in a while when you'd come to see Sleet at the cop house. Charley called me Peanut; maybe you remember."

"Yeah. Sure. Peanut. So what happened? Someone set Charley up on a frame?"

"Hard to see a frame in it. He gunned some guy down this morning."

"What guy?"

"Some guy in the courthouse, don't know his name. I'm not talking City Hall, you know, 'cause that's closed for earthquake repairs, but the temporary courtrooms they rigged up in the phone company building on Folsom. That's where it happened."

"Out front, you mean. Some sort of shoot-out on the street."

"Naw, this was inside. Judge Meltonian's court."

"Charley shot a guy in open court?"

"Yeah. Twice, is what I heard. First one missed high; second nailed him square in the back of the head. Popped like a muskmelon, I heard; dude was dead before he hit the carpet. So much brain spattered on the bench it looked like Meltonian chucked up his lunch."

My heart was beating so loudly I could hardly hear Glen Bittles's grating whisper over the troubled thumps within my ear. "What was it," I tried again, still struggling for a benign explanation, "some nut got a weapon past the metal detector and Charley had to take him out?"

"Naw, all he was was a defendant in a civil case. Sitting at the table with his lawyer, listening to the bullshit, and Charley ups and drills him. Court reporter took shrapnel in the shoulder—bullet must have fragmented."

"I don't . . . Did you see this go down, Peanut? You sure someone isn't playing with you?"

"I wasn't there but I know it happened. Joyce Yates told me. She was covering the case for the *Chronicle.*"

"So Yates saw the whole thing?"

"Happened right in front of her. Way she tells it, Sleet might have taken out the whole room except some guy grabbed his arm and wrestled him. By the time Charley shucked him off, he must have figured he'd done all the damage he needed to do, 'cause he tossed down his piece and dropped to the floor and waited for them to come take him."

"Anyone hurt besides the court reporter?"

"Naw. Meltonian made like a rabbit and scooted back to his chambers and the lawyers dove under the table. No heroes in that bunch, right? Some paralegal turned his ankle when he jumped in the jury box, is all."

3

"Where was the clerk?"

"Finnerty. Marjie. She stayed put. I hear she said she didn't think Charley had a beef with her, and if he did, he'd wait till after hours and take it up with her at Cafe Vince. Marjie's got more balls than most men, let me tell you. Cute as a cornflower; maybe you know her."

"I've seen her out there. Was a jury in the box?"

"Naw. Motion for summary judgment. Supposed to be over by noon."

"Who else was there? Anyone you know?"

"Not that I heard. Maybe some of the regulars—you know, the pension guys—but I don't know any by name. Marjie can probably tell you, she likes those old farts. There was some other media in there, too."

"Why all the media?"

"It was some sort of sex case. Sex brings out media like shit brings out flies."

"What kind of sex case?"

"Who knows? Someone probably cut something off, if you know what I mean." Peanut chuckled his way to an uneasy silence.

There were still questions to ask, of course, but Glen Bittles wasn't the person who could answer them, so I didn't make an effort.

As I clutched the phone in a sweaty hand and cast about for a plan of action, images flooded my senses. An image of Charley looming large over a fallen corpse was succeeded by a vision of Charley behind bars, being preyed upon by a gang of felons who had reason galore to wreak havoc with him. I waited for the pictures to penetrate to the regions of the brain that thin our terrors and dilute our dread, but for some reason they wouldn't sink.

"Where's Charley now?" I asked.

"Don't know for sure. Holding cell, most likely. Hall of Justice."

"Has anyone talked to him? Has he got a lawyer yet?"

"Don't know that either. Hey. I got to get going, my jury's coming back from break. Just wanted to let you know about Sleet, Marsh; figured you'd know why he done it."

"No idea."

"Yeah. Me neither. Well, I'll be seeing you, Marsh."

"Yeah, Glen. Thanks for the call."

Peanut didn't hang up. "You going down there? To see Sleet, I mean?"

I told him I probably was.

"Well, tell him I know whatever he did, he had a reason. I mean Charley's a good cop. He's not the kind of guy who . . . well, you know what I mean."

"Yeah, I know what you mean. Charley's not the kind of guy who blows somebody's brains out without a good reason."

I put the phone in its cradle and spent the next ten minutes trying to guess what that reason could be. When I didn't come up with anything I could make myself believe, I applied some psychological salve to the sting of my scalded emotions.

There are certain verities you count on: The sun will come up in the east; the Warriors won't get a big man; traffic on the bridges will get worse; Congress will toady to big business. But the surest verity of all is that Charley Sleet wouldn't hurt a fly unless the fly carried a virus that would wipe out the world if it was allowed to keep flying. Which meant what I'd heard from Glen Bittles was irrational and incomplete, suggestive of farce or incompetence; which made it, someway, somehow, wrong.

Of the people I know, Charley is the least likely to take a life. It's a revealing statement to make in his case, since, as opposed to most of us, his job presents him with the opportunity to commit homicide nearly every day. But time after time, in situations that would terrify or inflame a normal man, Charley passes on the prospect of violence and keeps his weapon holstered. Charley enforces the law with his courage and his wits.

His personal life is similarly pacific. He's opposed to both the death penalty and abortion, one of the few people who have consistent positions on those issues. He devotes his off-hours to counseling kids at risk; he donates more money than he can spare to homeless shelters and free clinics; he helps a buddy run a halfway house for Labrador retrievers that takes strays from the pound and finds them new owners. And suddenly this man guns someone down apropos of nothing? Not bloody likely, as the Brits would say.

My initial impulse was to try to make sense out of the nonsense Glen Bittles described, quickly enough so the nonsense wouldn't be regarded as truth, whether by the DA, or by the media, or by the Office of Citizen Complaints. The only way I could think of to do that was to put his conduct in context, and the only way to do that was to head for the Hall of Justice, to get a context from the horse's mouth.

CHAPTER

2

THE QUICKEST WAY TO THE HALL OF JUSTICE WAS BY CAB—I got lucky and hailed one in five minutes, at the corner of Columbus and Montgomery. The cabbie groused about traffic and the new mayor and the Warriors; I stayed silent and pissed him off. When he dropped me at Sixth and Bryant, I tipped enough to make amends for my dearth of municipal animus.

The Hall of Justice houses the city's criminal courts. As with all such buildings, there is an aura of doom about the place, a sense that violence is near eruption, that mores and morality are checked at the door, that no one gives a damn what happens inside the building because most of its customers deserve what they get and then some. I'd spent all the hours I cared to in the place, offering testimony, serving subpoenas, shepherding witnesses, even spending some time in the jail on the sixth floor when I was cited for contempt of court back when I was a lawyer instead of a PI.

Persons like Charley, who are under arrest and awaiting trial, used to be held in the San Francisco city jail in San Bruno, ten miles south of town. The Bruno jail is sixty years old and is under indictment from the Grand Jury, which declared it to be seismically unsafe, disgustingly unsanitary, and unfit for human habitation even by humans accused of criminal misconduct. It teems with rats, roaches, and raw sewage. Its heat and hot water come from a boiler on the back of a truck that is parked outside the building. And it's vastly overcrowded. To handle the surplus, the city fathers are reportedly considering putting inmates on barges, just like they do in New York.

Since prisoners are always going back and forth from San Bruno to court, the Hall of Justice needs a place to house them till their trial is called or their hearing comes up or their public defender drops by to touch base. The sixth-floor jail I'd inhabited after my allegedly contemptuous courtroom performance was still in operation, but now there's a brand-new jail adjacent to the hall, a glass-brick-and-stainless-steel structure that's a model of its kind, or so they claim. Given the public mood these days, being a model jail may mean they've brought back the racks and screws.

The third person I saw was a sheriff's deputy named Gil Harrison, who'd been a jailer for twenty years. Anyone who's been a deputy that long knows Charley Sleet and probably me as well, so he didn't have to be told why I was there.

"Shitty deal," he said without preamble.

"Yeah." I gestured at the door to the rear of his desk. "He back there?"

"Yeah."

"Bail been set?"

Harrison shook his head. "Not till arraignment."

"When's that?"

"Tomorrow, unless he gets a continuance."

"He going down to Bruno tonight?"

Harrison shook his head. "Not unless the arraignment's delayed. We'll keep him till he pleads."

"He seen a lawyer?"

"Nope."

"Anyone else?"

"Deputy public defender wanted to chat, but Charley wouldn't see him."

"He made any calls?"

"Nope."

"Anyone at all been in with him?"

"Just Gutters."

"Who's that?"

"Deputy that logged him in. Larry Gutters. New guy."

"Charley say anything to him?"

Harrison shrugged. "He asked if anyone was hurt, I guess. In the shooting, he meant. That was about it as far as I heard. He was Mirandized and all. Not that he needed it. Charley was a cop when the only Miranda was a tap dancer."

I smiled. "You talk to Charley yourself, Gil?"

"I tried."

"What'd he say?"

"Not much."

"How's his head?"

"Seemed real calm. I've seen lifers more on edge than he is."

I waited for elaboration but didn't get any. "Can you go back and tell him I'm here?"

Harrison shrugged. "I can tell him, but it won't do no good."

"Why not?"

"He ain't talking about what he did, he ain't seeing no one he don't have to, and he don't want nothing from the outside. All he's doing is staring at the walls and popping his knuckles."

"You sure he hasn't flipped out?"

"Sounds sane as Santa to me. Made a joke about the Simpson trial. Talked about the swill that passes for food down at Bruno. Talked about a guy we both know ate his piece last week, worked with Charley out in Ingleside way back when. But he wouldn't talk about the shooting and he wouldn't let me get anything for him—no candy, no smokes, no nothing. He's hurting a bit—kind of bent over and he limps some. Must have strained something when the civilian fought him for the gun."

I rubbed my eyes and looked around, as though help might materialize like Casper, as though an explanation might be written on the jailhouse walls, but all I saw was glass and steel.

"Anyone in the department have any idea why this went down?" I asked.

Gil shook his head. "No one I talked to."

I sighed and gave up. "Okay, Gil. Tell Charley I'm here, will you? Ask if he'll see me. If he won't, ask if he wants me to get anything for him. And ask him what lawyer he wants me to talk to. And if he wants me to call anyone else."

Gil shrugged. "I'll tell him, but it won't matter. It's like he's in a daze or something. Like his brain shut down and he don't know where he is or what he done to get him here. Only other guys I seen like that was the ones on death row back when I was a ranger in Texas, guys who'd been there so long their appeals was up and their lawyers had quit and they was about to be strapped in the chair. Scared half to death already, was what it looked like. Only Charley ain't scared, he's just . . . sluggish. I got a bird dog gets that way come spring. Vet says it's allergies, but I figure with Sleet it's something else."

With that bit of insight, Gil left me in the waiting room and disappeared down the hall beyond the doors that separated the good guys from the bad guys and their keepers. In the driveway outside, a row of prisoners filed out of the bus from San Bruno, herded by a silent sheriff, linked by a shiny chain. From the expressions on their faces, the system hadn't bought whatever they were selling it. One of them glanced my way. His cloudy expression said he wanted to kill me just for being alive: I was white and he wasn't; I was in civvies and he was in county coveralls; I could leave and he couldn't—plenty of grounds for murder right there. I wondered what could have put Charley Sleet in the same frame of mind.

When Gil came back, he was shaking his head. "No dice, Marsh. Says he's fine; says he don't need nothing; says for you not to bother coming back, to let things lay till they work themselves out."

"But—"

Gil held up a hand. "I know. You're his best buddy; you been through some shit together; you want to help him shed this. But he don't have to see anyone except the police or the DA and not even them if he lawyers up." Gil shrugged. "Sorry, Marsh, but he stays put till I get an order to let him go or bus him down to Bruno."

I got back to the office as ignorant as when I'd left it.

My first call was to Clay Oerter. "Ready to make a move into derivatives, Marsh?" Clay teased as he came on the line.

I usually plead poverty at this point, and say something about widows and orphans, but not this time. "Charley's in trouble," I said instead.

"What kind of trouble?"

I told him as much as I knew.

"That's nuts," he said when I was through.

"I know."

"But you're going to straighten it out, right?"

"I'm going to try. But I'm not sure there's much straightening to be done."

"Why not?"

"For one thing, there doesn't seem much doubt that he did it."

"What can I do to help?" Clay asked after he told his receptionist to hold his calls. Clay's a stockbroker; holding calls means missing commissions. It didn't seem to bother him.

"We're going to need money," I told him. "Bail money and lawyer money."

"What's bail likely to be?"

"Hard to say. The guy's dead, so they can't release Charley on recog. On the other hand, he's a cop, so that should cut him some slack. I'd say between a hundred and five hundred thousand, with bond at ten percent."

"How much for the lawyer?"

"If I can't convince Jake Hattie to consider his time as a tithe, it'll be fifty for a retainer at least. And that's just a down payment."

"So we're talking a hundred grand up front, maybe."

"Probably. Call the rest of the poker group. See how tough it's going to be to raise that much."

"It's not going to be tough at all. I can put up the whole thing if I have to."

My grip on the phone relaxed—I'd been more worried about the cash than I realized. "That's good to know, Clay, but there's no reason for you to front it all."

"No, but I can. And I will."

"Thanks."

"I can do something else, too."

"What?"

"Hire you to find out what the hell happened in there."

"I'm going to do that anyway."

"But now you don't have to do it for free."

I laughed. "I hope someone's recording this—we'd both be up for sainthood. Let's wait to talk money till we get to the bottom of things."

"Fine. But there's no reason for you to be the only one investing your capital in this."

"Or you either."

"Don't worry, I'll do what finance guys always do when they need to spread the risk."

"What's that?"

"I'll form a consortium."

We exchanged speculation on what Charley could have been thinking, then hung up. I took a minute to wonder if people would rally to me in time of need the way they were rallying to Charley. I decided that's something you never know until it happens.

My next call was to the office around the corner. "Hi, Lois. Marsh Tanner. Jake in?"

"He is but he's got someone with him."

"I'll be there in ten minutes. I'll need about that much of his time, as soon as he can fit me in."

"I'm sure he'll see you as soon as he's free."

"I'm sure that will be soon enough."

CHAPTER

3

SAN FRANCISCO HAS SPAWNED LOTS OF LEGENDARY CRIMINAL lawyers over the years—Ehrlich, Hallinan, MacInnis, and Belli, to name a few—but king of them all is Jake Hattie. Jake is sixty-seven and still going strong, both personally and professionally. He's been a trial lawyer for forty years. Although he used to pride himself on being a lone wolf, nowadays he comes to court with half a dozen young turks and turkettes in tow, all ready to charge forth at Jake's command to dispatch the forces of evil in the person of whichever state or federal prosecutor has the misfortune to be deployed against him. A criminal trial is a war of words and no one goes to war better armed than Jake Hattie.

On the personal side, Jake goes to dinner every night with a different blonde on his arm and usually goes home with yet another one; the gossip columns dutifully report each escapade and despite his age there are plenty of young women who still vie for the privilege of sharing his bed and his breakfast. Jake drives a Rolls, lives in a marble mansion in Pacific Heights, weekends on a horse ranch in Sonoma County, and vacations in a villa in

Tuscany, all in unapologetic excess. He makes Herb Caen's column once a week and the news pages almost that often. He's courted by socialites and bar committees and local politicians, all of whom want him to lend his name and his money to their various efforts, but since he has equal disdain for everyone but his clients, Jake declines most of the invitations.

Everybody knows Jake but not many admit to liking him, which seems to be the way he wants it. "The only friends I need are veniremen" is how he usually puts it. How his adversaries put it is "Jake's a world-class asshole, but if I fell in the shit myself, he'd be the one I'd call to fish me out."

Jake and I get along. I've worked for him from time to time over the years, mostly tracking down witnesses before trial, and I've done it well enough so he trusts me. I've worked against him a couple of times as well, usually in personal injury matters, with enough success that he respects me. But I was about to ask for far more than he owed me, so I was nervous and sweaty as I trotted down the stairs in my building and headed down the alley toward his sumptuous lair on Montgomery Street, in the shadow cast by the pyramid.

Jake's law office is on the ground floor of a historic brick building that once housed a Barbary Coast bordello. It's plastered with evidentiary souvenirs of his courtroom triumphs, festooned with gifts from his many admirers, and laden with antiques with impressive pedigrees, including a desk once owned by the junior Holmes. Locals and tourists stand in packs outside Jake's windows to watch him work—the windows are floor-to-ceiling and Jake never draws the drapes. I'm told they're about to do a movie based on Jake's life; I hear he wants Dustin Hoffman to star and Michelle Pfeiffer to play his first wife.

It was twenty minutes before he broke free. I spent the interim ogling Lois, his receptionist du jour. Jake's requirement for receptionists approximates Trump's requirements for wives. Although we engaged in some double entendre and mildly racy repartee, I took it as a sign of infirmity that I couldn't summon the optimism to ask her out.

Ten minutes later, Jake opened the door and beckoned. I waved good-bye to Lois, a gesture she acknowledged with a wink and a blown kiss, then joined Jake in his sanctum sanctorum.

He was dressed as usual—black suit and black boots and black hairpiece, all of which seemed derived from patent leather. Also as usual, the basic ensemble was brightened by a scarlet vest that seemed derived from a hurdy-gurdy man. Jake's the only person I know who's getting taller with age. I credit his boot maker with that miracle of measurement, but I don't give any credit at all to the guy who made the hairpiece.

When I got seated in a leather chair that seemed capable of reading my pulse and picking my pocket, I looked around. The amount of paraphernalia seemed to have trebled since the last time I was there but the clutter of paperwork had definitely diminished. Jake used to have legal documents heaped on the floor like stalagmites—pleadings and discovery motions and the fruits of subpoenas duces tecum—but now the office was neat as a pin. I gave credit for that improvement to the computers on the credenza behind him, their antic screen savers serving as a form of hyperactive art.

When Jake saw me looking, he smiled. "You on-line yet, Marsh?"

I shook my head. "Sounds too much like talk radio to interest me much. I can only take fanaticism in small doses."

He nodded. "There's a lot of zealots out there, sure enough, and the more fanatical, the less informed seems to be the rule. But if you pick your spots, the Internet can change your life."

"How so?"

"You know about the WELL?"

"The local bulletin board, or whatever you call it?"

Jake nodded. "Hell of a thing. I mean, you can get into anything under the sun on there. Met some horse people who've got me running a completely new feeding program with my two-year-olds. Met some other guy runs a shop called Meyer Boswell who's got me into investing in antiquarian law books. Plus, I'm here to tell you that sex on-line is better than the real thing. I've got three different WELL personas working for me—some cutie over in Emeryville thinks I'm a forty-year-old boxer with a cauliflower ear, an eight-figure bank account, and a pecker that can fire and reload six times a night."

I laughed. "That's what they call fraud in the inducement, isn't it, Jake?"

His grin was elfin. "Only if I can't perform as advertised. I really do have a bad ear."

"To say nothing of a big bank account."

Jake cackled happily, looking closer to twenty than seventy. "It's a brave new world, Marsh; that science fiction bullshit is finally coming true. I hate like hell that I'm not going to be around to see it all happen."

It was the first time I'd heard Jake hint of his mortality. I decided it was something I could use to my advantage. "I need a favor, Jake."

He sobered fast. "Do I owe you?"

"No."

"Just checking. Are we talking subsidy? Your balance sheet a little thin this month?"

I shook my head. "What I need is pro bono work."

"Get caught tapping a phone?"

"It's not for me, it's for a friend of mine."

Jake turned and flipped on a computer menu; I figured I had another ten seconds.

"The only pro bono work I do is for bookies and call girls," he said idly, as he scrolled some sort of text through his Compaq.

"This isn't a call girl, this is a cop."

"What the hell do you care about some . . . oh." He turned back toward me. "Sleet. Right?"

I nodded.

"He really do what they say?"

"Apparently."

"You happen to know why?"

I shook my head. "He won't talk to me."

"Where they holding him?"

"Hall of Justice. I tried to see him but he wouldn't give the okay."

"He tell you to come to me?"

I shook my head.

Jake thought it over. "He shoots square. Gave me some stand-up testimony in a brutality case I had awhile back. Made the uniform look bad enough so my man settled with the city for half a million." He glanced out the window at a corpulent young man who was pressing his nose to the glass and looking as though he'd seen God or at least Garth Brooks. The tourist waved but Jake ignored him.

"Any chance of me getting a book out of this thing?" Jake asked idly.

I shrugged. "No idea."

"You think he'd go for it?"

"Charley? A book deal? I doubt it."

"Not that his cooperation is essential."

I smiled. "You'd know more about that than I would."

"So how much of me can he afford?"

"Only your belt buckle, if you're talking your usual rates. That's why I mentioned pro bono."

"He got any rich friends?"

"A few."

"Can they cover my expenses?"

"How high are they likely to run?"

"Could be five; could be fifty times that. Depends on the defense. If we decide to go with insanity, experts can cost a fortune. And if we get into DNA, well . . ."

"I don't think Charley's insane, Jake."

"Sounds like it to me, given the stunt he pulled. And that's not the issue anyway. The issue is not what you say he is, the issue is what the jury says he is. And if they say he couldn't tell right from wrong when he pulled that trigger, he lacks an essential element for a conviction."

The idea that I might be contributing to such a rendition of the state of mind of Charley Sleet made me half nauseous.

"For whatever it's worth, Charley may not cooperate in his defense," I said. "I think he may be planning to plead guilty."

"Does that make any sense at all?"

"No."

"Then we've got a competency issue."

"A stubbornness issue, more likely."

Jake leaned back and crossed his arms above the bowling ball that champagne and caviar had made of his belly. "Remind me why I have a dime's worth of interest in this thing."

"Because when you get to the pearly gates, they're not going to ask about your girlfriends' bra size or the money in your stock portfolio or the time posted by your filly in the eighth at Bay Meadows last fall. They're going to want to know what you did for the good of the world or at least of San Francisco."

Jake laughed. "You think I believe in that hereafter shit, Tanner?"

I looked at the rosary that was looped over the framed picture of the pope that hung near the door. "I don't know. But I do think you're old enough to keep your options open."

Jake tried to shrug it off by lighting a lengthy cigar. "So this Sleet is some kind of saint, is that it?"

"He's not a saint but he's a good man. And for some reason, he did something completely out of character. I thought you might want to be the one who finds out why."

"You willing to handle the investigation?"

"Absolutely."

"Gratis?"

"Of course."

"When's the arraignment?"

"Tomorrow."

"How much bail can he make?"

"We can post a bond of fifty if we have to."

"You probably will. If we get bail at all, that is." Jake climbed out of his chair and offered a hand when I did the same. "I'll stand for him at the arraignment, then we'll see what's what."

"Thanks, Jake."

"Your appreciation is premature."

When I got back to the office, there were a dozen messages on the answering machine, each one asking about Charley, none from people who knew why he'd done it. The only one I returned right away was Ruthie Spring's.

Ruthie's husband, Harry, was my mentor in the PI business until he was murdered out in the valley almost twenty years ago. Ruthie had taken over his agency and in the process of managing our grief and pursuing our profession, we became close friends. Although we've had some friction from time to time, she's as close to me as anyone but Charley now that Peggy, my former secretary, is married and merry in Seattle.

Ruthie had been a combat nurse and a sheriff's deputy and a Texan before she'd married Harry, and she and Charley could trade war stories for hours if you kept the liquor coming and refereed the low blows. For a time, I thought she and Charley might get romantic after Charley's wife died, but Charley dawdled for so long that Ruthie hooked up with a rich guy.

"Ruthie? Marsh."

"Hey, hey, Sugar Bear."

"How's it going?"

"Not worth spit since I heard about Sleet. What the hell happened in there, Marsh? That gnarly old bastard finally lose his marbles?"

"He shot someone, Ruthie. That's all I know."

"Hell, even *I* know that much and I ain't been out of

the house. The news lady said it was some kind of sex case."

"They say anything more than that about it?"

"One of those child abuse things. You know, the kind they only remember later on. I think Daddy screwed me twenty years ago, even though it slipped my mind until now, and I want a million dollars to erase the pain I must have felt even though I didn't know I was feeling it."

Life made even less sense than before. "That was the trial Charley was watching? A sex abuse thing?" I didn't try to disguise my amazement.

"That's what they said. Charley drilled the dirty daddy right there in open court."

"What was Daddy's name?"

"Don't remember. Damn. Alzheimer's kicking in for sure. My goddamn brain won't hold on to anything longer than a frog's fart these days. I got to mark the calendar to remind myself that Conway and me are still fucking."

I sidestepped Ruthie's sex life. "What did this abuse case have to do with Charley? Did they say?"

"That seems to be an open question. Thought you might have ideas on the subject yourself."

"Not a one."

"Well, the only thing I know about Charley's love life is he's got himself a new squaw."

Finally, a revelation. "How do you know?"

"He let something slip one night when Conway and I ran into him at Kuleto's."

"Charley was at Kuleto's?" It was as unlikely as Willie Brown afoot at Taco Bell.

"Proof of the point, I'd call it. Wouldn't tell me who he was waiting for and Conway whisked me off to Slim's so fast I didn't get a chance to pump him. Conway can't get enough of that rockabilly." Ruthie paused for breath. "What are you going to do, Marsh?"

"Everything I can, Ruthie."

"I know that much. But what, exactly?"

"Get him a lawyer. Check out this sex thing. Find the

connection and try to come up with a defense that would excuse the shooting. I think Jake will represent him for free if Charley will let him."

Ruthie's voice grew weighty. "You know if you need anything, all you have to do is ask, Sugar Bear."

"I know that, Ruthie."

"Money. Legwork. Anything."

"Thanks. I may have to take you up on the money part if bail's higher than we think."

"Don't even hesitate. Conway's still got a pile. I've spent all I can on everything I can think of and he's still got more than Midas. Once you get rich, it's hard as hell to get poor, provided you stay out of Texas."

CHAPTER

4

I DIDN'T GET MUCH DONE THE REST OF THE DAY AND I DIDN'T get much sleep all night. I talked a lot on the phone to people who knew even less about the situation than I did and fended off newshounds fishing for dirt or worse, but mostly I thought about Charley. About what he'd done in the courtroom, about what could have brought him to that murderous point, about where he was now and what might be happening to him down there, about how to get him out of it. But mostly what I thought about was what Charley had meant to me over the years; mostly what I did was remember.

Charley and I do things together. We go to ball games, we play poker, we drink beer at the Bohemian Cigar Store, we bet on sports and politics and other vagaries of human behavior, we eat lunch at Chan's on Clement and Capp's in North Beach, but mostly we just hang out. On a thousand nights in a hundred places we've sat side by side on barstools, mourning lost loves, reliving lost youth, casting our triumphs in grandeur and our failures in pathos, chasing our whiskey with our dreams and our disappointments, lending aid and comfort to each other with and without the use of words.

Silence is a large part of what friendship is all about for men like Charley and me, the ability to feel so comfortable in someone's presence that there's no pressure to expend effort on conversation until there's something you really need to say. Charley could stay silent for hours, then mutter a single curse, and more often than not I would know the precise object of his ire whether or not he decided to expand on the subject.

Our friendship had a professional dimension as well. I don't think I could have made much of a living without Charley Sleet. The access to police data he has provided, the leads from the crime computer and the tips and hints and nudges that let me leapfrog ahead of the official investigation so I could get what I needed before the cops shut down the best sources, have been essential to my livelihood. We joke about the dinners I buy him in return for such favors, but Charley would do what he could for me even if I didn't pay for his pasta and wontons once in a while. He'd do it because we're buddies.

For a long time, I'd felt guilty because most of the favors had run one way, and now that I finally had a chance to even the score, Charley wasn't letting me. He was avoiding me and everyone else, as far as I knew, an attitude that in Charley's situation could literally be fatal. He had done something crazy and was still doing it—compounding the problem, threatening to make it insoluble. He was making me mad when he wasn't making me frightened. I spent the early morning hours the way I'd spent the night before, trying to imagine how all that could have happened to him, but by the time it was time for his arraignment I hadn't come close to an answer.

They brought Charley into Department 9 with six others, in handcuffs and waist chains and the orange jumpsuit they issue to miscreants. He looked straight ahead as he waited to take his seat in the jury box, then looked at his lap after he did so, avoiding me, avoiding the prosecutor, avoiding the world whose precepts he had so blatantly violated.

His huge bald head glowed like a golden orb of religious significance. His chest swelled like a cast-iron breastplate that could deflect a ballistic missile. Only the bulge of stress at the hinge of his jaw and the curve to his usually ramrod spine suggested the strain he was under and the storms that beset him, both from within and without.

Jake Hattie was seated in the front row, impeccably attired in charcoal flannel, surrounded by similarly suited acolytes, attracting stares and whispers. The guy next to me murmured, "If he's got Hattie on board, he's either real guilty or real innocent." Somewhere behind me someone said, "Only way he affords Jake is if he was on the pad." It was difficult to keep my hands at my sides and my butt on the bench; what I wanted more than anything was to punch someone.

The judge entered the room twenty minutes behind schedule. I'd hoped she would extend Charley the courtesy of calling him first and that's what she did, although probably for Jake's sake more than Charley's.

Charley stood when his name was called, his eyes polished pyrites in the caves of his skull, as blinkless and as fixed as twin rivets. Jake stood, too, but stayed behind the rail.

"Is defendant represented by counsel?" the judge intoned after flipping briefly through the slim file.

"No," Charley growled.

"I have that privilege, Your Honor," Jake announced simultaneously.

"Don't need him," Charley spat, moving only his lips.

"Have you engaged another attorney, Mr. Sleet?"

Charley shook his head. "Don't need one."

The judge frowned, then sighed, then patted her hairdo, then looked back and forth between the two men, trying to decide what to do.

"I'm not a fan of pro se representation, especially in criminal matters," she said finally. "From what I saw of the Ferguson case in New York, I'm more convinced than ever that the option should not be available regardless of the defendant's insistence on acting as his own attorney. However, I don't need to decide that issue this morning. You're willing to serve as Mr. Sleet's lawyer in these circumstances, Mr. Hattie?"

Jake bowed at the waist. "I am with pleasure, Your Honor."

"Fine. Mr. Sleet, for purposes of the arraignment and until further order of court, Mr. Hattie is appointed to serve you as counsel. Is the defendant prepared to enter a plea, Mr. Hattie?"

"Guilty," Charley blurted from between clenched teeth. The crowd buzzed; Jake shook his head; I stood halfway out of my seat before remembering that there was nothing productive I could do short of stuffing a gag in my friend's big mouth.

"The defendant is not guilty of the offenses charged, Your Honor," Jake intoned. "I ask that such a plea be entered."

Charley glowered; Jake preened; I was sweating like a pig in August. The judge was clearly uncomfortable and was just as clearly going to punt. "I'm entering a plea of not guilty on your behalf, Mr. Sleet," she said finally. "At some time in the future a court may entertain a motion for a change of plea, but for now I'm preserving all your rights."

"Thank you, Your Honor," Jake said.

"Do you waive time and reading the indictment?"

"We do, Your Honor."

"Fine." The judge turned to the prosecutor. "What are your thoughts on bail, Ms. Willoughby?"

A young woman stepped forward, tall, thin-lipped, short-skirted, clutching a stack of files to her chest. I wondered if she had any idea how unique the case she was about to engage was, or how magnificent the man she would be trying to imprison had been over the course of his life in the city's fractious streets.

"The people ask that bail be denied and that the defendant remain incarcerated pending trial," she declared officiously. "The charge is murder, Your Honor. Without provocation. Of a prominent person in this community."

"Mr. Hattie?"

Jake waded through the bar of the court and regarded the prosecutor with scorn. "I could easily usurp a month of the court's valuable time parading before it a host of witnesses to Lieutenant Sleet's matchless character. He is a much honored officer in the San Francisco police force, he is a donor of both time and money to a host of charitable causes, he has in past years served as the mayor's personal security officer and the community relations officer for the entire department. Had Ms. Willoughby spent as many years as I have in these courts, she would know that there is not the slightest risk that Detective Sleet will fail to appear for his—"

"I'm aware of Mr. Sleet's service to the department and the community, Mr. Hattie."

"I was certain you would be, Your Honor. May I make one additional point?"

"Briefly."

"Jail for any police officer, and particularly one as efficient and effective as Lieutenant Sleet has been, is much more than incarceration, it is a state of perpetual peril in a condition of cruel and unusual punishment. The cells surrounding Mr. Sleet's will bulge with felons placed there as the result of his skill and perseverance; the common areas will boil with cries for vengeance; the dining halls will echo with threats to his person. There is a far larger likelihood that he will not appear at trial if he is *not* released, because he may not *survive* till then. Literally. I know the court would not want a tragedy of that magnitude to be visited upon—"

"I'm not a cop," Charley blurted.

The courtroom froze; Jake's mouth stood agape; the judge frowned in confusion. "What did you say, Mr. Sleet?"

"I'm not in the PD anymore. Turned in my shield last Thursday."

I was shocked into bewilderment, but Jake was nothing if not nifty. "His present circumstance does not at all curtail the dangers that his past duties present to him, Your Honor. There remain many men in the city jail because Mr. Sleet has put them there. Their thirst for retribution will not be dampened by Mr. Sleet's recent resignation, if in fact that proves to be the case. I ask bail of no more than fifty thousand."

The prosecutor started to interrupt but the judge waved her off. "I have sympathy for your position, Mr. Hattie, whatever Mr. Sleet's employment status. On the other hand, I am not unmindful of the crime with which he is charged, the manner in which it was committed, and the strictures placed on me by recent amendments to the state constitution. Bail is denied."

"But, Your Honor—"

The judge shook her head and banged her gavel.

Charley smiled in triumph, then looked at Jake and then at me and muttered what I assumed was a curse. I stood up and tried to signal him with my hands and eyes—sympathy, encouragement, comradeship, something—but the message was garbled and in any event Charley was unreceptive. He shuffled out the door without acknowledging anyone or anything, his only expression a baleful glare that left no doubt that he preferred the roaches and rats of San Bruno to the company of the rest of us.

I waited for Jake in the hall. It took him so long to get there, I figured he must have been trying to talk some sense to his client.

"So?" I said when he strode toward me down the corridor, as cocky and crisp as a bantam rooster, his retinue nowhere in evidence.

"The guy's a zombie," Jake said, after making sure no

one was within earshot. "Won't talk; won't listen; won't say what happened or why."

"Is there any chance at all to spring him?"

"I'll make a motion to reconsider the bail ruling, but right now it's got no chance. I need facts."

"What kind of facts?"

"Find me a prisoner down at Bruno who threatened to kill him. Name and number. Fast."

I told Jake I'd do what I could. "So how's he seem?" I went on. "You know. In the head."

"He seems different."

"How so?"

"Distant. Uninterested. Fatalistic. Nihilistic."

"Even about himself?"

"Especially about himself. Something's happened to him, Marsh; something that's made him sociopathic. He doesn't give a shit; not about anything. You got any idea what it was that did it?"

I shook my head.

"Love life? Cop life? Anything at all gone south for him lately?"

"No idea. Except I heard he got a new girlfriend."

"Check it out. Maybe she dumped him. Maybe she left him for the guy he shot."

I nodded. "What else?"

Jake swore. "You're the investigator. You tell me."

"I find out exactly how Charley was connected to the guy in the courtroom."

Jake nodded. "I can help with that one." He opened his briefcase and pulled out a yellow pad and consulted it. "My people did some digging in the clerk's office. The case was *Wints* v. *Wints*. Jillian Wints was suing her father, Leonard, for sexually abusing her some twenty years back. Recovered memory thing. Asking five million plus. The case was in court on the father's motion for summary judgment."

"Who are the lawyers?"

"For plaintiff—Mindy Cartson. Andy Potter has the defense."

"Andy. Good. I know Andy."

"Me, too. He's a stickler for the rules sometimes, but there shouldn't be a problem in this case."

"Why not?"

Jake adjusted his hairpiece. "His client's dead. Most of the rules don't apply anymore."

CHAPTER
5

WHEN I GOT BACK TO THE OFFICE, I STARTED MAKING CALLS. Andy Potter was out and so was Mindy Cartson—I guessed their absence was more tactical than geographic. Joyce Yates wasn't at her desk at the *Chronicle* either. It seemed too soon to try to reach a member of the Wints family, since they were burying the victim that morning, so I was left with a source of information that was most likely both delicate and reluctant—the San Francisco Police Department.

Police people in general are closemouthed. Part of their reticence is legitimate, since with the advent of drug lords and gang-bangers and skinheads, policing has become a form of guerrilla warfare in which assaults and ambushes are carefully staged, complicated coordination is required, and success often depends on secrecy. Lives are at stake; literally.

Less commendably, some cops' silence is grounded in a sense that if people knew how they really conducted their business, they would be jailed on the spot. They're not as right about that as they used to be, but even in the nation's new compassionless climate, some police practices would shock the collective conscience if they received a public airing. For proof, consult the tapes of Mark Fuhrman. Some of the practices of pilots and politicians would shock the conscience, too, of course, which is why those people keep secrets as well.

Because I was a civilian, not a cop, I was starting out with one strike against me as far as the department was concerned. And since the beneficiary of my inquiry was Charley Sleet, the count was 0 and 2. That's because Charley is a maverick and always has been. He works mostly alone, mostly on special assignment from the chief's office or the DA, frequently undercover, and often in cooperation with Internal Affairs while investigating some form of his colleagues' corruption.

Although beloved on the streets of the Tenderloin and respected in the projects of the Western Addition, Charley has never been popular in the precinct. He knows too much, his skills are too refined, his ethic is too empathic and absolute, for him to fit with most of his fellows. What I needed to find was an exception to the prevailing wisdom, in the form of someone who owed Charley his life.

The colleague Charley mentioned most often, which was nonetheless infrequently, was a detective named Wally Briscoe. I'd met Wally a time or two—he'd joined us at Candlestick on occasion, which Charley endured even though Wally was a Dodger fan—and he seemed a genuine friend. He and Charley had worked the Taraval station early on in their careers, then pulled a tour in the Mission. It made them like combat buddies, Charley had told me one time, since most of their peers had either died or quit the force. What Wally had told me once, when Charley was out of earshot, was that Charley had disarmed a Filipino drug lord who was about to blow Wally into the bay one night, and Wally had felt beholden ever since.

It took me a while to track Wally down. When I did, he agreed to meet for an early lunch. Since he was working the Marina that morning, we rendezvoused at Judy's.

Wally was late. Cops are always late, even to most emergencies, which I suppose is why he didn't apologize when he got there and I didn't mention the slur.

I stood and shook his hand. He was a round man with a round face and a round body; even his nose and chin and earlobes were spherical. His hand felt like a water balloon when we shook, squishy and formless and silly. Sometime since the last doubleheader we'd attended, Wally had slipped past his prime. He probably thought the same of me.

When the waitress came, we ordered coffee and omelettes. "Hell of a thing," Wally began, singing the most popular tune on the hit parade.

"Yeah."

"He hire you to help Hattie get him off?"

I shook my head. "I'm on my own. Me and a few of his friends."

"Yeah. Friends. Charley always had lots of friends." He made it sound like having lots of lice.

"I'm wondering what might have made him do it," I began.

"Me, too," Wally said.

"You got nothing on it at all?"

Wally shook his head. "I asked around. No one knows nothing about this Wints guy."

"Then let's back up. Why'd Charley quit the force?"

Wally shook his head again. "Came out of nowhere. He walks into Chief Daniels's office last Thursday, plunks down his piece and his shield, and tells Daniels he's through."

"No reason?"

"No reason. None of the guys knew till he'd cleaned out his locker and was gone for good."

"What was he working on?"

"Nothing special that I could find out. I mean when you called, I figured you'd ask me, but I got to say there was nothing big on the board. Fact is, some of the guys told me Charley seemed to be slacking off lately."

"Charley? Slacking off?"

Wally smiled. "I know. Sounds crazy. Maybe they meant he was only working nine to nine instead of nine to midnight."

"Slacking off how?"

"Not around the station that much. Not putting up many numbers. Not the primary on anything hot. Not even second-guessing the rest of the squad, the way he always did."

"Any reason for that they could see?"

"Not that I could find."

"Did the Wints trial have anything to do with an active police matter?"

Wally waited for the waitress to deliver the omelettes, then sampled the fare before he answered. "There's no open file in that name, so I'd say it wasn't. Unless it was a special project; then I wouldn't be able to get at it."

"You mean a sting of some kind?"

"Or a task force project. Or a covert operation. Or an IAD investigation."

"If it was a special project, Charley wouldn't know about it either, would he?"

Wally shook his head. "Charley knew everything. I think he's got the place bugged." His laugh was brisk and uneasy; his brow bore a film of sweat. I wondered if Wally had fears he was the object of a special project himself.

"Charley might have been in on it," he added around a bite of Denver omelette after picking out the peppers. "The special project, I mean."

"If he was, would anyone else know about it?"

"Hell, no. No one down the chain of command, I mean. With Charley, information only traveled one way—in, not out." He looked up from the omelette. "Except you. I never could figure why he fed you so much of our product. I never saw what was in it for him."

"Maybe justice," I said, and watched while Wally shook his head and swore.

"Fucking peppers. Only ones who think it's about justice are the civilians."

"If it's not about justice, then what is it about?" I asked, just to keep things rolling or maybe just to give time for my omelette to cool.

Wally swallowed. "Control."

"How so?"

"Our job is to put enough of the swill away to keep control of the places that count. The rest of it is just politics. Some days politics says bust the whores; some days it says bust the dopers; some days the homeless; some days the street artists. Don't matter to us what we do, as long as we got the time and talent to keep control of what counts."

"Which is where?"

"Where we live and where we work. The rest of it don't mean shit."

I let his essay evaporate before it did any more damage to my ideals. "Was Charley into anything political recently? Did politics tell him to bust anyone in particular?"

Wally thought through another bite of omelette, then shook his head. "Don't think so. Like I said, the guys claim he was dogging it for some reason."

"How about in the department in general? Any rumors of something heavy going down in Internal Affairs?"

Wally put down his fork. "Only thing with priority as far as I know is that cop killing in Herman Plaza last week. But that's not IA, that's just a priority homicide—double shifts and the usual red-ball bullshit when one of the blue goes down. But I'm just a second grade in the North Station. I'd be the last to know about IAD or anything else that was sensitive."

I switched focus. "Have you seen Charley much lately? Personally, I mean."

"Only a few times in the last year—dinner at Capp's a

couple of months ago; lunch in the Mission some months before that. Why?"

"Was he acting differently? Nervous? Frightened? Anything?"

"Shit. Only time I ever seen Sleet frightened was when his wife was sick, and that was because he was afraid he couldn't live without her. For a while, I thought he was right."

I knew what he was talking about. After Charley's wife, Flora, had died, he'd crawled into a bourbon bottle for a year, incommunicado and inconsolable, as bereft as anyone I'd ever seen. But he'd climbed out, eventually, on his own, as usual, without the aid of psychotherapy or 12 Steps or even my friendship. Until now, I'd never felt as helpless as I had back in those days, watching him founder, knowing he wouldn't let me help him, hoping that he'd come around before it killed him or cost him his job, which in Charley's case would have been more fatal than cirrhosis.

"I hear he's got a girlfriend," I said abruptly, hoping to jar something loose.

"You mean that whore he visits down on Turk Street?"

I didn't know about the whore, but she didn't fit with Ruthie's peek at Kuleto's. "Someone new."

"Don't know anything about it. I hope so, for his sake. A good woman can turn it all around."

It sounded like Wally had gotten lucky himself.

I finished my coffee and looked up. "Is there anything at all you can tell me about this, Wally?"

He shook his head. "I thought about it a lot, and you know I owe him, but I don't know what the hell would have made him do something like that. I mean if he wanted to take someone out, there's cleaner ways to do it, and Charley knew them all."

"Jake says it would help if we knew someone down at Bruno who had a mad-on for Charley in a big way. Might convince the judge to set bail."

Wally nodded. "I'll check it out."

"And ask around some more. Especially the guys at the Central Station."

"Sure. Doubt if I get any answers, though. Lots of the guys got a grin when they heard Charley quit the department. Not all, but lots."

"Before this is over, I'm going to cram that grin down their fucking throats." My vehemence caused the woman at the next table to shake her head. I didn't blame her. Given the circumstances, the threat sounded juvenile even to me.

CHAPTER

6

IF YOU WANT TO FIND A LAWYER WHO DOESN'T WANT TO BE found, you've got to catch him in his nest. In this case, it was a she, not a he, and her nest wasn't a Financial District high-rise with a view to the end of the earth, it was in a nicely refurbished Victorian on Webster Street a block north of Union, with a view of St. Vincent de Paul.

If you need biographical information on a lawyer, you turn to Martindale-Hubble, the national legal directory. My set is a year out of date, since I get it gratis from my friend Russell Jorgensen when his firm receives the new edition, but in this case obsolescence didn't matter—Mindy Cartson was listed in the San Francisco section.

The entry told me that she was thirty-six, she'd gone to Mills, then on to Golden Gate, she'd been an editor of the law review and an intern at the Justice Department, then clerked a year for a federal district judge. She specialized in personal injuries and employment discrimination claims, with some domestic relations work on the side. She'd coauthored a CEB book on termination damages and was a member of a bar committee on discovery reforms. Based on her Martindale entry and her office address, I guessed she was one of the few who'd actually become the kind of lawyer they had planned to be on the day they entered law school.

The carved wooden sign on the door at the top of the stairs that carried me up from the sidewalk listed Mindy Cartson, Attorney-at-Law, a Professional Corporation, along with four other attorneys whose form of business association was unclear—I guessed they were sole practitioners who shared space and staff. The other occupants of the building included a massage therapist, a baseball card trader, and a swimsuit boutique. I was tempted to stop in and see if I could afford an original Duke Snider now that the Duke was a self-confessed tax evader, but somehow I knew I still couldn't.

A receptionist was waiting at a desk just inside the door. When I told her I was there to see Ms. Cartson, she asked if I had an appointment.

I shook my head. "I was hoping she'd see me as a walk-in since my situation is so . . . horrible."

She gave me the once-over, then wrinkled her nose with skepticism—she'd seen horrible before; I wasn't it. "What exactly *is* your situation, Mr. . . . ?"

"Tanner. And it's not me, it's my wife. She's weeks away from graduating from pharmacy school at Stanford and she got run down by a pizza guy three nights ago. They say she'll live, but she won't . . ." I swore. "They ought to do something about those maniacs," I snarled in a nasty conclusion.

It was about as low as I'd ever sunk; I had to keep Charley in the forefront of my mind in order to throttle an apology. For her part, the receptionist didn't fully believe me, but she couldn't afford to turn me away given the potential magnitude of my pseudo wife's pseudo damages, so she gestured toward a director's chair near the window. "Please have a seat. I'll see if Ms. Cartson has time for you." She walked through a door and yanked it closed behind her.

Time doubled back on itself as though crafting a second draft. I listened to a secretary type digits onto a disk; I listened to a printer laser forth a page; I listened to a fax print out an electric message—Mindy was doing well enough to afford the latest toys. In my day, all it took to practice law was a Correcting Selectric and a Xerox machine on lease.

The receptionist came back wearing the dubious frown she'd left with. "She only has ten minutes. If she feels you have a cause of action, you'll have to remain for an intake interview."

I told her that would be fine. She asked me to follow her. We went through the door and down the hall. "Mindy, this is Mr. Tanner. He's promised to be brief."

The receptionist looked at me one last time to make sure I had the message, then made space for me to enter her boss's domain. "Ten minutes," she repeated at my back; I think the reminder was as much for Mindy as for me.

The office was small and neat and unpretentious, with the usual files and law books and computer terminals on the desk and tables, the usual diplomas and admission certificates on the walls, the usual discount Danish furniture arranged around the room. What was unusual was the playpen in the corner with a baby in it. The baby was gurgling and tugging on its toes. I assumed it wasn't a client.

I smiled. "I've got one of those myself," I said, then wished I hadn't. "Sort of."

Mindy Cartson frowned. "How do you 'sort of' have a baby?"

"I have one, but I'm not raising it."

"Divorce?"

I shook my head. "It's a long story."

"It would have to be. But I only have time for one story this afternoon and I'd like it to be the one about your wife, the pharmacy student."

"I don't have a wife," I said.

"But you told Jackie—"

"I lied. I'm here because my best friend is in trouble."

She frowned, then ruffled through some papers on the

desk before gathering them into a pile; at best I had half her attention. "I don't have time for surrogate clients, I'm afraid. If your friend needs legal advice, have him make an appointment. Now, if you'll excuse me." She stood up and waited for me to depart, after a glance to see that the baby was well.

Ms. Cartson was blond and cutish; a little too plump, a little too pug-nosed, a little too pugnacious, but cute all the same. Her hair was short and shaggy, her face full and frank, her body fluffy and marbled and Gapped in tan blouse, white cardigan, and gray slacks. If she'd been a boy, she'd have played outside linebacker. High school, not college or pro.

Since she still seemed piqued by my confession, I hurried ahead with my story. "My name is Marsh Tanner. I'm a—"

She looked away from the baby and back at me. "Private detective."

I was surprised. "Right."

"You get some nice press from time to time."

"Not enough to get me a table at Masa's."

"Can you afford a table at Masa's?"

I shook my head.

She smiled. "Neither can I, especially now that you're not bringing me a pharmacist who's been disabled by a deep pocket."

"Sorry about that."

She shrugged. "I'll survive. What can I do for you? Some slimy divorce involving this friend of yours, I suppose. What's his name?"

Before I could set her straight, she dropped the papers she was holding and looked at me more intently. "Wait a minute. You're here about Leonard Wints. The cop in the courtroom—you two work together sometimes."

I nodded. "Like I said. My best friend is in trouble."

Her expression hardened and her voice took on a sarcastic edge. "So you're here to do what? Offer some sort of service to my client? Some inside info on the murderer? Selling your pal for a piece of silver?"

"I said he was my friend, Ms. Cartson. I'm here to find out how Charley Sleet is connected to the Wints case."

"So you can get him off, I presume."

"That's the plan."

"At least you're honest about it." She turned back to her chair and sat down. "Even if I knew of a connection, why should I tell you?"

"Because there's no reason why you shouldn't. It can't prejudice your client for me to find out why Charley killed her father. From what I understand of her lawsuit, it puts your client and Charley on the same side."

"You don't know that the murder has anything to do with my client."

"You're right. Do you?"

"No."

"There's no connection at all?"

"Not that I know of."

"Did you ask the Wints girl about it?"

"Not specifically. And she's not a girl, she's a woman. She was as stunned as anyone by what happened. If she knew this Sleet person, I'm sure she would have said something."

"I'd like to talk to her."

She shook her head. "She's in seclusion."

"Why?"

"Her father was murdered."

"She was suing him for everything he had. Seclusion seems an odd response."

She shrugged. "He was nevertheless her father. Emotions are complex in cases such as this."

"Cases such as what, exactly?"

She hesitated, then relented. "It's a matter of record at this point, I suppose. We allege that Leonard Wints engaged in a pattern of abusive sexual relations with his daughter Jillian over a period of several years when Jillian was a child, a course of conduct so repellent that Jillian repressed all knowledge of it until she was guided out of the darkness by her therapist."

"Recovered memory."

"Yes." She caught my look. "I take it you're one of those who've read some biased and simplistic research on the subject and have decided that daddies never abuse their daughters no matter what the little darlings say."

I shook my head. "I know sexual abuse exists, but I have to admit I get skeptical when the first one to suggest abuse is a therapist with an agenda and when the absence of memory of the event is considered proof of the fact it occurred. The last part gets to sound a little too much like *Alice in Wonderland.*"

Mindy Cartson reddened. "This is not that sort of case, not that it's any of your business. No one has an agenda in this matter except a desire to reclaim a badly damaged life. I think you should leave now, Mr. Tanner. I don't think it's in the best interest of my client for me to discuss this any further with you."

I smiled my most maddening smile. "You're a little defensive, aren't you, Counselor?"

Her face mottled with rage. "I'm not defensive at all. I believe something as vile as incest is often suppressed, both consciously and unconsciously, by the victim, and I am certain that my client did in fact suffer from such mistreatment. If necessary for full recompense, we will pursue our action against her father's estate." She walked to my side of the desk. "Now, if you'll excuse me, I have other matters to attend to."

I stayed put. "Whether your client was or wasn't abused is not my concern, Ms. Cartson. My concern is why Charley Sleet would care about it one way or the other. Care enough to blow someone's brains out."

She looked at her watch. "I really do have a place I need to be."

"And I really do have a best friend who's been jailed on a charge of murder."

She sighed and shook her head. "Since in my view Mr. Sleet did the world a favor, I suppose I'd like to be of help. But I have nothing at all to give you."

"Give me permission to speak with your client."

"Absolutely not."

"Why not? What's she got to hide?"

"She's not hiding, she's recovering. At this point her best course is to establish herself as an independent and healthy person, then put the past out of her mind and move on."

"That shouldn't be hard," I said.

"What do you mean?"

"She had it out of her mind until the therapist put it back in."

I'd made the statement in hopes of sparking a revealing outburst, but Mindy Cartson just growled with annoyance. "Who are you to challenge Jillian's experience? Did your father assault *you* sexually? Were *you* a prisoner of a man's desires when you were only eight years old? Of course not. Men don't *have* that problem."

It wasn't quite true but I wasn't there to debate perversion. "I'm not belittling child abuse," I said again, then glanced at the baby. "And I don't need to prove that it didn't happen in order to help my friend. You can sue to your heart's content as far as I'm concerned. But it would help me to talk to Ms. Wints."

"She's going to be out of the country for a while."

"Doing what?"

"Traveling. Relaxing. Getting her focus back."

"Can she afford to do that?"

"She can now."

"How so?"

"Through oversight or design, Jillian Wints is her father's primary heir. He was a wealthy man. As soon as probate is complete, she will finally get what's coming to her."

I waited till her eyes met mine. "Unless she hired Charley to bump him off."

It knocked her off balance. Her eyes scrambled across my face like insects. "Do you have any reason to believe that's the case?"

"No, but I'm going to look into it. And I'm more likely to get it right if your client cooperates."

She hesitated. "If you go public with talk about my client aiding and abetting Mr. Sleet, I'll recommend a suit for slander."

"Just let me talk to your client, Ms. Cartson. Not about her father, not about her childhood, just about Charley."

She looked at me for a long time. "I'll let you know," she said.

"I'd appreciate it."

The baby made a noise with a rattle. Mindy Cartson walked to the playpen and reached down and tickled it on its tummy. The baby smiled happily, waved the rattle once more, and drooled. When I asked what she called it, she told me her name was Flannery.

I guess that meant it was a girl. A girl with a brilliant talent and a complex measure of good and evil. Probably a lot like her mom.

CHAPTER 7

EVEN THOUGH I'D KNOWN ANDY POTTER FOR FIFTEEN YEARS, I had to use Jake Hattie's name to get through to Andy's secretary. She said her boss would see me as soon as he could, which turned out to be at six that evening. That left me with several hours to kill; I decided to kill them looking for motive.

Charley Sleet lived high within the curves and curls of Upper Market Street, in a small house tacked to a steep cliff with a tiny yard out front and a terraced garden that fell off the back of the lot the way water falls off Yosemite. The garden had been lovely when Charley's wife, Flora, was alive, but although Charley had labored for several years to maintain it in her memory, it had eventually gone to seed. It was still a good place to drink beer, though, and howl at the moon and swear at the fates and watch the fog tumble over Twin Peaks and shade the summer in swaths of gray bunting.

I parked out front but stayed in the car, impaled on the horns of a dilemma. There might be things in that house that could help me: hints of Charley's purposes, hints of a link to the dead man, hints of his secretive girlfriend, hints of a mental illness that was still my best explanation of what had transpired in the courtroom. On the other hand, it was Charley's house. His home; his castle; a private preserve that even the Constitution says can't be searched without cause. So I sat in my car and brooded, wondering if I'd forgive myself if I passed on the opportunity to gather knowledge, wondering if Charley would forgive me if I took advantage of it, wondering what the cops would do when and if they discovered I'd been there before them, assuming they got around to searching the place at all. Predictably, I placed my own peace of mind above both Charley's and the police department's.

There used to be a key in the mailbox. Since there wasn't one now, I assumed Charley had removed it, perhaps anticipating my snooping and forestalling it. Or maybe he'd given it to the girlfriend. I was left with a variety of possibilities for effecting abnormal entry, all of them arguably felonious. The one I chose to employ was to break out a rear window and unhook the sash, then slither into Charley's back bedroom the way an eel slithers into a reef.

It's odd being in someone's house when they're not there. You feel slimy and skulduggerous. You feel nervous that they'll return unexpectedly and catch you at something nefarious, even if the someone is in jail. You also feel excited by the prospect of learning something you didn't know before, something akin to what they would learn from your house if the roles were reversed. I began the effort gingerly, as though the secrets I was about to unearth came shielded within a curse in the manner of the treasures of King Tut, but within a few minutes I was going full speed, curse and Constitution be damned.

Since I was already in the bedroom, I started there. It was an oddly formal little room, still decorated more to Flora's taste than Charley's: The spread on the bed was chintz, the paper on the walls was floral, the rug on the floor was pink. The bed was an old four-poster that had belonged to Flora's mother, the dresser was from maple that had been carved to match. As I rummaged through its drawers, I caught my reflection in the dresser mirror. I wasn't charmed by the image.

You couldn't call Charley a neat person, in fact you might call him a slob, but he was neater than the bedroom implied. Clothes were scattered everywhere—bed, floor, chair backs, even draped over the lampshade and mirror. A three-foot pile of socks and underwear smoldering in the corner indicated a trip to the laundry was prudent. The jumble of shoes on the floor of the closet looked like the stock-in-trade of some charity. I ran some possibilities through my mind before deciding that the scene was more likely a slovenly symptom of bachelorhood than the product of a hasty search by person or persons unknown.

I was headed for the kitchen when an idea made me detour to the closet. Charley isn't a clotheshorse by any means, but he has a few favorite garments and one of them is a camel sport coat. He wears it twice a week in every month but October. But it wasn't there. At the cleaner's, possibly, but his canvas hunting coat wasn't there either, and the blue cotton pajamas that usually hung on a hook on the closet door were missing as well.

Another idea popped up and I looked in the night table next to the bed. The 9 mm Ruger that Charley kept handy for prowlers was missing, as was the 16 gauge Remington pump he kept in the closet for pheasant season. Which caused me to amend my initial decision. What I concluded at this point was that the mess in the bedroom was purposeful, most likely Charley's attempt to disguise beneath a blizzard of chaos what was missing from his personal effects.

A clue to where the clothes and the weapons had gone were the shoes—not the shoes that were there but the ones that were not. What was there were dress shoes, the brown ones Charley wore to work and the black ones he wore to church and to funerals. What weren't there were the scuffed and oiled Red Wings he wore when he went

hunting and the stained and stretched moose-hide moc-
casins he wore when he was lounging around the house
after hours. I sat on the bed and thought about it. What I
decided was that upon his release from prison, Charley
was intending to go to ground somewhere out of town
and that the somewhere was most likely rural and rustic
and remote. The question was: Why wasn't he out there
already? Why had he been determined to stay in jail if
what he planned was to hide out? I moved on to the
kitchen with only a faint hope of finding an answer.

In contrast to the bedroom, the kitchen was as ordered
as usual. Order in the kitchen was usual because Charley
never cooked anything except an occasional Sunday
morning pancake or Friday evening steak, taking the rest
of his meals on the run whenever there was a break in his
workday. But there was evidence of a contemplated
odyssey in the kitchen as well: The cupboards were bare
of the kinds of prepared and preserved and prepackaged
foodstuffs that are the staples of men like Charley and
me.

My taste runs to sugar and Charley's runs to salt. He
always has several boxes of Better Cheddars on hand,
with Triscuits and Wheat Thins on standby in case his
hunger turns heavy. Pretzels were also a favorite, but
there were none of them around either. And no beer in
the fridge or booze in the cabinet except for the gin and
vermouth he kept for the nights he was host to the poker
game and a martini drinker like Clay Oerter came by. It
seemed that Charley was planning to lie as low as
possible, even from the clerk at the grocery.

The living room was Charley's primary domain. The
rest of the house existed for essentials—sleep, eat, bathe,
brush; the living room was where he lived and lan-
guished, the only part of the house that bore Charley's
peculiar stamp. And a peculiar stamp it was.

For one thing, the walls were grass green enamel
because that was his favorite color and enamel was easy
to wash free of the smells of smoke and fried foods. For
another, the lights in the lamps were red, because the

glow they gave off reminded Charley of Christmas. For still another, the rug wasn't a rug, it was a sheet of clear plastic, so he didn't have to worry about staining the carpet beneath it, which was the last thing Flora had bought before she died. There were probably weirder things around as well, but most of me hoped I wouldn't come across them.

The furnishings were a brown leather chesterfield and matching chair that Charley had bought from a lawyer who'd used the proceeds from a contingent killing in a PI case to remodel his office and move it north of Market. The chair and chesterfield formed a rectangle with the fireplace on one end and the TV on the other. The bookcases on opposite walls contained biographies of political figures, technical works on crime scene investigation and interrogation methods, and pulp novels about cops and spies and private eyes: Charley's a big fan of Charles McCarry and Jim Thompson. The stereo system housed an eclectic collection dominated by black blues and military marches and Bach cantatas. The wall decorations were a print by Charles Russell, a knotty assemblage of rope and yarn done by the wife of a rookie cop Charley had dragged out of a firefight some years back, and a framed photograph of Charley in his blues shaking hands with Joseph Alioto during the years when Joe was mayor and Charley was his driver—Charley had worshipped Alioto and vice versa. But for my purposes, only the desk looked promising.

It had been ransacked much like the bedroom, with papers pulled from drawers, then perused, then discarded if outdated or irrelevant to some secret purpose. I collected what I could find and sat on the couch and looked through them. It would have been nice to find love letters from the girlfriend or hate mail from the dead guy or a forwarding address to the prospective hideout, but all I found besides promotional trash was a *Chronicle* clipping that had been crumpled and tossed in the wastebasket.

The clipping concerned the arrest of a counselor at a place called the Tenderloin Children's Project, which was a community services agency funded by city and federal sources that focused on problems of inner-city kids. The man's name was Lumpley. The charge was misappropriation of funds, with additional charges hinted at. The clipping was dated two weeks previously; Lumpley was being held on fifty thousand dollars' bail.

The name of the agency was familiar—I was pretty sure it was one of the places where Charley spent his off-duty time, doing what he could to help out. I imagine the prospect of official corruption especially pissed him off when the ultimate victims were kids. Nasty, but apparently irrelevant.

I folded the clipping and put it in my pocket and made a final tour of the house. What I was looking for was Charley's lockbox, the small fireproof case where he kept his important papers—deed, car title, marriage certificate, department commendations, and the like. Normally, he kept it under the bed, but now it wasn't there. The medication that lowered both his blood pressure and his sex drive wasn't in the bathroom cabinet either. I sat on the couch to think.

Charley had admitted his guilt in court and had apparently prepared for a lengthy absence in the event he was ever set free, but there was no piece of proof in the house that connected him to Leonard Wints, the man he had killed some twenty-four hours earlier. If my guess was correct, and he had in fact made plans to flee, it began to seem crucial that he remain where he was, even though where he was was in jail. And then I had a revelation.

Charley had done something crazy in that courtroom. If he wasn't crazy himself, the only person I knew who might have caused such conduct, other than maybe the new girlfriend, was Charley's dead wife, Flora. Maybe the evidence I was looking for wasn't connected to Charley, maybe it was something of Flora's. So I went back through the house looking for places that Flora might have used to hide secrets, then remembered that the house wasn't where she would hide them; the garden was.

I found them in the form of a small stack of photographs, bound with a rubber band, protected with plastic wrap, and stuffed in a rusted watering can in the potting shed that was rotting away at the low edge of the lot. Most of the pictures were self-explanatory—an impossibly young Charley and an impossibly beautiful Flora on their wedding day and their honeymoon in Hawaii; Flora in Golden Gate Park with an older couple I assumed to be her parents; a handsome Charley in his blues, arm in arm with a buddy at graduation from the police academy; Flora and a woman I didn't recognize; and Charley and the first Governor Brown, Charley and McCovey, Charley and Montana, Charley and Mel Belli. Fine so far, but two pictures were inexplicable. They were both of an infant, a newborn really, prone on a tiny blanket, sleeping and peaceful and bald.

Charley and Flora hadn't had kids, that much I knew. Or did I? What if they'd had one and given it up for adoption? What if their baby had evolved into Jillian Wints? What if they'd kept track of her over the years and when he'd read about the trial Charley had avenged his long-lost daughter in a fit of outrage at what had been done to her? Certain that I was finally on track, I put the pictures in my pocket and headed for the door.

When I passed the table with the telephone on it, I pressed the redial button on his receiver. It rang four times, then activated a machine:

"This is Marjie Finnerty. I'm not at home right now, but if you leave a message, I'll call you back *tout de suite*. Thanks."

Marjie Finnerty was Judge Meltonian's clerk, the woman who'd held her ground when Charley had opened fire and everyone else was ducking for cover. That Charley had placed his final call to her home made it likely that she was the woman Charley had squired to

Kuleto's, where he'd been caught in flagrante romantico by Ruthie Spring.

When I checked Charley's own machine, there was a single message in a woman's voice, saying "Hi" in a tone implying intimacy and enticement. I didn't need a voice print to know that it was an exact match to the one I'd just summoned with the redial button.

CHAPTER

8

I GRABBED SOME BREAD AND CHILI AT MacARTHUR PARK, then headed into the steel-and-glass forest of downtown.

Andy Potter's office was on the fourteenth floor of the Alcoa building, where he was a senior partner in the firm of Geer, Goldberg & Potter, Attorneys and Counselors-at-Law. The last I checked, Andy had more than fifty partners and almost a hundred associates helping him fight the good fight or at least the remunerative one. When he'd entered law school at Stanford, Andy had wanted to be a civil liberties attorney. The only liberties he worked for now were those of major capitalists, who had far too many of them already as far as I was concerned. I began to think more fondly of Mindy Cartson.

I'd gotten to know Andy in my first big case, which involved a client of his named Roland Nelson, who was the head of an advocacy organization called the Institute for Consumer Awareness. Nelson turned out to have a lurid past. Lots of things happened to him and to the rest of us before it all got straightened out, including the murder of Harry Spring, my friend and mentor, out in a valley town called Oxtail. I'd worked for Andy a few times since, but because his practice is more corporate than criminal, I don't get a call very often. Andy is one of the few blue-suit types I can abide, however—he doesn't think the be-all and end-all of the nation's soul should be pledged to business profits—so we stay in touch and meet for drinks and go to a game once in a while. Among the things I intended to ask was how he happened to end up in Superior Court representing a purported child molester.

We shook hands crisply. Andy was five-eight and stout, with a creaseless, guileless face that looked somewhat like Gene Autry's back when Gene had owned quarter horses and not baseball players. Andy had gone through a quick divorce, then married a lawyer who worked in the firm, and the last time I talked to him he'd declared himself fat and happy. So I was happy for him.

"I tried to call you after it happened," he said with apology in his voice. "But there was no answer and I didn't want to leave that kind of message. You know?"

"I know. Thanks for the thought."

Andy shrugged with helplessness and led me back to his office. The walls used to display abstract art and African masks and the furniture used to be chrome-and-glass, but now it was all Southwest—Navajo rugs and Hopi jars and lodge-style chairs and couches with coverings of saddle leather and joints wrapped with rawhide. The view was still the same, though, toward the Golden Gate Bridge and Mount Tam. As I waited for an invitation to sit down, I told Andy I liked the new look and asked what had prompted the change.

"Cormac McCarthy."

Andy looked surprised that I knew who he was.

After we took our seats, Andy shook his head before I even asked a question. "It was the damnedest thing I've ever been through, Marsh. There I was, taking notes, preparing some concluding remarks, listening to opposing counsel argue a minor point of procedure, and all of a sudden my client gets shot. Bam, bam; two feet away from me. I swear I heard the bullet, Marsh. I think I heard the first one fly by my ear and I *know* I heard the second one hit him. I'll never forget that sound as long as I live. I got *blood* on me, for God's sake. And *skull* fragments. I actually watched him die. I watched his eyes go dark, Marsh; I watched them fade to black just like in the movies."

He shook his head with puzzlement, still awash in mayhem. "And to think it was Charley. I don't know him as well as you do, but I *know* him. We played *poker* together. Christ. What the hell did he think he was *doing* anyway?" Andy bowed his head dolefully, as though the universe were coming unhinged, as though the gods and goddesses had taken leave of their senses and had dragged Charley along for the joyride.

"I suppose there's no chance he wasn't the one who did it," I said, just to start at square one. "I heard someone was struggling with him; I thought maybe what really happened was that Charley was trying to disarm the other guy."

Andy shook his head. "I turned around before that. He was still holding the gun, looking . . . I don't know, scared, or remorseful, or something. He was the shooter, Marsh. No question. I don't think he even recognized me," Andy went on. "I'm not sure he realized what he'd done."

"What makes you say that?"

"I don't know, he just seemed . . . confused, at first. Then he got this odd smile on his face, like there was something funny about it. Plus, he must have been hurt wrestling the guy for the gun, 'cause he was limping pretty badly when they hauled him out of there. I asked him if he wanted anything, but I don't think he heard me."

"Did he say anything at all?"

"Not that I heard."

"Was he the only one in the courtroom besides the litigants?"

Andy shook his head. "It was pretty crowded. The

case has had some publicity because of the nature of the claim and the prominence of the defendant. There were all kinds of people in there, most of them adverse to my client, I'm afraid. These abuse cases amount to feminist crusades in some circles."

"The sex abuse stuff isn't your usual cup of tea, is it, Andy?"

"No, but Leonard insisted I handle it at least through motions and discovery. I'd done his corporate work for years, and some commercial litigation as well, and we've become pretty close. When this abuse thing was filed, Leonard asked me to take care of it for as long as I could so he wouldn't face the embarrassment of discussing such matters with anyone else if he could possibly help it. Normally, I wouldn't have agreed, but the claim was such an obvious fraud, I was confident we could bounce it out before trial. And from the questions Judge Meltonian was asking, I think we would have prevailed on our motion."

"So this wasn't a trial?"

He shook his head. "Motion for summary judgment."

"Were you going to offer testimony?"

"Just Leonard and his daughter's therapist."

"How about the plaintiff? Was she going to call any witnesses?"

"Just the therapist and the daughter."

"Jillian."

"Right. A truly unfortunate human being."

"How so?"

Andy shook his head with sadness or at least with sympathy. "Jillian Wints is the most miserable individual I've ever seen, I think. Totally depressed, totally mercurial, totally suggestible, and totally victimized by this so-called feminist therapist who's convinced Jillian that everyone's to blame for her problems but Jillian."

"What does Jillian do for a living?"

"Works in a bookstore on Laguna, but only part-time. Mostly she borrows money from her mother, who in turn gets it from her father."

"Where does she live?"

"Why do you . . . oh. You're going to try to see her."

"Yep."

"I'd be more comfortable if you got that information from her lawyer."

"I tried that already. She wouldn't give me the time of day."

Andy avoided my glance.

"So where does she *live*, Andy? Your ethical comfort level is not my primary concern at this point."

"I don't know if I—"

"I don't have time to beg for this shit; just tell me where she is." My voice chilled the room as effectively as had the war chants of the men who had carried the weapons on the walls into battle a century ago.

I knew he would yield and he did. "Jillian has an apartment on Greenwich, just off Union." He gave me the number.

"That's not far from her lawyer."

"It's not far from her therapist either. She's on Union, too."

"What's her name?"

"Danielle Derwinski. She has an office across from the Metro Theater."

"She's a psychiatrist?"

He shook his head. "Feminist counselor, is how she bills herself."

"Ph.D.?"

"M.A."

It looked like I was going to be spending some time haunting Union Street. "About the lawyer," I said. "Mindy Cartson."

"What about her?"

"She didn't seem like a shyster to me."

"I didn't say she was."

"You said the claim was bogus."

"It is. But Mindy Cartson is a true believer. Anything women say is right; anything men say is either a deliberate lie or an unwitting denial. Mindy Cartson truly believes that Leonard Wints abused her client when she was a small child."

"And you're sure he didn't."

Andy reddened. "If I wasn't, I wouldn't have been in that courtroom."

I was about to ask the basis for his opinion when I remembered that Leonard Wints's veracity wasn't anything I needed to establish.

I stood up and walked to the window. The lights of Berkeley were beginning to twinkle on, as though someone had poked little holes in the city streets, allowing access to a subterranean light source. The traffic was the usual sludge, carriages of people fleeing the night stalkers of the inner city for the more tranquil and tranquilized inhabitants of the bedroom communities. The waters of the bay looked calm and collected; I wondered if Charley could see them from the jail.

"Here's my question, Andy," I said as I turned back toward him and crossed my arms. "Why the hell did Charley give a damn about this case?"

"I don't know."

"He never talked to you about it?"

"Never. Not even indirectly. I haven't seen Charley in months."

"And Leonard Wints never mentioned him?"

"No."

"Or anyone else involved in the case?"

He shook his head.

"The police never investigated the abuse charge?"

"Not that I know of. A civil action only."

"Okay, tell me more about your guy. Somewhere in his biography there has to be a link to Charley."

"What exactly do you want to know, Marsh? Because I'm not sure I can divulge—"

"He's dead, Andy. The privilege died with him."

"I know, but—"

"But nothing." I didn't try to keep the heat out of my voice. "Don't dance with me on this, Andy. Charley's behind bars in San Bruno and who knows what might happen to him down there. I need to come up with a defense, or at least a basis for bail, and to do that I need to know why he did what he did."

Andy bit back. "I'd give some serious consideration to a defense of insanity, if I were him. If you'd been there, you'd know how *crazy*—"

I was impatient and I let it show. "That's not for me to decide or you either. Jake Hattie is handling the legal stuff but he needs something to work with. So come on. Was Wints ever arrested? Did he have business or personal problems? Did he have any dealings with the cops at all?"

Andy leaned back in his chair and clasped his hands behind his head, implicitly calling a truce. "I spent most of the morning trying to think how Charley might be involved and I really haven't come up with anything. It's still a mystery to me."

"No domestic disputes? No traffic beefs? No dealing in illegal substances?"

"By my client? No. Nothing. Leonard Wints was a straight arrow."

"Then let's start at the beginning. Family, friends, business, clubs, the whole thing. If I have to talk to everyone in the city to get to the bottom of this, that's what I'm going to do."

Andy sighed. "Don't quote me on any of this. Okay?"

"Fine."

He looked out the window, then looked back. "Leonard was a city kid. Parents had a mom-and-pop grocery on the corner of Bush and Larkin; Leonard grew up in an apartment at Bush and Polk. Went to Lowell High, then to Berkeley on scholarship. Met a guy there who was a fanatic about pastry, and since Leonard knew something about the grocery business, they had enough contacts to start a small company that supplied bread and fresh pastry to groceries and restaurants all over the bay. His buddy was the baker; Leonard handled the marketing. They didn't make millions, but he made a nice living.

The bakery was down on Bluxome, by the Caltrains Depot. Bluxome Bread is what they called it."

"I remember it. Good stuff."

"Yeah."

"So how about the family?"

"Leonard married his college girlfriend, had two daughters, Jillian and Sandy, then divorced when the girls were in college. Several years later, he married a wonderful woman named Catherine and moved to Jordan Park. Leonard sold the business five years ago to the Langendorf people for big money; he still went to the office but only on a consulting basis. He was pretty much taking it easy till this lawsuit came along."

"The new wife upset about the lawsuit?"

"Of course she was."

"How do she and the stepdaughters get along?"

"Just adequately."

"How about the ex-wife? What does she say about the abuse?"

"She says she has no knowledge on the subject."

"But not that it didn't happen."

"She's not that strong about it but that's because she has lots of resentment left from the divorce. It's clear she wouldn't have minded seeing Leonard roughed up a little in court."

"Where does she live?"

"She rents a place on the Filbert Steps."

"How about the other daughter?"

"Sandy married a doctor. They live on Stanyan out by the Med Center. Great couple."

"Was she abused as well?"

"She says not."

"So in effect she's backing Daddy."

"That's right. It's the only good thing that happened to Leonard through all of this, Sandy's faith in him."

I thought over what Andy'd said. "What'd you find out about the therapist that made you decide to use her as a witness?"

Andy smiled. "Let's just say we were prepared to show that Ms. Derwinski's credentials are suspect—master's in counseling from Idaho State—and her practice is totally biased—calls herself a feminist therapist and refuses to counsel men—and her advice is predictable— at least four other clients have filed suit for recovered memory of childhood sexual abuse."

"You're not a big fan of Danielle's."

"No." Andy rubbed his face as though the experience of the past twenty-four hours was a smudge that could be wiped away like soot. "You've shot someone before, haven't you, Marsh? You shot Roland Nelson."

I nodded.

"And you've been shot yourself. That time up by Broadway."

"Yep."

"Did you ever get over being involved in something like that?"

"Not completely."

Andy nodded morosely. "I didn't think so."

CHAPTER
9

THE FILBERT STEPS ZIG DOWN THE EASTERN SLOPE OF TELE-graph Hill and constitute the only means of travel from top to bottom on that side of the promontory. The top half of the slope is a nest of private dwellings; the rest of the way down, it's a steep cliff. At the top the steps are wooden and rotting, overgrown with weeds and wild-flowers, but they nevertheless provide the only access to the funky little houses that cling like ice climbers to the side of the hill and boast the finest views in the city from a structure made of wood. At the bottom the steps are made of steel, with no claim to charm at all.

As I walked up the steps from Sansome Street, I had to make way for two guys lugging some Sheetrock to a remodel project high on the hill above me, still on the job in early evening, logging time and a half. They were already puffing and panting and cursing and there was a high pile of sheets left to go. I was puffing and panting myself and I wasn't carrying anything heavier than my waistline.

When I'd called to make sure she'd be home, I'd implied I was someone official. What I said was "My name is Tanner. I've been assigned to investigate the death of your ex-husband. I'd like to stop by and ask a few questions. Just routine. Background for the file."

Misrepresenting myself as a cop could cost me my license, of course. But I'd kept it fuzzy, and true in the literal meaning of the words, so I thought I'd be all right even if the woman decided to raise a ruckus.

The former Mrs. Leonard Wints lived on Napier Lane, on the top floor of a board-and-batten duplex that apparently stayed put only with lots of support from its neighbors. The knock on the door made the house shake. When I thought of the distance we would travel if something separated the house from its footings, I decided to make my visit short and sweet.

The woman who came to the door looked as though she lay awake nights worrying about the eventuality I'd just contemplated. Her hands trembled, her eyelids fluttered, and her hair looked tossed with salad forks. As though symptomatic of her insomnia, her body was thin to the point of alarm. The black leotard that encased it from neck to ankle was uninterrupted by curves or caves or bulges except for the crowns at her hips and the ripples at her ribs.

"I meditate," she began without prompt, as if that would explain everything.

"I'm Tanner. We spoke on the phone."

"Don't you have a badge or something?"

I glanced up and down the narrow lane. "Is that wise? Having me flash a badge in front of the neighbors?"

A trembling hand traveled to a quivering lip. "I suppose not."

"If we can step inside, I'll try to be brief."

I looked beyond her at the staircase that led to the second story. "Follow me," she said finally. "Would you like some herbal tea?"

"No, thanks." If I thought she had any handy, I would have asked for a beer—the thought of hauling all that Sheetrock made me thirsty.

The inside stairs led to a living room that was sparsely

furnished primarily in wicker and rattan, with oak floors and pine shelving and art on the wall that was evocative of delusional states of mind. A big pillow lay like a soft blue rock on the floor in front of the large front window; I guessed it was where she meditated. What she saw when she opened her eyes were the Levi Strauss offices and the Fog City diner below, then the piers of the waterfront and the edge of Treasure Island alongside a strip of the Bay Bridge, then Berkeley and Albany and El Cerrito on the far side of the water, shimmering in the distance like dream states.

When I walked to a wicker chair and sat down, the house wobbled under my weight. It made my heart do a tap dance but it didn't make the former Mrs. Wints any more nervous than she was when I got there.

She lowered herself to the pillow as though its hide was as prickly as cactus and crossed her legs in the lotus position. It's easy to do when you don't have much fat or muscle; I couldn't get in the lotus position with a crowbar.

"How can I help you . . . Sergeant? Is that what you are?"

"That's close enough. But you can call me Marsh."

"Marsh. For Marshall. The Marshall Plan."

"Chief Justice Marshall, not General Marshall. And the only plan I have right now is to get back down those steps without having a heart attack."

"They are a chore, aren't they? I seldom go out anymore. Luckily, most of my needs can be delivered."

"By Jillian?"

Her hand rose to her lip again, like a hummingbird on its way to a trumpet vine. "Jillian seldom comes here. We haven't been close, especially since this lawsuit business. Apparently she intended to sue me as well as Leonard until her lawyer advised her against it. Mothers aren't as easy targets as fathers, apparently."

I got out my notebook and flipped it open, the way cops do in the movies. "When's the last time you saw your ex-husband?"

"Why I . . . let's see. A month ago, I suppose. He came by to ask me to assist his defense of the lawsuit."

"And what did you tell him?"

"That I was remaining neutral."

"Could you have helped him if you wanted to?"

"I don't know; I'm not sure what kind of help he was looking for. I wasn't in a position to swear it never happened, if that's what you mean."

It was close enough. "Did you keep in regular touch with your husband after the divorce?"

She pivoted on the pillow and looked out across the bay. "Shall I be frank?"

"Please do."

"I keep in touch when I need money. Leonard keeps in touch when he wants me to do something to curb some aspect of Jillian's behavior."

"What kind of behavior was that?"

"Hysterical rages; depressive funks; desperate alliances with men who exploit her for money then quickly discard her. My daughter has been a trial in almost every respect you can imagine, Mr. Tanner."

That seemed like possible evidence of abuse to me, but as Mindy Cartson had pointed out, what did I know about it? "How long have you been divorced?" I asked.

"Ten years."

"And how often did your husband want you to do something about Jillian?"

"At least once a month."

I couldn't keep from asking. "Even though you're remaining neutral, do you think Jillian's claims have merit?"

She swiveled away from the window toward me. Her arms crossed above her stunted breasts and her hands made fists that lolled like mollusks upon her narrow thighs. "You mean did I marry a sex pervert and live with him for twenty years while he was violating the flesh of my flesh? No, Mr. Tanner. I don't believe that happened."

"But you weren't going to testify for him."

"Only because I had nothing to say. On the one hand, I never saw anything improper take place. On the other, Jillian is profoundly disturbed. I can't swear that nothing untoward occurred during the time she lived under our roof, although I doubt very much that it was sexual. In the circumstances, it seemed wise to remain above the fray."

I smiled. "That's nice work if you can get it. But sometimes a subpoena gets in the way."

She unhooked her feet and drew her heels against the backs of her thighs so she could rest her chin on her knees. "What I don't understand is why you're here. There's no mystery about who killed Leonard, surely. The papers say all kinds of people saw your colleague shoot him."

I flipped a page in my notebook. "We do have a strong case, but Mr. Sleet isn't talking and we haven't come up with an explanation of why he did what he did. The DA likes to give his jury a reason, particularly if the suspect pleads not guilty by reason of insanity."

Her eyes widened. "Is is that what he's doing? Claiming he was insane?"

"Not yet, but it's still a possibility. We're hoping you can tell us that Lieutenant Sleet had reason to be angry with your ex-husband. Something that would make it look more like vengeance than madness."

She looked at me for several seconds. "Do you know Officer Sleet, Mr. Tanner?"

"Yes, I do."

"Is he a friend?"

"If he was a friend, I'd have been taken off the case. What can you tell me, Mrs. Wints?"

"Nothing."

Like the small sloop that was bobbing out in the bay, I jibed in another direction. I leaned forward and asked the only question I could think of that might yield the glimmerings of a motive, and maybe even an excuse. "Was Jillian your husband's biological daughter?"

She frowned. "You mean was she adopted?"

"Yes."

"No. Of course not. She was his. Ours."

I put away the notebook. "This is important, Mrs. Wints. It will be to everyone's advantage for you to be absolutely candid. Is there any question of paternity at all? Could Charley Sleet be the father of your child?"

"You mean did I . . . was I . . . ?" She looked around the room, her nose wrinkled as though she smelled something burning. When her eyes returned to mine, they were as bright as the sea in the sun. "Just because I pursue an unconventional spirituality does not mean I'm promiscuous. I was faithful to my husband in every minute of our marriage. Although at his insistence the vows we took were Christian, I honored them as though they flowed from my own belief system."

"And what system is that?"

She hugged herself tightly, as though the truths in her life were all served cold, then wriggled farther into the pillow. "It's a system of my own devising. Since I doubt very much that it's relevant to your inquiry, and since I don't sense any real interest in the subject on your part, I'd rather not go into it."

"Suit yourself," I said. "Was your husband as faithful to you as you were to him?"

"No."

"Did it bother you?"

"Of course it did."

"How did you deal with it?"

"I spent as much of his money as I could, I overindulged in every way I could imagine until I gained eighty pounds, and when that didn't erase my shame and humiliation, I divorced him and renounced worldly goods." She slid her hands along her flanks. "Meditation is so much more satisfying than sex. I don't know why more people don't pursue it."

Like a lot of other faiths, this one seemed to have essentially pathetic origins. "Why did you wait so long to divorce your husband?" I asked.

"Because I thought the girls needed a father."

"Then why did you do it at all?"

"Because their father stopped loving them not long after he stopped loving me."

"Why did he stop loving them?"

"I don't know."

"Why didn't you ask him?"

"By that time, words had become weapons—every time he spoke to me, it hurt. After a while, I couldn't endure it any longer." Her eyes glazed and her lips thinned. "Jillian says it began when she was eight. Can you imagine? Having sex with an eight-year-old child? There are people in the world who do, I know, but what kind of mind would . . . ?" She couldn't finish the sentence and I didn't want her to.

"Can you tell me what role Charley Sleet played in all this?" I asked when her anguish had cooled.

She blinked and looked at me. "I know of none."

"You never heard his name before the shooting?"

"No."

"Back before your divorce, did you or your family have any dealings with the police at all?"

"I don't think so. Why would we?"

"Domestic disturbance. Burglary. Lost dog. People call cops for lots of reasons."

"I don't recall any such event."

"Were your daughters ever in trouble with the law?"

"They were disciplined at school on occasion, but nothing that involved the police." She unhooked her legs and stood up. "Wouldn't you have a record of this, Mr. Tanner? If you really are a policeman?"

I shrugged it off. "Sometimes an officer investigates a complaint but decides not to write up a report. Mr. Sleet, in particular, was prone to informal suggestion rather than official sanction. And juvenile records are often sealed, as you know."

"Well, if any of that happened, I wasn't aware of it."

I stood up and faced her. This time I tried a grin and a nudge. "You can tell me, Mrs. Wints. Weren't you and Charley Sleet lovers?"

Not for the first time, my charm was ineffective; her lips folded in firm rebuke. "The circumstances are crude enough without you making them more so. I'm afraid I must ask you to leave."

I fished in my pocket for the snapshots of the infant on the blanket I'd found in Charley's garden and held one out to her. "Isn't this Jillian?"

She glanced at it and shook her head. "No."

"Are you sure?"

"A mother knows her child, Mr. Tanner. You can't be much of a policeman if you don't even know that."

Her voice was thick with disgust. She stood by the door till I used it.

CHAPTER

10

I GRABBED A BITE AT A PLACE IN NORTH BEACH THAT Charley and I had never frequented, so my mind could stay oriented toward the future instead of lolling in the past. But a half hour of pondering didn't get me much beyond the dead ends I'd encountered so far, so before heading home I stopped at City Lights to browse in the groves of psychology. After being amazed by the number of titles on the subject of childhood sexual abuse, I bought a couple that focused on the area of interest, which was the recovery of repressed memories of such trauma, then trudged up the hill to my apartment.

Before delving into the evening's research, I called the Wints's other daughter, Sandy. When she came on the line, I told her who I was and what I did for a living.

"This isn't about the malpractice case, is it?"

I suppressed a laugh at the glimpse of a private terror. "No, this is about your father."

"Oh. That. What about him?"

"I'm looking for information on the man who killed him."

"Why?"

"So I can learn why it happened."

"Why do you care?"

"Because someone is paying me to."

"Who?"

"Can't say."

"Well, I'm not talking. Not to you, not to Jillian, not to her lawyer, not to anyone. The idea that my father was having sex with my sister is so . . . well, let's just say I'm not talking."

"What about Mr. Sleet?"

"What about him?"

"How is he connected to your family?"

"I haven't the faintest idea."

"I've been told you and Jillian were adopted."

Her laugh was brutal. "Whoever told you that is full of shit. God. Can anyone say *anything* in this world and get away with it? Next we'll be lepers, I suppose."

"Then have you heard Mr. Sleet's name in any connection at all?"

"The man murdered my father. Isn't that connection enough for you?"

She hung up with a bang. I fixed a fresh drink and returned to my chair and asked the question I'd asked Wally Briscoe over omelettes that morning: Had Charley seemed different of late? The more I thought about it, the more I realized I hadn't *seen* him much lately. He'd canceled a couple of lunch dates, skipped the last two poker sessions, and begged off a weekend jaunt to San Jose to watch hockey. As far as I could recall, for at least two months, roughly since Christmas, my conversations with Charley had been confined to the phone.

His excuse was always work, of course. Since crime is the only phenomenon as inexhaustible as Charley's energies, and since at that point I hadn't known there was a woman who might compromise his devotion to his job, work always seemed a good excuse. But now I wondered. Was it my imagination, or did Charley seem less immersed in the world the last time I saw him? Could he, in fact, have fallen in love and become happy without my realizing it? If that was what had happened to him, and I hoped it had, the engine of the transformation would seem to be one Marjie Finnerty. I called her again but got the message I'd gotten when I'd called from Charley's house, courtesy of the redial button.

I fixed another drink and retired to my books, both of which were devoted to the phenomenon of the recovered memory of childhood sexual abuse. One was pro, the other con. One cited case after case of tormented young women who suffered a range of afflictions—depression to bulimia to frigidity and worse—and who experienced a sudden surge of repressed memory in response to a seemingly benign stimulus. Over time, these women would narrate, in increasingly vivid detail, incidents of sexual and psychic abuse, usually committed by a member of their family, most often by their father. Once brought to light and reacted to with appropriate outrage—once the youthful feelings of pain and shame and confusion were allowed to be expressed—the women reported a lightening of burdens that had hobbled them for years, and progress toward inner peace. The sheer quantity of incident and anecdote collected by the authors made it difficult to doubt that such transformations had occurred, and in large numbers.

The antithesis, offered by people of equally lofty credentials and experience, claimed that the mind didn't work that way. These writers assert that the phenomenon of repression of traumatic memory lacks scientific support, that such experiences are not buried in the brain only to emerge years later with perfect accuracy in the way the believers claim. Rather, a continuing pattern of abuse is usually recalled from the date it occurs, and over time its particulars are blurred and altered, often in significant particulars, just as less inflammatory and more recent memories are.

In contrast to the unreserved acceptance of their

patients' claims by the pro-abuse counselors, the skeptics point to the phenomenon of false memory, in which wholly fanciful recollections have been created by suggestion in experimental settings, in both adults and children. The implication was that suggestions by therapists who look for abuse and expect to find it, and push their patients until they start speaking in those terms, can create entirely fantastic recollections that lack foundation in fact. In extreme cases, the prodding of therapists has led people to spin out increasingly bizarre descriptions of events that could not have occurred— satanic rituals of gang rape and human sacrifice, for example. Since such bizarre memories almost always lack empirical evidence to support them—scars of abuse are absent even when the claim is of ritual sexual torment—the contras find no support for the claim that a recovered memory of sexual abuse can surface years after the trauma took place.

What was amazing to me was that expert opinion could differ so widely on such an important issue. At one extreme were therapists who found sexual abuse at the root of every claim of dysfunction that walked through their door. At the other were those who argued that recovered memories of abuse long after the fact are never accurate, no matter the suffering of the victim or the relief of symptoms after the recollection is voiced. In the middle were those who said that it didn't matter—if a patient believes she was abused and if in the process of discussing "recovered memories" she experiences therapeutic improvement, what difference does it make if the memories are real or false?

As with most controversies, the dispute has moved to the courts, where the tide seemed to have turned against the women who claimed to be victims. In Napa, one accused father won a malpractice verdict of half a million dollars against the therapist whom he charged had created memories of abuse in his daughter that were false. The case that brought the phenomenon to public attention in the first place—a woman who accused her father of murdering her childhood friend when she was eight years old, based on a recovered memory of the incident—was reversed by a federal court because the jury wasn't told that all of the facts recalled by the daughter, based on a purportedly recovered memory, had been available in media reports of the crime.

On the other hand, provable cases of incest and abuse, cases that have been all too well remembered over a period of many years and are supported by both physical evidence and witnesses, have reached epidemic proportions, suggesting that at least some of the recovered memory cases must surely be based on fact. But apparently no one can agree on how to tell the difference between true and false in this heated atmosphere. The dilemma has existed from at least the time of Freud, who initially felt that women's hysterical neuroses arose from childhood instances of incestual seduction, then changed to a theory that women only *wished* for such relations to have occurred, an amendment that many women now regard as treason.

By the time I finished reading, I wasn't much further along than when I started when it came to deciding what had really happened to Jillian Wints. But whatever the validity of her claim, I didn't see how it could relate to my friend unless Charley Sleet, and not Leonard Wints, was her father, something that her mother and sister quite adamantly denied. It was time to talk to Jillian.

The first thing in the morning, I drove to the Greenwich Street address that Andy Potter had given me. Jillian's apartment was on the top floor of a converted town house. There was music coming from inside—something airy and monotonous and New Age—but the shades were drawn and the windows were closed and no one came to the door when I knocked. When I dialed her number on my cell phone, a phone company robot told me the number had been disconnected.

Next I drove by the bookstore on Laguna and asked if Jillian was expected at work any time that day. A man who was hairless except for his beard told me she was on extended medical leave. Blocked at every turn, I opted to call on the widow.

CHAPTER

11

THE WINTS HOUSE WAS ON COMMONWEALTH AVENUE NEAR
the Church of St. Gregory the Illuminator in a tranquil
section of the city known as Jordan Park. It was a large
boxy structure, with wide wood trim, beige stucco walls,
a deeply shaded porch beneath the two front dormers,
and a garage to the side in the back. The lawn was
immaculately tended, with an ornamental plum in one
corner and a sculpted shrub in the other. Only the black
drape above the door reminded me to be sorry for
intruding like this.

Which is exactly what I said when the widow answered
my ring. She was wearing a simple gray dress and
sensible black shoes and the hair on her head was wound
as tight as her nerves. Her eyes were dyed to match her
outfit but they were clear and inquiring, not clouded
with grief. She seemed aristocratic by nature, not by
affectation, with strong bloodlines and good manners
that held up even in trying times. I liked it that she was
brave enough to talk to a stranger two days after her
husband had been murdered.

She stuck out a hand when I introduced myself. "I'm Catherine Wints." Her hand was the first sign of stress—despite her apparent savoir faire, I'd felt warmer flesh on fish.

When I repeated my apology for intruding, she waved it away and glanced back toward the house. "Please. It's a relief to have an excuse to be out of there for a while. May we sit over on the glider? For some reason, my family doesn't feel I should be seen at a time like this." She smiled gamely, and perhaps a little flirtatiously. "If you tell me something that will make me cry, I'll have to go back inside. I don't want to upset the neighbors."

"I'll try not to do that," I said truthfully.

She met my eye and smiled. "It may be easier than you think."

She led me to an old-fashioned glider, covered with a flowered oilcloth and a tattered blanket, hidden behind a web of wisteria lying in wait for spring. We sat side by side and began to rock, ever so slowly, ever so pleasantly. The breeze rattled the vines and the smell of baking bread slid out of the house and joined us. It was cool and quiet and peaceful; even the squeak in the glider's joints was musical.

"Who are you, Mr. Tanner?" she asked after a moment.

"I'm a detective."

"A policeman, you mean?"

"A private detective. I'm investigating your husband's death."

"Why?"

I opted to remain obscure. "I have a client who's hired me to look into it."

She thought it over. "One of the lawyers, I imagine. They're the only ones who would think of such a thing as a private detective."

I shrugged. "I'm afraid I can't reveal the name of my principal, Mrs. Wints."

"Call me Catherine."

"Only if you call me Marsh."

She nodded to confirm the deal, then pushed with her foot to keep us going. "This is nice," she said after a while.

"Yes, it is. This is a lovely home. I always wanted one just like it."

"What kept you from it?"

I laughed. "Money, mostly."

"We paid seventy thousand for this back in 1974. My first husband and I, that is."

"It must be worth ten times that now."

"Much more, I'm told. Several realtors called once the obituary appeared."

"They tend to do that."

"Human behavior is so frequently disappointing, don't you find?" she said. I didn't know if she was talking about the realtors, or me, or her dead husband, or Charley, or herself. Maybe all of us. "It's quite like a cave back here, isn't it?" she went on. "I used to explore caves when I was a child in Kentucky. When something like this happens, that's what I think of doing—finding a cave to hide in. Away from the peekers and poachers and gossips. Away from the ones who claim to love you but enjoy your humiliation nonetheless and hope to turn it to profit." Her eyes traveled briefly to the house.

"Are you talking about your stepdaughter's lawsuit, Mrs. Wints?"

"Among other phenomena."

"The lawsuit isn't really my concern. We don't have to talk about it if you'd rather not."

"Talking about it isn't the problem. *Thinking* about it is the problem."

"I assume you believe Leonard was innocent of the charges."

She hesitated. "Not necessarily."

I recrossed my legs and angled my torso so I could look at her. "Are you saying he did it, Mrs. Wints?"

She stared at the street as though bad wrecks and

terrible riots had occurred out there. "I don't know if he did or didn't. How could I? It's not the kind of thing that takes place at the dinner table, after all."

"You could know if he told you about it."

She shook her head. "He didn't. He denied it, in fact."

"Or if he'd done something similar to others."

"I know of no such behavior."

"Then what makes you equivocal?"

She shoved the glider several times before she answered. "Leonard wasn't a believable man. He lied about many things over the years; big things and little things. He wasn't a bad man but he was a man who was very afraid of being criticized. Of being considered ignorant. Of being found to be wrong. Almost invariably, he said what he thought people wanted to hear, rather than what he truly believed. It made him look ridiculous, at times, trying to bluff his way out of sticky situations, and even those that weren't so sticky." She looked at me defiantly. "Men are so very vain, don't you think?"

"Some men," I amended. "The lawsuit must have been devastating for both of you."

"More me than him, somehow. Leonard seemed to be energized by it, actually. His anger made him more dynamic than he'd been since before he sold the business. His friends rallied around him, too, whereas most women saw me as this pathetic little creature who was too stupid to know that she'd married a pervert."

A car rumbled by, its driver glancing briefly at the porch, then quickly looking away. Catherine Wints laughed, lowly and cynically, as though she knew a secret about him.

"What do you think of Jillian?" I asked after a moment.

"Have you met her?"

"No."

"I think she's stark raving mad."

"Why?"

"Because of what she did. Even if Leonard did what she claimed he did, why would she make it public? What possible good will it do for her to parade this filth through the courts? Doesn't she know she'll never be the same again? Doesn't she know they'll never let her live it down?"

I tended to agree with her and told her so. "I'm looking for the connection between Charley Sleet, the man who shot him, and your husband, or your step-daughter, or you, or anyone else involved in the case. Can you provide one?"

She shook her head. "I'm sorry."

"Think about it, please. Mr. Sleet is a policeman. He lives on Upper Market. His wife's name was Flora. He's active in community action programs, particularly down in the Tenderloin. Does any of that ring a bell?"

"I'm afraid not."

It was the answer that I'd expected her to give. What I didn't expect was the hesitation that came before she delivered it.

"I'm an experienced investigator," I said after we'd rocked a moment more.

"I'm sure you are."

"I've developed a pretty good instinct for when some-one is lying to me."

"I imagine you have."

"My instinct just poked me in the ribs."

Her tone became blasé. "Did it?"

"So now I'm wondering what you and Charley Sleet had in common."

"I'm sure I couldn't tell you."

"Did your husband ever tell you that Jillian was adopted?"

The glider screeched to a halt. "Adopted? No. She wasn't, was she?"

"I don't know for sure. But I think it's possible."

She thought it over. "If she was, it might explain some things."

"Like what?"

"Her behavior, for one. She was very unlike Leonard."

"How so?"

"Jillian was so very extreme. Leonard was so very . . . normal."

"Except for the lies."

"I think lies by men are *quite* normal, don't you, Mr. Tanner?"

"I don't think men have a monopoly on them."

"I suppose not. But men's lies do far more damage."

We rocked a while longer. "I'm going to have to talk to Jillian," I said after a minute.

"That's of no interest to me one way or another. But I'd be surprised if she proves to be helpful."

"Why?"

"She seems to be impaled on fantasy. She's been mesmerized by this Derwinski person. Nothing she says is remotely trustworthy."

"Ms. Derwinski is the therapist."

She nodded. "Although she seems to deal more in torment than therapy."

"I'll be talking to her as well, of course, but I'm sure she won't help me get to Jillian."

"No. I suppose not."

"I haven't been able to find her. I've tried her apartment and her job but there's no trace. Plus, her phone's been disconnected."

She crossed her arms. "I don't know if I should say anything."

"I just want to talk to her. Not about sexual abuse—it's going to take a skilled counselor to get to the bottom of that. Just about why Charley Sleet would want to kill her father. I promise that's all I'll go into. Give me some background, some leverage, something."

Catherine Wints kept rocking.

"If you don't talk to me, I'm going to start digging into the whole Wints story," I said heavily.

"You're *already* digging, aren't you?"

"I haven't dug around you. Until now."

She didn't say anything but she was worried.

"If you think you've been under a microscope before,

let me assure you you haven't seen anything yet. You could end up a witness in a murder trial."

She closed her eyes. "It would be unfortunate if that came to pass."

"So what do you have to tell me?"

She stopped the glider with her foot. "Nothing, I'm afraid. I have secrets, matters I pray will remain private, but they have nothing to do with this."

"A week from now you'll wish you'd talked to me."

She stood up and strolled toward the door, toward whoever was waiting for her in the house, leaving me swinging on the glider.

"I've wished for many things in my life, Mr. Tanner," she said softly when she'd grasped the knob with her elegant hand. "Very few of my wishes have been granted and the ones that have tended to create disillusion." She gestured at her surroundings. "It might not seem like it, but I've endured a great deal of suffering over the years. I am looking desperately for signs that it's come to an end."

She opened the door and looked back a final time. "Jillian used to spend hours sitting on the Marina Green, watching the boats go by. I imagine she still does."

"Do you have a photo of her I could borrow?"

"I do but I won't be able to give it to you. Once I go back in that house, I will not be allowed to return. My family is easily scandalized."

I discovered I was sad that she was leaving me and taking her secrets with her. I wondered what they were. I wondered if it was smart or foolish of me to take her word that they didn't have anything to do with Charley.

CHAPTER

12

I HAD NO IDEA WHAT SOMEONE IN JILLIAN WINTS'S POSITION would do in her circumstances—mourn and withdraw or party till the cows came home because her tormentor had been dispatched to his doom. I must have been hoping for the latter reaction, though, because a half hour after Catherine Wints went back to her house and her family, I was loitering on the fringe of the Marina Green, keeping an eye on the benches and walkways and playing fields on the chance that Jillian would show up for another tonic from a look at the bay and the boats.

An hour later, I was beginning to think I'd have to look elsewhere, except I'd already tried the only elsewheres I knew of. I looked at the boats myself for a while, remembering the last time I'd been on one, courtesy of my friend Russell Jorgensen, thinking with pleasure about the child who had been a by-product of my involvement in that case and was now the shiniest badge on my life.

When Jillian finally showed, what I recognized was less her physiology than her psychology—Andy Potter had said Jillian Wints was the unhappiest person he'd ever seen, and the woman trudging across the grass of the Green in my direction fit that description to an unfortunate T.

Her gray leotard was overlaid with men's boxer shorts and a plaid flannel vest that didn't disguise the fact that she was rope-thin, with stumps and bumps of bone protruding to a disturbing degree from chest, shoulders, elbows, and knees—Jillian made her mother look portly. Her eyes were countersunk into her skull, so far removed as to seem diseased. Her skin was pocked and bruised and decorated with an unattractive combination of makeup and tattoos. Her hair was tangled and bristly and forbidding. The shorts and vest were formless and outsized, glen plaid clouds within which she hoped she could hide from the world. A tattoo of a black rose climbed the side of her arm, complete with stem and thorns, and one of a narrow chain circled her neck like a noose. As I moved to intercept her, I could see the line of black drops that fell off the rosebud. I wasn't sure if they were blood or tears or dewdrops. I don't suppose it mattered.

Her gaze was down, her focal point barely in front of her feet. As she heard me approach, she raised a furtive glance and seemed to flinch, as though she expected me to strike her or be critical of her conduct in some way. When she saw I wasn't menacing, she edged by as if I were a maharajah and she were an untouchable, scraping against an adjacent light post to put maximum distance between us.

I waited for her to pass, then turned and watched her go. The sag in her shoulders and the slump in her posture suggested she hadn't slept for days. The scuff of her heels through the grass was indicative of self-loathing and despair. Andy Potter was right; Jillian Wints was a mess.

"Miss Wints?" I called out.

I might as well have taken a shot at her—she spasmed so badly she almost fell down. When she recovered her balance, she kept moving at a faster pace.

I followed her at a distance. "Jillian? May I talk to you a minute? About what happened in court on Tuesday?"

She didn't stop and didn't look back but she did shake her head in refusal.

"Please. It won't take long. I just need some information."

Her arms pumped for more speed. Her gait became awkward and ludicrous, a gangly new giraffe scampering across the veld in Doc Martens and baggy black tights.

Her destination seemed to be a portable plastic rest room plopped on the northeast edge of the Green. I hurried to catch her before she reached it. I didn't doubt that once inside, she would stay there till I left the area, even if it took a month.

This time I opted for truth. "The man who shot your father was my best friend. I need to know why he did it. I need to know why he gave you that gift."

That stopped her flight so fast she staggered from the shift in momentum. She was paralyzed with uncertainty for a moment, hands fiddling with her shorts, eyes glancing up and down the greenbelt at the joggers and skaters and bikers who were ignoring imperfects like us.

"You call that a *gift?* Sabotage is more like it." Her voice was raw and disparaging, as though we'd been arguing for hours. Her eyes had turned wild and peremptory, her body was tensed against an anticipated assault.

Jolted by her own outburst, she backed against a car fender to reassemble her mood. Her confusion gave me time to join her.

I stuck out my hand when I reached her. "My name is Tanner. Can I buy you some coffee? Or lunch? I'd like to talk for a few minutes."

She blinked and panted and looked everywhere but at me. "I can't. I have to be somewhere."

"Are you still at the bookstore?"

She inhaled as though I'd broached a deep secret. "Who have you been talking to about me? No one's supposed to *talk* about me." She was about to run but I made sure she knew that I would do what it took to stop her.

I smiled as warmly as I can manage; it's not my best trick. "I've been talking to anyone who would listen."

"Are you police? Are you going to arrest me for something?"

"Do you deserve to be arrested for something?"

She shook her head. "But that's what they do. They do everything in their power to silence us."

"Silence who?"

She dropped her arms and thrust her jaw, which was pointed enough to draw blood. "The survivors."

"Survivors of what?"

"Of childhood sexual abuse." Her chest swelled; her fist clenched. She seemed proud of her precision.

When I didn't dispute her, she decided to elaborate. The words were as rehearsed as the Pledge of Allegiance. "No one dares hear the truth; no one wants to see our anger dance. White male America cannot stand for its crimes against children to become known. Each truth teller is in jeopardy."

"From whom?"

"From assassins like you and that policeman."

She started to walk away, then stopped. "Anyway, my lawyer said I didn't have to talk to anyone if I didn't want to."

"Why wouldn't you want to talk about the man who went to jail for you? The man who removed the biggest obstacle in your life."

She was nonplussed by my rhetoric, but only momentarily. "You can't fool me. He is as much my enemy as you are."

Her hostility was puzzling. "But he must have believed what you said about your father. Why else would he have killed him?"

She shook her head with impatience. "To keep the case from proceeding, of course. Don't you see? Now I am silenced. My enemy is destroyed, so no one will hear my story. The forces of perversion have won once more. The woman cowers alone with her torment."

I felt like I was talking to an oracle, one with a single song. I examined her face more closely, looking for Charley or Flora or a combination of the two of them in there, but emaciation had reduced her features to the nub. It was like trying to find a family resemblance in a skeleton.

"Who was the policeman working for if he wasn't helping you?" I asked when my inspection was unavailing.

"The CMI, of course."

"The what?"

"The Corrected Memory Institute."

"What's that?"

"The deniers, the excusers, the aiders and abetters."

"How do they go about the aiding and abetting?"

"They call us liars or fantasists; they call our guides manipulators and exploiters; they call our pasts hysterical and unreal. They will not rest till we are silenced; they will not be satisfied unless our pain goes unrelieved and our life remains unbearable."

"And you think Mr. Sleet was working for them."

"Of course he was. My guide says that he was probably one of my ritual abusers himself."

"Charley?"

"If that is the man in the courtroom."

Her easy accusation made me furious. "If he wanted silence, why didn't he shoot *you?*"

I expected her to be frightened or insulted but instead she seemed delighted. "That would be too obvious. Don't you see the scheme? They pretend to love us. They pretend they want to help us; they pretend they seek the truth. They can't attack directly or their charade will be exposed, so to achieve their goals they block all means to relief. Mindy said it was happening already, that the deck was stacked against us."

"By relief you mean money? From the lawsuit?"

She shook her head vehemently. "It's not *about* money; it's *never* about money. But in this society money is the only way you can make yourself heard. The only way the system will let you use its power to heal and not destroy is if you want *money* from someone. *Then* they will listen. *Then* they will provide a forum."

"If it's not about money, then what's it about?"

"It's about admission and confession. Atonement and apology." She met my eyes for the first time. "It's about giving me my *life* back."

"And because of what Charley did you can't get it back?"

She blinked away a tear. "My guide says I can but it will take much longer. Except I don't know if I can *take* it much longer."

She shuddered so violently I thought she was going to collapse. I softened my tone and leaned against the car myself. "No one's abusing you now, are they, Jillian?"

"I'm abused every night of my life."

"By whom?"

"By my memories." She hugged herself as though her innards were septic and aflame, as though her memory was an infestation.

"Your guide is Danielle?" I asked when she seemed a little better.

She blinked and blushed. For a moment, I wondered if the alliance with her therapist were partly sexual. "Do you know her?" she asked eagerly.

"Not yet. But I'll need to speak with her."

"About me? She won't *talk* to you about me. She can't. It's the law."

"I don't need to know about you, I just need to know about Charley."

"She doesn't know anything about him."

"I thought you said she told you that he'd abused you."

"She said probably. He *probably* abused me."

"When did she say this?"

"Right afterward."

"In court?"

She nodded. "She was there to speak out, to publish my truth. That's why they sent him. Don't you see? If that other man hadn't grabbed the policeman, I'm sure he would have murdered Danielle as well."

I didn't know whether to laugh or cry. "Why did the CMI pick Charley to do their work? Did he know you from someplace? Did they think he could get to you easier?"

She shook her head. "They used him because he was an agent of the state. He could do what he did and get away with it. He was immune to the law, just like the others."

I wanted to tell her that Charley *was* the law, for me and for lots of people, but that didn't fit with her fantasy. "Did Danielle tell you anything else about him?"

"Just that they use the system to enforce the silence and hide behind it. They have people at all levels of power; the judges and the politicians are almost all abusers themselves. They will do anything to maintain their defenses."

I still didn't see a link to Charley, no matter what Jillian and her guide might think. "Were you abused in a ritual manner, Jillian?"

She lowered her eyes and nodded. "At the end. Before I got away, I was the plaything of my father and his friends."

"Do you know who the friends were?"

"I know the faces but not the names. I see them in my nightmares. I hear them seduce me; I feel them rape me; I smell them as they debase me with their urine and their excrement."

"Where are they now? These friends."

She shuddered. "Everywhere."

"Did these men abuse anyone else that you know? Your sister? Your friends?"

"I'm sure they did. They are never satisfied. They use children like parlor games, they play with us until they get bored, and then they pass us along to others until finally they dispose of us. I'm lucky I escaped before they slaughtered me."

"Did Charley Sleet know any of the other victims? Do you think he could have been trying to help them?"

"He was helping the CMI."

"The Corrected Memory Institute."

"Right."

"Who runs the CMI?"

"They are a worldwide organization because the abusers are in all nations and are in constant need of protection. Their directorate includes several famous heads of state. Here in the city, the chief terrorist is a man named Kirby Allison. His office is on Beale Street. He tried to get me to go there once, supposedly to help me. He was trying to dispose of me, I think."

"You mean kill you?"

She nodded.

"Did Charley say anything to you after he shot your father, Jillian?"

"No."

"Did he look at you? Smile? Frown? Nod? Anything at all that might indicate why he did it?"

She thrust herself away from the car. "I've told you why he did it. Now, really, I have to go."

"Can I tell your guide it's okay for her to talk to me?"

"She won't believe you."

"Why not?"

"You're a man. Why should she believe you? You're probably an abuser, too."

CHAPTER
13

I WAS NEAR UNION STREET ALREADY, AND SHE WOULD probably be coming back from lunch and might have some time to kill before her next appointment, so there was no reason not to try to see her. No reason at all, except my reluctance to confront someone I suspected was a liar, and a menace, and my enemy, the probable perpetrator of a charade that was wreaking havoc all around and had somehow ensnared Charley Sleet in its metafiction.

Her offices were difficult to locate. It took three passes before I finally figured out that the number I was looking for was down a covered alleyway that led to an inner courtyard that served as a showroom for an espresso bar and an upscale plant store. The plant store featured the type of stuff that looks like it grows on the bottom of an ocean or the top of a mountain, stuff that's weird and kind of creepy, stuff that makes you wonder.

The ceiling was a tangle of vines and hanging plants that seemed to drip with a form of translucent blood. A gentle waterfall seeped out of one wall and bubbled across some mossy stones before disappearing beneath a bank of ferns, the spitting image of an idyllic glade in some crevice of the rain forest. Flowers of all shapes and sizes and shades were arranged around several wrought-iron tables and chairs that looked to be cool and inviting. I expected to see Puck at any moment, dancing to the accompaniment of lutes and panpipes. That Danielle Derwinski's office opened onto such an exquisite environment suggested that after some time with her your inner world would become as soothing to you as the world outside her office.

The door to the waiting room was Dutch, its top panel opened to the pleasures of the pocket garden, the bottom locked against intruders. The secretary's desk was small and unobtrusive, as was the woman who sat behind it. Eyes closed, hands clasped and resting on the desk, she was listening intently to a headset that was clamped over her coiffure like some postmodern chapeau. When I buzzed the bell, she opened her eyes and looked at me, then pressed a button that let me in. As I neared the desk, she lurched for the keyboard and began to type furiously, as though the headset had just emitted the solution to Fermat's Theorem or a great recipe for quiche. I had to cough and carry on before she paid attention to me.

"Sorry," she said in a rush as she lifted the headset off her ears. "Are you from building management?"

"Never have been from management; never will be from management."

"Oh. I was hoping you were here about the mildew problem."

"Sorry. But I am a bit of an expert on the subject if it has anything to do with shower curtains."

She shook her head. "Carpets."

I shrugged. "Can't help you."

She brushed some light brown hair away from her earnest face, punched some keystrokes into her computer as tenderly as if she were feeding it a snack, then rolled her chair back to the wall again and looked at me. "How may I help you?"

"I'd like to see Ms. Derwinski."

"Professionally?"

"Sort of."

She shook her head as though I'd done something indelicate. "Danielle is a feminist therapist. She doesn't counsel males."

"I'm not here to be counseled, I'm here to be informed."

She lifted a brow. "Then you're a reporter? Danielle only does media by appointment, after written submission of the questions and a guarantee of the amount of airtime or column inches the interview will occupy. She doesn't share space and she doesn't do survey pieces."

I laughed. "I'm impressed that she's carved out a philosophical position on the subject of personal publicity, but I'm not a reporter. I'm a detective."

That took her down a peg. "Has there been another threat? I thought Detective Jamette was handling the other one."

"I'm not police, I'm private. What kind of threat are we talking about?"

She was still preoccupied with my occupation. "Private. Then we aren't required to speak with you."

I met her look. "Only morally."

That took care of it as far as she was concerned. She plugged the earpieces back in place, punched the button on the deck, then typed the next piece of transcription. I reached over with both hands, tugged the headset free of its notches, and let the earpieces flop against her temples.

"Let me tell you what I'm going to do if your boss doesn't see me in the next five minutes," I snarled in my second-best snarl. "I'm going to collect all the complaints that have ever been lodged against her—police, DA, medical examiners, Better Business Bureau, and civil damage suits—and I'm going to write them up in a pretty brochure and I'm going to sit in that garden and sip espresso and hand my brochure to everyone who even thinks about coming in here."

Her face got as red as a ruby. "You can't do that. That's libel. That's harassment. That's—"

"Free speech," I interrupted. "I'm here about the guy who shot Leonard Wints in court on Tuesday. Tell Danielle I need half an hour of her time."

"But she—"

I raised my hand in a carefree wave. "See you in the garden."

"We'll get a restraining order. Do you know what lawyers *cost?* Do you know how quickly you can spend ten thousand dollars on—"

"My lawyer won't cost a dime," I interrupted.

"Why not?"

"Because my lawyer is me." I dug out my bar card and showed it to her, though not long enough for her to read the word "Inactive."

She removed her headset and shoved back her chair and gave me an involuntary glimpse of thigh as she slipped her feet into some red high heels, then pivoted out of her chair. "I'll be back in a second." She vanished through a door at her flank.

Negotiations on strategy and tactics took several minutes; I spent the interlude girding for battle. It was a given that Danielle and I were not going to get along. She would be one of those man bashers, one of those women who blame everything from migraines to menstruation on the male of the species, who find females without blemish and men without merit, who misuse statistics and overreact to imperfection, who further their own cause far more effectively than they do their clients'. I'd run across more than a few of her type in my life and it was always a depressing experience.

Plus, even though there wasn't any need to get into a debate on sexual abuse and recovered memory with her, get into it I was sure we would. Women like to fight. Not all of them, or maybe even most, but enough so there's an argument any way you turn these days. However benign the subject, it accelerates to gender warfare if it sparks a smidgen of disagreement that touches even tangentially on the differences between men and women. Generalizations are lobbed like mortar rounds and gripes and grudges are sprayed with the firepower of Uzis. I had a lot of preconceptions about Danielle Derwinski, in other words; it took a while before I realized that most of them were wrong.

Her look, for example. I expected Birkenstocks and faded Levi's and a colorful ethnic overlay, with wire-rim eyeglasses and steel gray hair rolled into a forbidding bun, all in the service of an aggressive denial that physical appearance had the slightest role to play in human relations. What I saw instead was a handsome woman whose figure was definitely defined by tailored twill slacks and an orange silk blouse and hair that was stylishly molded to curl toward the front and angle across the brow. Her lips were orange also, her eyes were lined in black and blue, her nails were long and lacquered, and her neck and wrists were agleam with golden chains. My mood picked up, the way it always does around an attractive woman, until I remembered that she'd accused Charley Sleet of sexually abusing her client.

In contrast to the pillows and batiks and incense I had envisioned, her office was sterile and impersonal. A sleek rosewood table served as her desk and faced a pair of thickly upholstered leather chairs that looked comfortable enough to linger in. The rug was a brown Berber weave, the walls a creamy yellow satin, the decorations subtle splashes of pastels sponged directly to the wall surface rather than brushed onto framed canvas. The mundane matériel—file cabinets, computer, video library, recording equipment—were partially hidden behind a freestanding screen.

There was piano music in the air, Chopin maybe. The only item on the desk was a pad of yellow paper. There was nothing on the paper and there was nothing in Danielle Derwinski's eyes when she reached across the desk and shook my hand—not warmth, not hostility, nothing. I wondered if she was ever thus, a blank page that became imprinted only with her patients' troubles.

"I don't appreciate threats to my staff, Mr. Tanner," she began before I could introduce myself.

"I'm sorry. It seemed the only way I could get over the moat."

Her voice was stern and richly modulated. "There are good reasons for our security measures, I assure you. Anyone who counsels women in abusive relationships must eventually deal with . . . well, I'm sure you can imagine. Or maybe you can't. In any event, it's not me toward whom your apology should be directed."

I met her candor with some of my own. "I'll take care of it on the way out, unless you want to call her in and have me do it now."

"Upon your leave-taking will suffice." She glanced at a clock on the wall. "Which will occur in exactly six minutes. I have a client coming who is much more in need of my time than you are."

I smiled. "How do you know?"

"For one thing, her nose is broken."

She gestured to a chair; we sat across from each other and took stock. My guess was we both sensed that something interesting could happen in the next six minutes, and then we both decided not to let it.

"I'm here about the shooting," I began.

"What about it?"

"For one thing, what makes you think Charley Sleet sexually abused Jillian Wints?"

"I don't think that or not think that. I just think it's possible that Leonard Wints was not alone in this."

"No, it isn't. Not if you're talking about Charley Sleet."

She raised a brow. "I'm not inclined to take your word for it, I'm afraid."

"Why not?"

"Because you haven't proved to me that you're not an abuser yourself."

"Guilty until proven innocent, is that it?"

Her eyes sparked hot and mean. "Oh, yes, Mr. Tanner. That is exactly it. Where the welfare of my clients is concerned, men are indeed evil until they establish otherwise."

"You find that an equitable approach to take, do you?"

She brushed at her hairdo as though to dislodge some snowflakes. "I find it an essential approach. In the first years of my practice, whenever I gave men the benefit of the doubt I almost always regretted it. Almost as much as my battered clients did."

Our eyes did mortal combat for a moment, then retired to neutral corners. "Why did it happen?" I asked. "The shooting, I mean."

"I don't know. If you want me to hazard a guess, I'd say it was because Leonard Wints inflicted psychic and physical damage on someone else to the degree that he inflicted it on his daughter."

"And Charley Sleet was an avenging angel."

"Yes."

"Do you know that specifically?"

"No." She shrugged. "On the other hand, I know a great deal about Mr. Wints. I know he was a sexual predator, I know he was a liar, I know he cared more about his image and his income than he did about his daughter's mental health, and I know he was on the verge of facing a sizable judgment of money damages for the harm he had done to my client."

"You're certain you would have prevailed in court?"

"Quite certain."

"I heard it was going the other way."

She made a face. "We had yet to introduce our evidence. Whoever told you that had only heard one side of the issue."

Her confidence was beginning to get to me. I decided to take it down a notch. "You aren't bothered by the case in Napa where the father won a malpractice suit against the therapist for implanting false memories?"

She swore in disgust. "I know little about the particulars of that case and I care even less—judges aren't immune to denial. What I do know about is Jillian Wints. She has suffered an immense wound to her selfhood and that wound began to be inflicted upon her when she was a young child. And it continues to this day." She crossed her legs and shook her head. "Why are men like you so defensive in these matters, Mr. Tanner? Why do you wish to see the guilty go unpunished? Have you abused your own daughter, by any chance?"

A vision streaked through my mind, an image of a child named Eleanor whom I regarded as my daughter, an image soon coupled with a blur of a hulking faceless force that was assaulting her obscenely.

Sweat broke on my brow; I crossed my arms and took a breath. "That's a cheap shot," I said around my fury. "Apparently it's typical of the way you conduct your business, given your ludicrous charges against Charley Sleet."

She was unfazed by my outrage; I suspected she had encountered it countless times in the faces of men like Leonard Wints. "Do you deny that such atrocities occur?" she asked levelly.

"Of course not."

"Does it surprise you that the victim of sexual abuse finds it impossible to lead a normal life in later years?"

"No."

"Then why are you disturbed that Jillian Wints is seeking some small recompense for her many injuries?"

"It doesn't disturb me at all if the crime was actually committed."

"Why do you doubt that it was?"

"Because, as I understand it, there's no evidence to support it other than these new memories she's come up with."

She arched a brow. "It happened twenty years ago in the privacy of a small child's bedroom. What kind of evidence would you expect there to be at this point?"

"There are people who say that if the abuse was continuing, the victim would remember it. That such things don't disappear from consciousness the way you people claim they do."

"You've been reading Professor James."

"Among others."

"Well, she's wrong. She's not evil, at least I hope she's not, but she's mistaken." She stood up and walked around the room, then gestured toward her desk. "If someone like Professor James sat in that chair for a week, and listened to the horrors that tumble out of the mouths of my clients and heard the screams and saw the tears and felt the pain of the violations she so casually dismisses well up until they warp the features and blind the eyes and cramp the muscles and convulse the gut until . . . well, I don't think she could so easily declare it as fantasy, Mr. Tanner. I truly don't."

Danielle was genuinely agitated. She brushed away a tear, looked past me toward the window that opened out onto the courtyard, let the little garden work its magic, then returned to her chair and sat down. I was tempted to tell her that I could paint an equally anguished picture of a father who had been falsely accused of molesting his daughter, but I decided not to. Not yet.

"I'm sorry. It's been a difficult week. I wanted Mr. Wints to be called to account for what he did but I didn't want him to pay with his life. I don't know why someone would do something like that."

"The man who shot him was a policeman."

"So he said."

"Who?"

She opened a drawer in the desk and fumbled through some papers. "Hilton. Detective Gary Hilton. And the newspapers say the same, of course."

"Charley Sleet is my friend," I declared for what seemed like the hundredth time, although somehow I wasn't getting tired of it.

"And you want to see him exonerated."

"If it's appropriate. Yes."

"How can it be? A dozen people saw him do it."

"Not all homicide is punishable. Some of it is justified."

"In what circumstances?"

"Self-defense, for one."

"That hardly seems applicable—Leonard had his back to the man."

"Defense of another, then."

"Of Jillian, you mean."

"It's a possibility. What was the connection between them? Charley and Jillian, I mean."

She shook her head. "The police asked the same question, but I could be of no help to them."

"Jillian never mentioned him?"

"I can't disclose what Jillian may have mentioned."

"You could blink three times if she did."

She didn't blink but she smiled. I didn't know the import of either phenomenon.

"Do you think Leonard Wints abused other children besides his daughter?"

She shrugged. "I have no idea. He never agreed to meet with me, even in the early stages of Jillian's treatment when I offered to hear his side of the story. The statistics are all over the place. Sometimes the obsession is confined to their own child and the incest taboo is part of the attraction. Sometimes the child is only the first step in a lifelong pattern of pedophilia, and sometimes the sex drive is undifferentiated and they prey on anyone who can satisfy it—young, old, whomever."

"Did Wints ever work with young people? Scouts? Police Athletic League? School or church groups? Community centers?"

"Not that I'm aware of."

"Was he ever in trouble with the police?"

"Not that I know of."

"Was Jillian?"

"I can't answer that."

I shifted gears. "Is there any question of Jillian's ancestry?"

She frowned. "I don't . . . oh. That it would explain it, wouldn't it?"

"Yes, it would."

"I have no knowledge on that subject, but a DNA test could tell for sure."

"I know. Would you mind if Jillian were tested?"

She hesitated. "I'd have to think about it and I would guess that Mindy Cartson would require a court order. Are you planning to seek one?"

"I'll let you know." I cast about for a fresh focus. "This case has gotten lots of press. Has anyone come forward to tell you that Leonard Wints assaulted them as well?"

"If they did, I couldn't tell you about it."

"If they did, you could blink three times."

She didn't blink and this time she didn't smile either. She just looked at the clock.

"How did Wints react when you sued him?"

"He denied the charges, of course. Vehemently."

"Convincingly?"

"To some, perhaps, but not to me. Convincing denial is quite common to perverts."

"To innocent people as well."

She met my look. "Presumably."

"The irony doesn't bother you?"

"No."

I laughed. "What's this CMI organization I've heard about?"

"The Corrected Memory Institute. Their mission is quite simple—they are bound and determined to erect a safety barrier around the child abusers of the world, to demonize therapists such as myself who dare reveal their crimes, to make it impossible for the truth to be heard and the victims to be healed."

"Have they made threats to you?"

"Only in general. Exposure of my methods, reprogramming of my clients, that kind of thing."

"What about the threat the police are investigating? Are they behind it, do you think?"

She frowned. "How did you know about that?"

I decided not to rat on the secretary. "Just a shot in the dark."

"It was an anonymous call. Threatening to cut my heart out. I get them frequently, but for some reason this one chilled me. I fully believed he would try it."

"Do you know who it was?"

"No idea."

"Are you taking precautions?"

"Yes, I am."

I was tempted to make some suggestions, then decided she wouldn't listen. "Did Mindy Cartson take Leonard Wints's deposition?"

"Yes."

"Was it revealing?"

"Not at all."

"How did this lawsuit change his life? Did it bankrupt him? Cost him friends? Turn him into a basket case? What?"

"What does it matter? And how would I know in any event? He's not my client; Jillian is."

"I'm looking for friction, Ms. Derwinski. Cases like this do lots of damage. It's the kind of thing that could make a guy do something that might provoke a similar response."

"Like doing something that would make a man like Charley Sleet want to kill him."

I nodded. "The only absolute truth I know in this world is that Charley Sleet wouldn't shoot anyone unless he deserved it."

Her smiled was chilly and arch. "Leonard Wints deserved to be shot, Mr. Tanner. He just didn't deserve to die. He should have lived for years in intense and disabling pain, exactly the way his daughter is living.

That's what he deserved. Your friend let him off the hook."

She sighed, then rubbed her arms as if to ward off a sudden chill, then stood up. "I'm afraid I have a patient to see. I've given you far too much of my time."

I was about to launch one last line of questions when the phone on her desk buzzed once. She picked up the receiver and listened. Her face reddened and her hand became an ugly pink claw around the white receiver.

When she hung up, she looked at me. "How dare you confront Jillian without my permission? How dare you interrogate her in a public place?"

"It's a free country, Ms. Derwinski."

Her voice became operatic. "Don't do it again. Do you understand? If you talk to her again, you'll regret it."

I know a threat when I hear one, too.

As I left the office, a young woman was coming through the door. She was young, and black, and ethereal; if her nose was broken, it didn't show. She said hi and I said hi; her smile was as bright as chrome. She seemed far too chipper to need anything a therapist had to offer.

At my back, the receptionist gushed, "How *are* you, Tafoya? It's so good to see you." The contrast to my own welcome couldn't have been more marked. But I couldn't help but wonder whether Tafoya's bright smile would survive an hour spent with Danielle Derwinski.

CHAPTER

14

THE OFFICES OF THE CORRECTED MEMORY INSTITUTE ON
Beale Street were several blocks south of Market on the
second floor of a commercial complex known as Bayside
Village. The receptionist welcomed me extravagantly,
presumably because I was male and thus a potential
victim of uncorrected memories. When she asked me my
business, I told her I wanted to see Kirby Allison. When
she asked the purpose of my visit, I told her with a
degree of truth that I was having a problem with a claim
of recovered memory.

She preened with satisfaction. "I'm sure we can help
you, Mr. Tanner. We've helped countless others in that
situation and we can help you, too. Voodoo therapy is on
the run."

She seemed as pleased as if she were winning at
Pictionary. I sat where she told me to sit and waited
while she checked to see if Mr. Allison was free. When
she returned moments later, she had a man in tow.

He was husky and hearty, with a salesman's mien, a
convert's zeal, and a drill sergeant's haircut. As we shook
hands, he hauled me to my feet. "Step right this way, Mr.

Tanner. And let me compliment you on your decision to consult the CMI. You won't regret it, believe me; we can lift the burden that has been so unjustly heaped upon you. We can support you in your grief and we can show you how to turn the tables on your accusers."

With a pudgy palm he beckoned me to follow, then led me toward the rear of the building. Along the way we passed a series of small offices in which men and women were manning phones and feeding Xerox machines and typing truth into laptop computers. As he passed them by, Allison issued various signs of encouragement, as if we were in a locker room just before game time. The players looked willing and able to go out and win one for Kirby.

Allison's office was bureaucratically plain and philosophically low-key, in contrast to the frenetic activity in the cubicles down the hall. He motioned for me to sit on a small tweed couch, then took the vinyl chair across from me. He clasped his hands in his lap and leaned forward as he began to speak, to make certain I wouldn't miss a word. For a moment, I was afraid he was going to take my hand as a symbol of his devotion to my well-being, but at the last minute he held off.

"Let me begin by saying that I have been where you are," he said softly, in the manner of preachers in the early innings of a sermon. "I want you to know that up front. I have felt the hurt, the shock, the outrage, the frustration. I have lain awake nights trying to imagine how my child could tell such lies about me, I have wondered what would cause my darling daughter to even *think* such things, let alone make such charges against me or anyone. I have asked myself what kind of person could encourage a woman to invent such hateful false-hoods and then to compound the lie by making them public. In response to the charges, I have considered suicide, I have considered violence, and I have considered litigation, all as a means of relief from the tortures I have suffered.

"So I have been where you are," he said again, this

time more intently. "Every man in this building has been, as have others you will never know of. There is a man in city prison right now being victimized in absentia by a therapist who is bent on persuading his daughter to charge the foulest possible . . . So you are among friends, Mr. Tanner. Even though you don't know a single individual in the building, you are in the presence of the dearest friends you will ever have."

When he had finished his invocation, Allison leaned back and looked at me. He smiled till his eyes swelled shut, pleased with himself, pleased with whatever he saw in me that was responding to his call, pleased with the ways he would please me.

I had to admit I was moved, at least in some sense of the term. Although I had not been accused of child molesting, I had been unjustly accused of other things over the years, quite often by myself. The idea that someone understood and sympathized, and forgave me my impurities, struck a surprisingly grateful chord.

I tried to break the spell. "How much is this going to cost me?"

Allison crossed a stubby leg and shook his head with sadness. "Only what you feel you can afford. Quite frankly, we are as much in need of your time as we are of your funds."

"Who supports the place, then?"

"The founding families—there are three of us, six people in all—put our life savings in the association in order to get it off the ground. That was four years ago. More recently, contributions from grateful clients have covered virtually all of our expenses."

It didn't sound much like the worldwide cabal Jillian Wints had described. "What is it you do, exactly?"

"It depends on the circumstance. If there is litigation pending, we provide access to attorneys and experts in the field of recovered memory who are familiar with the issues and can show such claims for the fabrications that they are. We also maintain a file of judicial precedents that indicate recovered memory cases are increasingly being found to be without merit by the courts. If there is only the informal charge of abuse, without litigation, we provide grief counseling to the family, a list of therapists who can reorient and rehabilitate the person making the claim, and suggested courses of action to counter such brainwashing as has already occurred."

"Deprogramming, in other words."

For the first time, he clouded. "That is not a term we use at the Institute. Nor a method. Have you been named in a lawsuit, Mr. Tanner? Or only slandered by your offspring and her therp?"

"Therp?"

"It rhymes with perp as in perpetrator, and refers to her therapist. We find it an apt analogy."

I smiled. "No lawsuit."

"That's fortunate. It doesn't mean your struggle will be less painful, necessarily, but it does mean it will be less expensive."

"Good. I hear one of your people is particularly effective in getting the accuser to see the light. I was hoping I could work with him."

"What person is that?"

"Sleet, I think his name is. Charles Sleet."

Allison frowned. "I don't—"

"I don't think he's full-time; I think he just handles certain special projects."

"Sleet?" He shook his head. "The name is not familiar to me."

"Do you have a personnel list of some sort? I did hear that this guy really went to bat for people. He's the reason I came here, actually. I'd be willing to pay a premium to work with him."

Allison thought about it, then abruptly left the room.

It had been a gamble and it didn't pay off. When he returned, the bonhomie was gone. "Who are you working for, Mr. Tanner? The Cartson woman?"

I shook my head. "I'm not working for anyone."

"I don't believe you. You're trying to link the CMI

with the man who shot Leonard Wints. Well, it won't wash. We were in Leonard's corner; we were not opposed to him. The idea that we would want him dead is ridiculous. If you come here again, or make any attempt to interrogate our staff, we'll seek a restraining order and take whatever additional steps that are necessary to be rid of you."

I held up a peaceable hand. "I admit I got in under false pretenses. But I think we're on the same side in this thing. If you were working with Wints, you must have an interest in who killed him and why."

Allison hesitated. "So?"

"So is there anything at all you can tell me about Charley Sleet and Mr. Wints? Maybe if I could talk to the person who counseled him."

"I counseled Leonard myself."

"Was there anything unusual about the case?"

"Only the virulence and scope of the charges against him."

"You're convinced the charges were bogus?"

He met my look. "Did you know Leonard?"

I shook my head.

"He was a great guy. A truly kind individual. He was as devastated as any man could be by his daughter's hysterical allegations. He became a recluse. His lovely wife despaired for him. Only in recent weeks, when he had finally become convinced that he would win in court and be exonerated, did his outlook begin to brighten."

"How about the police? Were they called in on this case in any respect?"

Allison shook his head. "Not in its current posture, at least. If they made an inquiry at the time the abuse took place, I'm not aware of it." He rushed to correct his implication. "And how could they? Since it didn't happen."

"Have there been any other instances of accused abusers being killed mysteriously, Mr. Allison?"

"There was the woman from Sierra who shot the man

who abused her son. But he wasn't a parent, he was a teacher, and recovered memory wasn't an issue. That's the only one I know of."

"So you can't help me."

"I'm afraid not. But we have plenty of others whom we can help, I can assure you. The degree of witch-hunting in this field is phenomenal. The Spanish Inquisition had nothing on these so-called Recovery Therapists."

The ghost of Torquemada went with me out the door.

CHAPTER

15

THERE WERE A COUPLE OF COPS TO CALL, SO I WENT BACK TO the office and called them.

One was in and one was out. The one who was out was Gary Hilton, the guy who'd talked to Danielle Derwinski about the Wints shooting. The one who was in was Earl Jamette, who had investigated the anonymous phone threat to the selfsame woman.

When I asked him about it, he swore sarcastically. "The woman makes her living telling people to leave their husbands, quit their jobs, call the cops on their fathers, and cut themselves off from their families. In other words, she pisses people off. When people get pissed off, some of them piss back; she's lucky no one's planted a bomb."

The word summoned images of Oklahoma City, the way it would for anyone. I put them out of my mind, though not without difficulty. I asked Jamette if he'd come up with a list of suspects.

"How could I? She wouldn't give me her client roster. She wouldn't give me shit," he expanded grumpily.

"Sounds like she's not all that worried about it."

"She's worried enough to hire private security to watch the place all night. Worried enough to pay five large for a home alarm system and a bunch of yard lights at the house on Baker Street. Worried enough to get a permit to carry a piece."

Suddenly I took the situation more seriously. "What kind of threats were they? How were they delivered?"

"Phone, is all I know."

"Traceable?"

"Booth by Union Square. Hundred people a day use that thing. When it's working."

"No leads at all?"

"Plenty. But they're all inside her head." Jamette paused, then went on. "You ask me, I think she knows who did it. Know something else? I think she wants him to make a try for her. I think she wants to take him out."

"Personally? With her weapon?"

"With whatever. Last time I talked to her she was real relaxed about it. I think she's ready to waste his ass."

When I tried to imagine who that someone might be, the only name I could come up with was Kirby Allison of the Corrected Memory Institute.

"How long ago was the last threat?"

"Three weeks."

"Where do things stand now?"

"I call her once in a while to let her know I'm still on it, but what I'm really doing is waiting for it to happen again."

"You mean you want him to try to make good."

"Hey. Don't act like I'm some sort of sadist here; I got nothing else to work with. She knows it but she won't do nothing about it. She calls it ethics; I call it dumb-ass. But what can I do? No court's gonna order her to talk to me, that's for sure. So is that it, Tanner?" he concluded gruffly. "I got some statements to take."

"What does the guy want Derwinski to do?"

"Hard to say. Says he's going to kill her. Perforate her privates."

"For something she's already done?"

"Sounds like it."

"This the first time something like this has happened to her?"

"Says it happens all the time. But this is the first one she took serious."

"Charley Sleet involved in any way?"

"You mean as Investigating Officer? Naw. We're working this out of Northside; Charley only comes out here to play cards." He paused. "Wait a minute. I got a bell ringing all of a sudden. This is the shrink who was in court that day. Right? When Charley took out the civilian."

"She's the one," I agreed. "Know any connection?"

"Naw. Me and Sleet weren't all that tight, tell you the truth. I think he thought I was dirty."

"Are you?"

"Fuck you. I'm so clean you could use my piss as perfume."

I laughed. "Any chance Charley was the one who threatened the Derwinski woman?"

"Doesn't sound like him, but what do I know? Damnedest guys turn out to be psychos."

"Anyone in Northside have anything cogent to say when they heard Charley got busted?"

"Cogent, huh? Not really. Someone said he was glad when any Internal Affairs guy went down, but Sleet ain't been IA for a long time."

"Any word why Charley quit the department?"

"Naw. These days you don't shit on the guys that quit, you pity the fucks who stay on. Most of the guys been talking about the Walters case anyhow."

"Who's he?"

"Clifton Walters. Shield that got smacked in the plaza last week."

"What's the word on it?"

"Official word is that the department is devoting all its resources to finding the perp. Unofficial word is that Walters was a rogue with a crack habit and the department is better without him. Me, I don't see it that way."

"How do you see it?"

"He got set up. Someone he trusted lured him down there, then blew him away when he wasn't looking."

"Any idea who?"

"Could be anyone. Walters worked the streets for thirty years. Had a lot of friends; had a lot of enemies."

I thanked Jamette for his time and left a message with him to have Hilton call me when he got in. My next call was to the *Chronicle*. Joyce Yates, the *Chron*'s longtime courthouse reporter, came on the line a minute later.

"Yates."

"Joyce, this is Marsh Tanner. Maybe you remember me from the Arundel case."

"The PI. Yeah. How you doing?"

"Good. You?"

"Still pissed that I didn't get a shot at O.J."

"Literally or figuratively?"

She laughed. "Both. What can I do for you, Marsh?"

"Talk about Charley Sleet."

"Yeah. Jesus. That was one for my memoirs, let me tell you."

"He do or say anything at all that gave a hint of why the hell he did it, Joyce?"

"Naw. Didn't say . . . wait. He said, 'Two for one.' That's what it was. See, I noticed him when he stood up. He got this weird smile on his face and said, 'Two for one.' Then he pulled his weapon and started shooting. I didn't have a chance to do shit." She paused. "At least that's what I tell myself." Her guilt sizzled through the line like a power surge.

"Two for one what?" I asked.

"I haven't the faintest idea."

"Anything else? Anything at all?"

"Sorry, Marsh. I hope to hell he gets out of this, but right now it's hard to see how. On the other hand, there's O.J."

I'd had more than my fill of O.J. "Did you dig into that recovered memory case very deeply, Joyce?"

"Not really. Just there to see how it turned out, basically. There's lots of action on that front these days. A bit of a reaction has set in, what with the case up in Napa and some TV documentary stuff that made some of these therapists look like quacks. My editor thought we should monitor the active cases in the area and report how they went."

"How do you think this one was going?"

"Looked to me like the judge was leaning toward the defense."

I thanked Joyce for the information and punched up Jake Hattie's number.

"I'm getting nowhere with this thing, Jake," I confessed when the lawyer came on the line. "I can't link Charley to anything that was going down in that courtroom."

"Neither can I," Jake said, without his usual gusto.

"You got any brilliant suggestions what I should do next?"

"Not really. Guess I'll have to employ the last resort."

"What's that?"

"Jury nullification."

"You mean like Johnnie Cochran did in—"

"Hell, I was getting my juries to ignore the law when Johnnie was just a bulge in his daddy's pants."

"I'd still like you to lean on your client if you get the chance. It would help a lot to know what Charley thought he was doing in there."

Jake laughed. "That's going to be tough to do."

"Why?"

"He won't see me. Has the boys at the door primed to keep me out."

"What about his right to counsel?"

"At this point it looks a lot like he's waiving it."

"This is life and death, Jake, goddamnit. You need to take it more seriously."

"It's his life and his death, Tanner. I'm taking them as seriously as he'll let me."

CHAPTER
16

IN SOME CASES, THE SCENE OF THE CRIME IS EVERYTHING—
physical evidence both tells the tale and provides proof
for conviction. Since I don't do forensics, at such times
my job is peripheral. The crime lab provides the who; at
most I can sometimes provide the why.

In other cases, the crime scene is irrelevant—the only
thing it has to offer is the fact of death. When I work such
a case on behalf of a suspect, part of the job is to come up
with everything necessary for the conviction of someone
else—motive, means, and opportunity that link that
other someone to the homicide. In many cases, none of
those elements can be found at the place where the
killing occurred.

There is a third kind of crime, however, where the
crime scene yields nothing solid—no prints, no hair,
no fibers, no DNA, no blood—but it nevertheless con-
tains something useful. That something is often
insubstantial—an aura, an ether, a nimbus, an invisible
indication of what transpired that lingers in the atmosphere and transmits a host of messages that become
distinct only if you prepare yourself to receive them. I'm

normally without mystical inclinations, but I've seen more than one case in which the crime scene told all without really telling anything.

I got to the Pacific Bell building that had been converted into a courthouse just before five. The directory informed me that Judge Meltonian held forth on the sixth floor. The elevator got me there nonstop.

Most of the rooms were empty of judge and jury, including the one Glen Bittles attended in his capacity as clerk. Luckily, Peanut was still behind his desk in the well of the court, reassembling some documentary evidence the attorneys had laid waste to earlier in the day.

When he saw me in the doorway, he waved. I joined him at his station below the bench. "I was wondering if you could tell me where Charley was when it happened," I said.

"Sure. How's he doing?" Glen asked as he led me to Department 5 down the hall, a smaller chamber than the one we'd just been in, its makeshift furnishings clean and bright and functional but lacking the faded grandeur of the decrepit City Hall. The ambience was more fitting for a church social than a court of law.

"Haven't talked to him," I said.

"He's clamming up, huh?"

"So far. At least with me."

Glen muttered a curse at Charley's nonsense, then pointed to a chair at the rear of the courtroom just to the left of the center aisle. "Way I heard it, Sleet was sitting about here. This chair or that one, I'm not sure. Then all of a sudden he stood up, pulled his piece and fired, and fired again, then wrestled with some guy nobody knows, then tossed the piece on the floor and lay down by that bookcase and waited for them to come get him."

"How about the other seats? Were they full?"

"Pretty near, from what I understand. Can't swear every single chair had an ass in it, though."

"Where was Leonard Wints?"

Peanut pointed to the defense table. "Andy Potter was sitting closest to the aisle, I think; Wints was in the middle and a paralegal or some such was on the other side."

"How about the plaintiff? Where was she?"

He pointed to a chair at the table that was nearest the jury. "The Cartson woman was next to her. Just the two of them."

"How about Danielle Derwinski? The expert for the plaintiff? Any idea where she was sitting?"

Peanut shook his head. "Don't know anything about her." He looked at his watch. "You need anything else, Marsh? I got to run for my bus. I miss this one, the next is full of people babbling about the fucking Internet."

I thanked Glen for his time and he left the room in a hurry. After a lengthy survey of the surroundings, I sat in a chair in the jury box and closed my eyes and imagined the scene as Peanut had described it.

I could see it easily enough, the players and their roles in the drama. What I couldn't accommodate was the mind of Charley Sleet. What I couldn't come close to was a rationale that let him believe that what he was doing was right. The man had devoted his life to law enforcement, to following the rules, to going by the book even to the extent of investigating malfeasance by his fellow cops. Now he'd become a vigilante. As his best friend, I should have some idea of why it had happened, but I didn't have a clue.

I opened my eyes and surveyed the room once more, then went through the bar of the court and inspected more closely. What I was looking for were bullet holes. What I found was a single perforation in the wall above and to the left of the witness stand at slightly above eye level. When I sighted from there to the chair where Charley had supposedly been sitting, the ghost of Andy Potter seemed to get in the way.

I tapped on the door behind the bench that sported a sign that read CHAMBERS. After a second knock, a voice told me to come in.

As I'd hoped, the voice belonged to Marjie Finnerty, Judge Meltonian's clerk. She was sitting behind a nameplate and a computer at a desk in a tiny anteroom that had formerly been a broom closet, looking alternately at the screen and a law book. Stacks of legal papers surrounded her the way a doughnut surrounds a hole.

Her hair was brown and tousled, her eyes brown and slightly fuzzy, her features pleasant but taxed, as though her weekend guests had overstayed their welcome. She was more attractive than she knew, I guessed, always surprised at the amorous attentions of men. Her beige dress was plain and serviceable, brightened only by a gold pin at her collar. The pin was in the shape of a trout. I bet Charley had given it to her—he used to give fish stuff to Flora all the time.

She raised a brow and scratched her nose. "Judge Meltonian is unavailable. Court resumes at 9 A.M."

"I'm a friend of Charley Sleet's," I said. "I'd like to talk with you about him."

She touched her pin. "What makes you think I—?"

"How explicit do you want me to be?"

She examined me more closely. The fog floated off her eyes, to be replaced by the gleam of a wary intelligence. "You're Marsh Tanner."

I nodded.

"It's nice to meet you finally."

"Same here."

"Charley talks about you all the time."

"Wish I could say the same."

She colored. "Why do you think I know anything you don't already know about this?"

"Just a hunch."

I smiled my sweetest smile and for some reason it infuriated her. "Is your hunch going to get him *out* of it? Is your hunch going to bring Leonard Wints back to life? Is your hunch going to tell me why Charley *did* such an asinine thing?" I could have roasted marshmallows on her cheeks.

"None of the above," I said affably. "Maybe we could go somewhere and talk."

She shook her head. "I've got to get these orders in

limine to the judge before he leaves." She glanced at the door to her left. "That's soundproof, if you're worried about privacy," she added, then punched some key-strokes with a hint of martyrdom, as if working late were par for the course and she was getting tired of it.

She rubbed her cheek and then apologized. "I'm sorry. You're here to help him. I know that. I thought of calling you myself but I knew you'd get involved anyway. Charley admires you more than anyone he knows, I think."

"That's nice to hear. The feeling is mutual."

I took a seat and crossed my legs. "You and Charley were lovers, right? I'm sorry to be so blunt, but I think we need to move quickly on this."

She met my look defiantly. "What makes you think we were in a relationship?"

"His redial button and his answering machine."

Her eyes widened. "You searched his house?"

I became equally self-righteous. "Of course."

"Why?"

"To find out why the hell this happened."

"And did you?"

Although the question was sarcastic, my answer was candid. "Not even close. I was hoping you could enlighten me."

She debated a moment, then sighed. "I would if I could but I can't."

"No ideas at all?"

She shook her head.

"Have you heard from Charley since he got arrested?"

She hesitated, then nodded.

I experienced a rush of jealousy that I hadn't been granted a similar indulgence. "What did he say?"

"Just that he was all right. And was sorry for what he'd done. And . . ."

"What?"

She blinked at a tear, then dabbed it with a Kleenex. "That I should forget about him and get on with my life."

"Do you plan to do that?"

"No."

"Good. Did he give you any hint at all why he thought the world should be rid of Leonard Wints?"

She shook her head, then yielded to her anxieties. "I don't know what to do, do you? I mean they can't just let this go. There's been too much heat about police brutality in this city already. They'll put Charley away forever just to show they're taking steps to address the situation, even though Charley is the least violent man I've ever known."

"Until two days ago," I corrected. "Did he say anything at the time of the shooting that might indicate what he was thinking?"

"I've gone over it and over it, but there's nothing. Actually, I thought he was there to see me," she added miserably. "I was hoping he'd take me to lunch."

"How about the Wints case?"

She blinked. "What about it?"

"You must have read the files and maybe even the depositions."

She nodded. "But I can't talk about it."

"Why not?"

"Because Judge Meltonian is very strict about the privacy of litigants."

"This is a lawsuit. The files are part of the public record. Litigants surrender their privacy when they decide to go to court."

"But there's a gag order in the Wints case. I'd be fired in a minute if he knew I'd said anything to you."

"I'm not trying to get you fired, Marjie. But until I find a link between Charley and Wints, I can't help Jake Hattie mount a defense."

"You're working for Jake?"

"I'm working for Charley. So is Jake. So are a lot of people who cared about him. Except you, apparently."

It was mean and unfair, a product of my panic. Justifiably, she lashed back. "I care about him so much I can't eat or sleep or breathe. I care about him so much I fell to my knees when he called and begged him to let me come see him."

She lapsed into convulsive sobs. Her arms hugged her chest; her head dropped so low that her tears spattered the pages of the *Pacific Reporter*. The computer gurgled periodically, in a vain effort to divert attention from her suffering.

"What else did he say?" I asked softly.

"He told me to leave it alone, that if I loved him I'd keep quiet and forget I ever knew him. As if anyone could forget Charley." The impossibility of obeying his command made her chuckle.

She wiped her tears away as best she could, then blotted them off the law book and finally looked up at me. "Sorry."

"Don't be. I feel like crying myself."

"Maybe you should."

"Maybe I will."

We stayed silent for a time, then I made a final plea. "Look at it this way for a minute. Charley isn't acting rationally; he wouldn't have done what he did if he was thinking straight. Which means telling you there's nothing to be done, to let it be and forget him, isn't rational either. Right?"

"Right."

"Then talk to me."

"About what?"

"To start with, how did you and Charley meet?"

She blinked to quash a lingering tear. "He was in court on some domestic violence thing. You know how it goes, we got behind and he kept having to come back day after day, and we started talking, and laughing, and having a good time, and finally I asked him to take me to dinner."

"You asked him?"

She nodded. "I made it sort of a joke, you know, but I knew that if I didn't make the first move there wouldn't *be* a move. So that's how it started."

"And how far did it go?"

She frowned. "Do you want the spicy details?"

"I want to know if he loved you."

"Why?"

"Because if he loved you, you're the one to convince him to help us get him out of this thing."

"He does love me, I think. He said he did, at least. And he acted like he did." Her voice fell to a whisper and her eyes softened like chocolate in the sun. "He's very gentle for a big man. And very kind. And very needy. I was surprised how much he seemed to need me, once he believed I truly cared about him."

"Charley's been lonely for a long time."

She nodded. "Since his wife died. I know. He talks about her as though she's sewing in the next room."

"Does it bother you?"

"Not now. Maybe later it will. If there is a later."

"How long has this been going on?"

"That's a song title, isn't it? Gershwin, I think. About four months."

"Were you making plans? Talking about marriage and a life together?"

"Sort of. I think mostly it was him trying to see if I had a problem sleeping with him without a ring on my finger. I didn't," she added quickly. "Have a problem, I mean."

"The fact that he'd fallen in love makes it all the more inexplicable that he put himself in jeopardy like this."

She nodded. "That's why I was so stunned when it happened. I just thought: Why are you *ruining* things for us?"

I paused and looked at her. "Can you help me at all, Marjie?"

"With the case files?"

I nodded.

She shook her head. "But there's nothing there. I went through every piece of paper to see if he was mentioned."

"And he wasn't."

"No. Not even in the depositions."

As if he'd been eavesdropping, the door opened and Judge Meltonian stood gazing down upon us like a disapproving chaperon. He was barely forty, tall and thin, slickly groomed and egoistically imposing, looking every bit the skilled trial lawyer that he'd been before going on the bench two years back. "I need those orders, Marjie."

"Sorry, Judge," she said, then turned to me and shrugged.

I stood up. "Did he say anything about me?" I asked.

She nodded. "He said to tell you not to worry. He said to tell you to give up the boycott and go down to Arizona next spring and enjoy yourself." She smiled with fondness at the memory of the conversation. "I haven't the faintest idea what he was talking about."

"He was talking about baseball," the judge told her with a kindly smile.

I regarded it as an opening, so I introduced myself and we shook hands. "I'm here about Charley Sleet," I said.

Meltonian nodded. "An unfortunate situation. And apparently inexplicable."

"I agree. Unless you have some ideas on the subject?"

The judge shook his head. "I'm afraid not. I'm just glad no one else was badly injured."

"Who was on the stand when it happened? Do you remember?"

"We hadn't gotten to the plaintiff's testimony yet. The movant had rested and the plaintiff had asked for a judgment on the record. I was just about to rule when the shots were fired." He looked at Marjie. "If I'm going to make that play, I need those orders."

I made a last pitch to Marjie myself. "We need to talk some more. I need to know everything Charley said and did in the past month."

She nodded vaguely and began to type. The judge slid back to his chambers without bidding me good-bye. On the way out of the building, I began to wonder if I had journeyed to another planet, where cause and effect were inoperative, where every act was random and inexplicable, where everything was upside down. What I wondered, at bottom, was whether what Charley had wanted was simply to get himself locked away in jail where no one could get at him, where the world would be the size of a sandbox.

CHAPTER
17

WHEN I GOT BACK TO MY CAR, I LOOKED AT MY WATCH. There was still time to catch Eleanor before her bedtime. I drove west on Fell Street faster than the law allowed.

Eleanor is my daughter. At least I think she's my daughter. Her biological mother is a woman I've spoken to on only three occasions, two of them when she was purportedly serving as a surrogate mother carrying the child of a wealthy couple named Colbert who couldn't conceive by normal means. For reasons grounded in her personal history with the future father, the surrogate decided to abort the Colberts' implanted embryo and replace it with one produced by the two of us, my part of the production being entirely unwitting.

At least I'm pretty sure that's what happened. The little girl who showed up nine months later is being raised by the contracting couple as if the surrogate contract had been fulfilled and the implant had proceeded to term. They don't know about the abortion or my probable relationship to the child. Although I'm not on the scene in an active capacity, I regard Eleanor as my offspring and I monitor her progress as best I can. To the Colberts, I'm a godfather manqué who stops by once or twice a week to check on his charge. In reality, I'm a more than middle-aged man who never expected to have a child of his own and is awestruck by the windfall that has graced him.

When I found out that the surrogate had made me a parent without my consent, I had no idea how to react. Based on some unnerving experiences with other people's children over the years, I didn't expect to feel much more than dutiful toward the infant, and perhaps not even that, since I had not planned to conceive a child and in fact had protected against conception, which had occurred only because the surrogate had sabotaged the method of birth control I'd employed. I expected my reaction to be tepid going on cool, and I was as wrong as I'd been when I'd predicted that Clinton would make a great President.

From the moment I first held Eleanor in my arms, I was a slave to her—bewitched, enchanted, and enthralled. Watching her evolve from an awkward lump of pink putty to a grinning, grasping, impish infant became the major miracle in my life. Every time I saw her, she was someone new. Every time I saw her, I hated to leave her all the more. Every time I saw her, I kicked myself for not doing it the right way years ago, with a wife and a marriage and a house and a dog and a baby I could hug whenever I got the urge to.

Usually I drop by when Daddy isn't home. Daddy is Stuart Colbert, a women's clothing magnate, scion of a notorious San Francisco family, the man the surrogate replaced with me. Stuart and I don't despise each other, quite, but we don't have much to say to each other either, once we quit talking about the weather.

Mommy is different. Mommy is Millicent, and for the most part I'm happy that Eleanor is in her charge. Because the Colberts are rich, Millicent doesn't go off to work every morning and she has help with the soiled sheets and dirty diapers. I'm not sure I approve of that, actually, but she's a good and earnest mother and I'm glad she's around most of the time tending to our daughter's business, so I keep my irrelevant mouth shut. Millicent also makes use of a nanny on the days when she golfs or plays cards or dines with society swells in the company of her sullen husband. I know I don't approve of that, but I'm not in a position to say so. A dozen years from now, we'll probably be engaged in open warfare over the rules and rights of parenthood, but for now, it seems as good as it can get, given the circumstances.

The Colbert house is in St. Francis Wood, a tony section of the city out near the ocean, straight up the hill from Stern Grove. The best thing about the tony sections of town is that there's always a place to park. The worst thing about them is they make you ashamed of your car.

Millicent was glad to see me and I was glad to see her. She was tall and slim and attractive and more exuberant by a factor of five from the first time I'd seen her, when her hopes for a child had seemed doomed. Now that things had worked out, she was a bundle of energy and enthusiasm; I was invariably cheered when I stopped by the house and gratified that I had been granted what amounted to an open invitation.

Because Millicent knew my interest in Eleanor was real and deep and lasting, she kept track of things for me; every time I came calling, she brought me up to date. True to form, after I rang the bell she let me in with a gush of greeting, then launched the next chapter of Eleanor's slim biography—what she'd done and eaten and worn and said since my last visit, which had been six days before.

"She said a complete sentence yesterday," Millicent concluded. "Really. She said, 'You my ball.'"

"'You my ball.' Byronic. Definitely. She'll be a lyric poet."

Millicent slugged me on the arm. "Don't make fun."

"I'm not making fun, I'm having fun."

"Good." She took hold of my sleeve and dragged me toward the nursery.

Eleanor was sitting on the floor in the center of a colorful patchwork quilt, clutching a fuzzy pink bunny, wearing the little blue flight suit I'd bought for her when I was up in Seattle on my last case. I'd also gotten her the bunny, on the occasion of her six-month birthday. I felt ten feet tall, as Millicent knew I would. I liked her for setting the stage for me.

When Eleanor saw me, she smiled, I think, and dropped the bunny and reached out her hand. I gave her a finger to squeeze, then sat beside her on the quilt and picked her up and perched her on my knee and said the stuff you say when you want a child to like you. That I was actually talking baby talk at this stage of my life was a never-ending wonder.

We played with the bunny and then with a ball. Then we stacked foam-rubber blocks and then she unwrapped the present I'd brought—a green rubber frog that made a noise like a burp when you squeezed it. Then I lay on my back on the quilt and put Eleanor on my tummy and poked and tickled and nuzzled and kissed her while she drooled all over my shirt.

I was having a wonderful time until it occurred to me that at some point it would become wrong. At some point putting her in my lap, or letting her flop on my belly, or tickling her ribs and itching her nose and playing piggy with her toes will be inappropriate and even harmful, at least in the view of some.

How was I supposed to know when that time had come? How was I supposed to know when touching could turn criminal? How was I to protect myself and how was I to protect Eleanor? And what if I made a mistake or was misinterpreted? What if someday someone like Danielle Derwinski convinced Eleanor to bring a criminal charge against me, asserting I was her child-hood abuser?

I shuddered so hard that Eleanor froze for an instant, as if some atavistic memory had given her a precocious glimpse of future struggles with the opposite sex. In the dark grotto carved by such thoughts, I wondered yet again if Jillian Wints had ever had a friend or a father named Sleet, because if someone ever did to Eleanor what Leonard Wints had allegedly done to Jillian, I would blow his head off, too.

A moment later, Eleanor found a stuffed dinosaur that was far more fascinating than I was, and Millicent and I repaired to the tea table and drank coffee and talked about our common passion. At such times I wonder if Millicent is far wiser than she appears, if she knows the genes within her daughter come from me and the surro-gate and not from her and her husband. To her credit, I don't think it would matter. When I kissed them both good-bye twenty minutes later, I was back to being glad to be alive despite what Charley Sleet was putting me through.

I stopped for dinner at a hole-in-the-wall in China-town, then headed up to my apartment looking forward to some peace and quiet, my mind more on Eleanor than Charley. I was on my third drink and my second sitcom when the phone rang.

"Marsh?"

"Charley?"

"Yeah."

"Jesus Christ. Where the hell are you?"

"Jail."

"I hope you're going to tell me you're ready to let us bail you out of there."

"Forget about it." His tone was the one he used whenever a suspect got an inkling to resist arrest.

"So how are you?" I asked him, as though there was nothing in the air but plans for the weekend.

"Fine."

"Great. What can I do for you? A news summary, maybe, since you've been out of touch? The Warriors dropped one to the Lakers tonight—Sprewell got twenty-eight. Weather will be clear and cool with periods of rain. Newt still wants to take from the poor and give to the rich and Clinton seems to want to let him. They call it welfare reform. Sort of like calling cancer health-care reform."

"Give it up, Marsh."

"The news flash?"

"Looking for ammunition for Jake."

"Why?"

"Because there isn't any."

I shut my eyes and turned off the light and sat in the room in the dark. Somewhere near Charley, a truck roared by. Somewhere near me, a car alarm went off.

"We've been friends a long time, Charley."

"True."

"I've done you some favors over the years."

"Not as many as went the other way."

"But still."

"What's your point?"

"My point is, I think that gives me a line of credit."

"Maybe. A short one."

"I'm drawing on it, Charley."

"How?"

"Tell me why you shot him."

"So you can run to Hattie and he can start up some phony media campaign about how I'm being railroaded by the department and the system is being used for political purposes and the rest of his usual tap dance."

"*Are* you being railroaded, Charley?"

"Hell no."

"So you shot him."

"Does anyone say otherwise?"

"Not that I can find."

"Good."

"Come on, Charley. Let me in on the game. This thing

is fucking with my mind—I keep wondering what I missed and why I missed it. I keep finding stuff out about you that I didn't know."

"Like what?"

"Like Marjie."

He laughed without humor. "She told me you dropped by."

"She's upset, Charley. She loves you and she knows you're in trouble and she's upset because you're setting yourself up for a fall."

"Well, there's nothing I can do about it."

"You can let me help you get out of this thing."

"That's the problem."

"What's the problem?"

"I don't deserve to get out of it."

"Why not?"

He paused. Another truck went by. This time a woman laughed, raucously and loudly.

"You son of a bitch," I said.

"What?"

"Where the fuck are you?"

"I told you."

"Bullshit. They've got lots of things down in Bruno but they don't have truck stops and sassy women. Where are you really?"

"Never mind," he said, then paused for so long I thought he'd hung up. When he spoke again, his tone was grim and incriminating. "This is all you get. What I was doing didn't have anything to do with the Wints girl. All that abuse shit. It wasn't about that."

"Then what was it about?"

"It doesn't matter."

"Sure it does. I been busting my butt trying to find a link between you and Wints."

"So what?"

"I didn't find one."

"I know you didn't."

"So it occurred to me that maybe you killed the wrong man."

Charley's laugh was harsh and arrogant, the way he laughed when he collected a big pot at poker. "Doesn't matter," he said again.

"It does if you're still trying to get it right," I said, but I was talking to a dial tone.

Five minutes later, I tracked down Jake Hattie. "I was just about to call you," he said before I could say anything.

"I figured as much," I said. "How'd you convince him?"

"Convince him to do what?"

"Accept bail."

"I didn't."

"The hell you didn't. He's out of jail, Jake. He just called me."

"I know he's out, but he wasn't bailed out, he was let out."

"What?"

"You heard me."

Sweat leached onto the surface of my skin, cool and warm simultaneously, suggestive of terror and tropical illness. "You mean they dismissed the charges against him?"

"I mean someone helped him break jail."

My stomach knotted large, like anchor rope. "You're kidding."

"I don't kid when the meter's running."

"Charley broke jail?"

"Yep."

"Who helped him?"

"No one knows. Most of the guys down there owe him big, I imagine. Or he has something on them, more likely. And there's something else."

"What?"

"When they saw Sleet didn't make dinner, they had a lockdown to look for him and they found a dead guy in the john."

"Who was it?"

"I don't know yet. They're not talking at this point."

"What makes you think Charley had—"

"Come on, Marsh. Don't get soft on this thing. Coincidence doesn't fly that far."

"What's the dead guy's connection to Charley?"

"Who knows? I thought if you had some time you might look into it."

CHAPTER

18

THE FIRST THING IN THE MORNING, I WAS ON THE PHONE TO Andy Potter. "I need a favor," I told him.

"I may not have time for a favor."

"I need you to draw a picture of the courtroom. I need to know where everyone was sitting when Charley pulled the trigger. Particularly spectators."

"This wasn't vaudeville, Marsh. I had more important things to do than count the house."

"Just do the best you can."

"Why?"

"Because he may have shot the wrong guy."

"What?"

"I don't think he was gunning for Leonard Wints."

"Who *was* he gunning for?"

"He wouldn't tell me."

"You talked to him?"

"Yeah."

"From jail?"

"Nope. He's out."

"Out? Since when? Where is he?"

"He won't say. He didn't have a beef against you by

1 3 6

any chance, did he? He swings the muzzle two inches right and you're the one hosting the funeral."

Andy's laugh was tense and terse. "Don't be ridiculous. How soon do you need this map thing?"

"Now."

"I'll fax it to you by noon."

"I don't do fax. Send it by messenger. I'm going to try to get the poker guys together tonight."

"I'm not sure that's particularly appropriate."

"Not for poker, Andy; for brainstorming. See if anyone knows where he is or why he did it. Can you make it?"

"I don't think so."

"Try."

"Where and when?"

"My place. Eight."

"I'll come if I can," he said, and hung up.

My next target was the plaintiff's team. Mindy Cartson couldn't be bothered to speak to me even when I told her secretary that Ms. Cartson couldn't be ruled out as the target of Charley's wrath. When I asked if there were any other cases in the office connected to him, she said she'd ask her boss about it and hung up.

Jillian Wints still hadn't hooked up her phone, probably on the advice of her therapist. Which left me with the selfsame Danielle.

For some reason, she came on the line even after she knew who it was. "I'd like to see you," I said. "It won't take long, but it's important."

"Is this personal or professional?"

I was more intrigued by the question than I should have been. "Professional. Unless you want to make it otherwise."

"Thanks but no thanks."

For some reason, I decided to flirt. "But you're tempted, aren't you? Just a little? I saw a look in your eye yesterday."

She laughed like bubbles in a watercooler. "Even if I was, it wouldn't matter."

"Why not?"

"How can I expect my patients to forgo temptation if I can't do it myself?"

"With patients, it's for their own good."

"The same with me," she said, then laughed again, this time with real merriment.

Although the duration of my current siege of celibacy tempted me to delve deeper, I opted to leave it alone. "When would be a convenient time to get together?"

"I suppose you'll hound me until we do this."

"Count on it."

She sighed. "After work I have an hour before a dinner engagement."

"Personal or professional?"

She hesitated. "Personal."

"So only some temptations are off-limits."

She laughed. "It's not that personal. We were in grad school together. We had a fling for a while, but he married his hometown sweetheart, so now we mostly talk shop."

"Such as?"

"Sexual deviancy evaluations. Trance states. Stuff like that."

"Sounds delightful."

"It can be."

"Too bad."

She paused. "Do you want to come by the office later on?"

"Not particularly."

"Then where? I need to be at Postrio by seven."

"How about the Postrio bar at six?"

"Six-thirty."

"Great. I'll be the one with the frayed collar."

"And I'll be the one with the décolletage."

After we said good-bye, I called Wally Briscoe at the North Station. When he came on the line, I asked if he could widen his focus to see what connections he could come up with between Charley and any of the lawyers or witnesses or anyone else in the courtroom. I gave him as many names as I had. Then I asked if he knew that Charley was out of jail.

"The whole department's heard; there's a manhunt on for the guy. He made the jail deputies look bad and some of them have friends in the PD. Could get dangerous out there."

"You involved in the hunt yourself?"

"Not really."

"They know you and Charley were close?"

"Not really."

"Any idea where he might go in this situation?"

"Not really," he said again, then heard himself and laughed.

"You can't talk, right? Because of who's around you?"

"Something like that."

"Could you help me out if we met somewhere?"

"I don't think so."

"I want to show you a picture."

"Of what?"

"Charley and a guy he went to the academy with."

"What does that have to do with anything?"

"I don't know," I admitted.

"I don't think I can make it," he said.

"This is Charley we're talking about, Wally. Like you said, if I don't find him pretty quickly, it could get dangerous out there. Including for anyone who tries to bring Charley in."

Wally paused, then murmured something to someone else, then spoke so softly I barely heard him. "I was thinking of the delta thing."

"The fishing cabin."

"Right."

"Is there a phone up there?"

"Not the last I knew."

"Any neighbors you could call who could tell you if anyone's using it?"

"Nope."

"I've only gone with him once. Remind me how to get there."

"Just a minute."

Wally waited, presumably for someone to leave the room, then gave me some quick instructions on how to navigate the complicated series of roads that led to a shady spot south of Rio Vista on the Sacramento River delta. Charley fished there sometimes, along with some buddies from the old days, buddies that are mostly long gone; it was as likely a hideout as anywhere I could think of.

I gave Wally my home number and asked him to call if anything else occurred to him. "Also," I added, "if the manhunt is closing in, I'd like to know it ahead of time."

"Why?"

"I might be able to bring down enough heat to make sure Charley doesn't get killed."

"Heat? You?"

"Not me. Some people I know."

"Friends in high places."

"A few."

His chuckle implied I was having delusions of grandeur. "I'm not in the loop on this thing," he said, "but if I hear anything I'll let you know."

I thanked Wally for his help and dialed another number.

"Anything new?" I asked when Detective Earl Jamette came on the line.

"On menacing the shrink? Naw. She still won't open her files."

"Been any new threats?"

"Not that she said."

"Check Charley Sleet's active case log. See if there's a link between him and Derwinski in connection with someone other than Leonard Wints."

"But Wints is the guy he shot."

"That might not have been the guy he was aiming for."

Jamette thought it over. "I still need a list to match against, don't I? If the shrink won't fork it over, I don't see how it gets me anywhere."

"Maybe her name's in one of Charley's files. Screen them for psych cases first."

"They're all psych cases; it'll take weeks to narrow it down."

"Maybe you'll get lucky."

"I ain't been lucky since my ex-wife remarried."

"And have Gary Hilton call me," I said before he hung up.

"I'll leave word. But he don't always return his calls."

"How does he get any work done?"

"Who says he does?"

Jamette's laugh was bitter and derisive. I wondered what had gone down between him and Gary Hilton.

I called the poker group one by one—the broker, the pathologist, and the restaurateur—and set things up for eight that evening. I told them to rack their brains in the meantime for any connection between Charley and players in the drama other than Leonard Wints, and also for any ideas of where he might be hiding. They promised to give it a go.

I was about to head for San Bruno to see what I could learn about Charley's escape from jail when someone entered the outer office. I ambled over to the coffee machine, where I could look at him without being seen.

He was wearing a gray worsted suit, shiny black loafers with tassels, and a shirt as white as rice. He looked like a haberdasher but what he was was a cop.

When I went out to greet him, he stuck out a hand. "Gary Hilton. Detective Sergeant. SFPD."

I did what I was supposed to do with his hand. "Marsh Tanner." I gestured for him to come in my office and sit across from my desk, then I assumed my throne. In the time it took to get there, I decided to be careful with him.

"I know you by reputation," he said with easy friendliness. His hair was trim and razor-cut, his flesh was tanned and healthy, his body was sleek and fit, his jewelry was golden and plentiful. I'll bet Charley hated his guts.

"I've followed some of your cases in the *Chronicle*," he went on. "Shutting down that Healthways operation was good work."

"I manage to get it right on occasion. What can I do for you, Sergeant?"

"Gary. Can I be frank, Mr. Tanner?"

"Sure, Gary." He seemed amused that I didn't invite him to use my given name.

"I assume you know that Sleet broke jail."

"If someone opens the door and lets you out, I'm not sure it amounts to a jailbreak."

Hilton shrugged. "Whatever. What I'm wondering is if what you're doing now is hiding him."

We stared each other down for several seconds, the cocky young cop and the grizzled PI. No one cried uncle, but no one raised their arms in triumph either.

"I don't know where he is," I said finally.

Hilton smiled around nicely capped teeth. "And I'm supposed to just leave it at that?"

I shrugged. "Why not?"

His eyes strayed to the painting on the wall behind me. "Nice art."

"Thanks."

"Klees cost a fortune."

"Not this one."

"Lucky you."

"Lucky me."

He waited for an explanation but he didn't get one. For the millionth time, I gave thanks to the client who'd given it to me.

"I'm thinking that even if you knew where he was you wouldn't tell me," Hilton went on.

"That's certainly possible."

Hilton stood up and began to pace. I stood behind the desk and watched him.

"There's a lot of heat on to find the guy," he said when he got to the window.

"I imagine so."

"The sheriff and the department don't look so good in this."

"No, you don't."

"So you'd be earning big points by helping us out. Points that could come in handy down the road."

"I'm sure they could."

"Then there's the personality part of it."

"What part is that?"

"Some of the guys working this thing wouldn't mind seeing Sleet cut down."

"All the way down, you mean."

He nodded. "If I get to him first, I can keep that from happening."

"Or you could take him down and win points with the guys yourself. Provided you're good enough to take him."

Hilton's smile ossified. "Except I wouldn't want to do that."

"How would I know?"

"Because I said so."

"And I'm supposed to leave it like that?"

He didn't like his words thrown back at him. His voice darkened. "I asked around. What I heard is that if anyone knows where he is, you do."

I shrugged and thought of an exception in the person of Marjie Finnerty. "Even if it's true, it doesn't mean I know anything."

"You're saying you don't?"

"That's exactly what I'm saying."

"We can make life real complicated if we find out you're holding back in this."

"If I was holding back, I imagine I'd be worried about it." I glanced toward the door to show Hilton I'd had enough with badinage. "What if we turn it around, Gary? If you let me be the one who finds him, I could give someone like you the kind of answers I've given Charley over the years. It hasn't hurt his career any."

Hilton shook his head and rebuttoned his jacket. "We're not getting anywhere, Mr. Tanner."

"You're right, Sergeant Hilton."

"You could change it with a phone call." He tossed his card on my desk.

"So could you," I said, then told him I was in the book.

CHAPTER
19

I SPENT THE NEXT TWO HOURS HIGH IN THE HILLS ABOVE SAN Bruno, pleading my way through the gate, begging access to as many jail personnel as would talk to me, but getting nothing out of anyone. If they knew how Charley had gotten out, they weren't talking. If someone was suspected of helping him, they weren't telling me who it was. If they knew where he was going, they didn't say. If they wanted my help in finding him, they didn't ask for it. If they suspected him of killing a prisoner, they didn't let on.

Discouraged and downhearted, I drove back to the office and looked at the courtroom map Andy Potter had sent over. I didn't find anything helpful there either. In as bad a mood as I can muster, I trudged up to my apartment to freshen up for my meeting with Danielle.

My wardrobe is in the nature of a natural disaster, so I was surprised that fifteen minutes went by before I settled on the ensemble that seemed appropriate. What was appropriate was not too sharp and not too scruffy, a shade above neutral but several shades below avid, a statement of interest but not a confession of lust. I had a tweed jacket that hit it just right, but true to my word, the only shirt that matched the coat was fluffy at the collar and cuffs. Maybe she'd think it was satire.

I got to Postrio early and was on my second scotch by the time she swept into the room. Since most of the walls were mirrors, her entrance created a stir. All the masculine eyes in the place were popped as wide as windows and all the females were squinting down their powdered noses in the manner of distaff assassins. Danielle hadn't been kidding about the décolletage.

"Mr. Tanner." She extended a bejeweled hand. At its tip her nails were the color of eggplant, a match for the gloss on her lips.

I stood up, took her hand, and kissed it.

She smiled at our turn of burlesque, then settled into her chair the way cats settle into their baskets. The waiter was there in a flash—he must have had seniority. She ordered a Campari and soda and shook her head a single time when he eagerly proffered a menu. His expression was a precise definition of crestfallen.

After he'd gone, I told Danielle I liked her dress. It was more a gown than a dress, crushed velvet in a dark kelly green, as far off the shoulder as it could slide, with a trim of burgundy satin at the bodice and hem. The gold chain at her neck supported a pendant in the shape of the universal sign for women that glowed like a brand just below the crevasse that was formed by her breasts. The college chum was going to get an eyeful and probably an earful as well. I was glad to be an hors d'oeuvre.

"You keep the glamorous part of yourself nicely under wraps at the office," I said, just to get things underway.

"At the office I see lots of women who have had sex used against them like a bullwhip. In public, I like to help reclaim our share of the playing field."

"You've claimed about ninety percent of it in the place."

"Thank you. I do what I can."

The waiter brought the drinks and we made a silent toast to whatever each of us wanted the fates to deliver to us. At the moment what I wanted was more women like Danielle Derwinski in my life. What she wanted was probably close to the polar opposite.

A breeze blew in the door, unseasonably balmy and romantic. As if on order, a jazz piano tinkled to life somewhere down the block in a decent imitation of Garner.

"Why are we here, Mr. Tanner?" she asked after she licked the taste of Campari off her lips.

"I'm here to find out whether my friend Charley Sleet wants to kill you." I made it sound as if I was there to chat about snack foods and laundry products.

I'd hoped to jar something loose but she didn't bat an eye. "Who says he does?"

"He does. Sort of."

She raised a brow. "By which you mean . . . ?"

"That he wasn't avenging Jillian Wints. I think he was gunning for someone else."

"Me?"

"I don't know, but you seem a likely target."

"Why?"

"Because you wreak so much havoc in the world."

Her smile was easy and arch. "Is that what they call it these days?"

"Who?"

"The CMI. I would have thought they'd dredge up a stronger term."

I smiled. "That's not from them; that's from me."

"So they've persuaded you I'm the Antichrist? Or at least the Great Emasculator?"

"They haven't persuaded me of anything except that there's lots of pain connected with this recovered memory business. I was holding a little girl in my lap yesterday and it occurred to me that someday someone might call it child molesting. I didn't like thinking about what my life would be like if someone ever did that."

"*Were* you molesting her?"

"Of course not."

"Then what's the problem?"

"The problem is that doesn't seem to be the issue anymore. What really happened doesn't count. What counts is what some therapist *assumes* has happened."

She shook her head. "What the patient *feels* has happened."

"If you feel it, it must be true?"

"What other explanation is there?"

I harked back to my reading. "Transference. False or implanted memories. Hypnotic suggestion. Invented explanations to give the therapist what she wants."

"But why would someone invent such a thing if it wasn't true?"

"Because they want someone to blame for their misery. Because they've been told men are evil. Because sex is so scary it's an easy answer for everything. And on the therapists' side, because if you create the problem, you control the cure."

Her smile was as icy and imperious as she could render it. "Or could it be because sexual abuse of children is rampant in all cultures of the world and will continue to be until its victims unite and fight back? You want women to suffer in silence, Mr. Tanner, the way they have always suffered. You want to deny them the right to compensation from their victimizers for the wounds inflicted on them."

"Don't misunderstand, Ms. Derwinski. I only want to deny compensation if the memories are fake and the dads haven't done anything wrong."

"But the memories *aren't* fake."

"What about the people who say there's no scientific proof that the repression of trauma *ever* occurs?"

"Those people are simply wrong. In one recent study, a researcher looked back at the hospital records of abused children—children who had suffered actual physical abuse when they were young and had been medically treated for it at the time. Then she asked these people as adults what they remembered about the abuse. A large percentage of them *didn't remember it at all*. The *entire experience* had been repressed, in some cases even

the fact of hospitalization itself. An experience that was
fully documented in hospital records was entirely absent
from memory of a significant number of the subjects.
What more proof do you need?"

"But what about the therapists who want the world to
believe that every single patient that walks in their door
has suffered from sexual abuse."

She raised a sculpted brow. "And you're qualified to
say they haven't?"

I remained the devil's advocate. "Yes, I am."

"Based on what?"

"Probabilities and logic."

"How probable is it that the leader of the CMI himself
was arrested twice for abusing his daughters? Two ar-
rests; one conviction on a plea of nolo contendere. But
he doesn't nolo now, does he? He claims such allegations
are the result of a conspiracy hatched by witches like
me."

I'd been knocked off track but it seemed advisable to
stay there. "Let's change the subject."

"To what?"

"You and Charley."

"If he was trying to kill me, as you suggest, I can't tell
you why."

"Can't or won't?"

"Take your pick."

"What do you know about the Tenderloin Children's
Project?"

She shrugged. "Nothing pertinent to this discussion,
I'm afraid."

"Does the project have anything to do with the Wints
case?"

"Not that I know of."

I laughed at the dead ends I was accumulating. "He's
out of jail, you know," I said finally.

"Who?"

"Charley."

For the first time, she seemed nonplussed. A bead of
sweat was a bright new gem at the curve of her thorax.

"It's not impossible that he'll try again to do whatever he was trying to do in the courtroom. Charley's nothing if not persistent."

She shrugged, then adjusted her bodice. "Are you offering to be my bodyguard, Mr. Tanner?"

"It wouldn't be the worst move you could make."

Her smile was vague and indecipherable. "I have a feeling it might be."

I took it as a compliment but I didn't know what to do with it. "So what are those sexual deviancy evaluations you mentioned?" I blurted to fill the silence.

She blinked at the shift in focus. "What?"

"That's what you told me you'd be discussing with your dinner companion. I take it there's some sort of test that tells if you're a pervert or not."

"Yes, there is."

"So what do you think about them?"

"I feel they identify important proclivities; Jed, my dinner companion, feels the science is so soft and the risk of a false positive so great that they should be discontinued. I've got some new data I'm going to spring on him in an effort to change his mind. Why do you ask?"

"Just making conversation. For the record, I agree with Jed. No one should be called a pervert on the basis of a test."

"Have you ever taken one?"

"No."

"Do you know anything at all about it?"

"Nothing."

"Then why are you opening your mouth on the subject?"

"This is America. I've got a right to be ignorant about anything. If you don't believe me, just listen to KSFO."

She shook her head with mellow exasperation and settled back in the seat. We sipped our drinks and flirted with our eyes for a time; at least that's what I hoped we were doing. Maybe we were just being bored.

"Let's talk about something else," she said after a minute.

"Okay. Let's talk about us."

"Us? When did we become 'us'?"

"I was wondering if we could work on it. See each other on a personal level sometime."

"Why would we want to do that?"

"You know damned well why *I'd* want to do that. Among other things, it's what the dress is for, isn't it?"

"You flatter yourself, Mr. Tanner."

"Do I?"

"I'm afraid so."

"Then I apologize. What is it for?"

"The dress?"

I nodded.

"One thing it's for is to show you and Jed and the CMI that I'm not against fun, or sex, or men, or any of the other phobias you might assign as motives to mislead my patients about their pasts. Which means what it's really about is getting people like you to take me seriously when I tell you that Jillian Wints was sexually abused by her father to the point that she will be emotionally impaired for the rest of her life, no matter what therapist she sees."

"I'll take you seriously on that score if you take me seriously when I tell you that Charley Sleet may be trying to kill you. If that's what he wants to do, that's what he *will* do, unless you give me enough information to stop him."

"How will information help? Wouldn't hiring you to protect me work better?"

"I can't protect you from Charley."

"Why not?"

"Because he's better than I am and he's better than anyone else is, too. Which means if he wants to take you out, he will. All I can do is convince him not to try. And the only way I can do that is to know why he wants to."

"I see."

I looked at her. "You know, don't you?"

"Know what?"

"Who he was trying to kill."

"I don't know if I do or not," she said, then hugged herself for warmth, then looked at her watch, then abandoned me for her date in the restaurant beyond the door in the rear of the room.

CHAPTER

20

THEY WERE THERE BY EIGHT-TEN, PRETTY MUCH A RECORD ON the promptness meter.

Clay arrived first, dressed immaculately as usual, as eager as an agent, also as usual. Poker night is some sort of sacrament for Clay, although I'm not sure quite why; I think it has something to do with his wife. Then came Al Goldsberry, the forensic pathologist. Al isn't aging well—he's too thin, too toothsome, too bald, and too weary. He plays cards with less and less enthusiasm with fewer and fewer grams of his intellect, which means he's a loser almost every time these days—I expect him to drop out before long. And finally came Tommy Milano. Tommy is short and fat as befits the owner of an Italian eatery, and he's the newest addition to the group. His restaurant is out in the avenues, which means it's too far away for the rest of us to frequent very often, which we wouldn't anyway because it's not that good. But we like Tommy because Tommy likes life and because Tommy brings the wine and the bread and the pasta.

Usually there's lots of sparring before we get down to the cards, riffs and variations on several standard themes: Tommy is accused of poisoning countless customers with his sauces, Al is accused of doing autopsies on live people and practicing necrophilia, Clay is accused of bilking widows and orphans and trading on inside information, I'm accused of alcoholism and keyhole peeping. And Charley is accused of graft and brutality. Since we've gotten better and better at the gibes, more and more blood gets drawn, not always in good humor. But tonight the rapier wits remained in their scabbards because the mood in the room was more fit for a wake than a roast.

We gathered our food and drink and took our usual seats at my dining-room table. After they directed some silent sentiments toward Charley's empty chair, they turned their eyes toward me. I made sure everyone was up to speed on the case, including the fact of Charley's jailbreak and the ensuing manhunt by the cops, then gave them a summary of who I'd talked to and what I'd learned to date, which amounted to half a dozen dead ends. Then I showed them the snapshots I'd retrieved from Flora's watering can. They went from hand to hand like a smokeless narcotic, provoking smiles and murmurs and remembrances, but nothing more concrete.

By the time I was done, everyone was shaking his head with frustration or muttering a helpless curse. "Cops'll gun him down, you watch," Tommy muttered. "He's got the goods on too many of them. Told me once he didn't know a single man on the force who hadn't committed a felony. They been wanting a way to get rid of him."

"Charley'd eat a round himself before he'd let them take him," Clay murmured, the hard-boiled jargon oddly brutal in the mouth of such a placid man.

Al looked my way. "So what do we do, Marsh? Is there a chance to get him out of this? I mean realistically?"

I avoided the question by saying that was up to Jake Hattie to estimate. "Jake needs input on three issues," I continued, to turn them from moaning and groaning toward recollection and speculation. "First, what was Charley trying to accomplish in that courtroom, and maybe in the jail? Second, assuming he had some sort of grudge to settle, why would a guy who worked with the system for thirty years all of a sudden become a vigilante? And third, where the hell is he? Let's take the last one first," I said when no one took up the slack. "Where's he gone?"

"The fishing cabin," Tommy said quickly.

I nodded. "I thought of that, too. We need to check it out. Can anyone run up to Rio Vista this week and look it over?"

After some hesitation, Clay and Al raised their hands. "This is a bad time for me," Tommy murmured in expiation. "My chef quit on me Saturday."

"Chef," Al repeated darkly. "That's the guy who makes the meatballs in his armpits, right?"

"Fuck you and the corpse you rode in on," Tommy replied. "Asshole didn't like my recipe for marinara. Can you believe it?"

We could but we didn't say so.

"What do I do if he's up there?" Clay asked me, to get us back on track.

"Call me and let me know. Keep him in sight till I get there."

"And then?"

I shrugged. "I try to talk him in off the ledge."

"What if he doesn't want to come?"

I had no answer that was comforting. "We let him jump, I guess."

Clay lowered his eyes and made crumbs out of a hunk of French bread. "Without telling the cops where he is?"

"That's right."

"But that's a crime, isn't it? Accessory after the fact or something?"

"Aiding and abetting a fugitive, too, I imagine. So what? This is Charley we're talking about."

I didn't give Clay a chance to rebut my rhetoric or question how Charley would be better off if all of his friends were in jail. "Where else could he be?"

No one offered a suggestion. I wondered if they really

didn't have any or if they had suddenly turned leery because I was so cavalier about Clay's concerns. I decided it didn't matter.

"Anyone know anyplace else Charley hung out, especially out in the country?"

"Why the country?" Al asked.

"Because he seems to have taken his hunting clothes with him."

"To do what?"

"Hunker down, I'd say. Live off the land and stuff."

"He hunted pheasant out by Modesto," Tommy offered.

"He shot a deer up by Quincy once," Al added.

I laughed. "And he was so upset about it he sold his deer rifle the next day. Anything else on his whereabouts?"

All of a sudden I got a tidal wave:

"He liked the lodge at Yosemite."

"He took Flora to Carmel every Easter."

"He went duck hunting up in Oregon once."

"He bought a car from a guy in Tracy."

"On Halloween he bought pumpkins for the Tenderloin kids over at Half Moon Bay."

I finally perked up. "What kids are those?"

"Down at that center," Al Goldsberry said. "The place on Ellis Street, near Glide Memorial. The Tenderloin Children's Project, it's called. Charley spent a lot of time there. I went with him a couple of times to give physical exams to some kids he thought were being abused."

"Were they?"

"I think one of them was. At least I told Charley it was possible."

"What'd he do?"

"He said he'd take care of it."

"Aren't you supposed to report something like that?"

"Yeah, but Charley asked me not to."

At one time or another we had all bent the rules for Charley because he had bent the rules for us.

"What was the kid's name?" I asked.

Al hesitated.

"Come on, goddamnit."

"Tafoya."

"What?"

"Tafoya Burris. Why?"

"Nothing."

But it wasn't nothing, it was the first real link I'd found between Charley's personal life and what had gone down in the courtroom. The clipping in Charley's house described misdeeds at the children's project, plus I was sure Tafoya Burris was the young woman who had entered Danielle Derwinski's office just as I'd been leaving and had been greeted as a prodigal by the receptionist. The name couldn't have been a coincidence.

I asked Al who was in charge of things down at the children's center.

"The one I met was a guy named Morrison. Hank Morrison. Heavy dude. Seemed to run the show."

"I'll follow up on that one," I said. "Anything else on where he might be?"

No one offered anything.

"Then let's move on. Under the heading of why the hell did he do what he did, if no one has any thoughts I'm going to need some legwork." I looked at Al. "You're the man for the job."

"Fine with me. What job is it?"

"I want you to check all the hospitals in the city."

"Why?"

"I want to know if they have any record on our boy."

"You think he's in a hospital?" Tommy asked.

"Not now probably, but recently maybe."

"What makes you think so?" Al asked.

"Nothing specific, but he's been acting crazy and I've been thinking maybe some sort of medication got to him—Prozac, Halcion, something like that. Or maybe something is really wrong with him, something that fucked up his head. Like a stroke."

Everyone in the room seemed jolted by the prospect of a defect in Charley's massive physique. If Charley's body could go bad, anyone's body could go bad.

Al was the first to speak. "I'll get on it right away, Marsh. It'll take a while to cover them all, but I'll try to get some help with it."

"Did he ever say anything to you along medical lines, Al? Ask for a free diagnosis?"

He shook his head. "Not since the time we talked vasectomies. But that was years ago."

"Charley had a vasectomy?"

"I don't know if he went through with it, but he sure as hell asked me about it. That was the first time we met, I think. He had some questions on a tox report on a murder victim and after we went over the drug numbers he started asking me about getting clipped."

"When was this?"

"Long time ago. Twenty years, maybe. Maybe more."

It seemed relevant, somehow, the talk about sterilization, but I didn't know quite why.

"The subject of children brings me to the next item on the list, which is the baby in the snapshot. When I found the thing, I got a feeling the baby was Charley's and that that's what this has been about in some way. I can't prove it's true, but that's what I think. Any ideas?"

No one said anything.

"Anyone ever hear Charley hint that he'd been a father way back when?"

Everyone shook their heads.

"Charley loved kids," Clay said finally. "He's been involved with them in a major way ever since I've known him. My brokerage firm funded a T-ball team one summer Charley coached in the PAL."

"That cuts against him putting the baby up for adoption," Al pointed out.

"Did I miss something? What does adoption have to do with it?" Tommy asked.

"I thought it might explain things if Jillian Wints is Charley's daughter."

Tommy shook his head. "He'd never do that. Put a kid up for adoption. Neither would Flora."

"Plus, he told you it didn't have anything to do with the Wints girl," Clay reminded.

"Which might mean that it did and he's trying to shove me off the track. Charley's not above a fib when it serves larger purposes."

I took out a sheet of paper and read the names I'd written on it. "Andy Potter says these people were in the courtroom that day. Anyone know any of them?"

"Meltonian used to come in the restaurant once in a while," Tommy said. "Had a sister lived out my way, I think. Haven't seen him in years, though."

Al and Clay exchanged wry smiles. I could taste Tommy's marinara sauce until I took another sip of beer.

"And Andy, of course," Al said. Andy played poker with us on occasion.

"Anyone know of any trouble between Andy and Charley?" I asked. "Andy was supposed to drop by tonight but I guess he had other plans."

Everyone shook their head.

"Marjie Finnerty and Charley were lovers," I said. "Been hot and heavy for four months. She's Meltonian's clerk."

That one brought another round of murmurs and at least one trill of satisfaction.

"Maybe she dumped him," Clay said. "Or maybe she just made him crazy. A woman could drive the greatest guy in the world insane."

There came Clay and his wife again. What the hell was going on with them?

"I didn't think there'd ever be anyone for Charley but Flora," Tommy said softly.

"Me neither," Al agreed.

"Speaking of Flora," I said, "I seem to remember a sister."

"Right," Tommy said. "Charley brought her to the restaurant one night. Long time ago, though."

"Remember her name?"

"Ellen. No. Emily, I think. Emily . . ." Tommy's brow wrinkled at the effort to dredge up a surname.

"Fulton," Al said. "At least that was Flora's maiden name. Flora Fulton."

"What a wonderful woman," Clay said. "Poker's never been the same since she quit making those brownies. No offense," he added sheepishly, after a brief glance at Tommy's scowl.

"Anyone know where the sister lives?"

"I think Concord," Al said. "Charley talked about going out there once. He hated his brother-in-law, I remember."

"Right," Tommy said. "Gus in the discount carpet business. A suede shoe guy. Hookley was his name. That must be the sister's name, too. Emily Hookley."

"Anything on anyone else in the room? Cartson the lawyer? The judge? The court reporter? The *Chronicle* woman? Anyone?"

No one had anything to say.

"Think about it for a while," I said.

We finished our food and our drinks in silence broken only by laments about the Niners and curses at the cops. Then Clay reminded us of the time Charley had won a huge pot with a ten high. And then came the deluge—Charley and his clothes, Charley and his bleeding heart, Charley and his courage, Charley and his wife, Charley and his job. Everyone had an anecdote; everyone paid a tribute. But by the time the guys had left, memory had been superseded by reality and I was haunted by the possibility that I would never see Charley again, at least not outside the silks and satins of a coffin.

CHAPTER

21

THREE MEN WERE RECUMBENT ON THE SIDEWALK, UNCON-
scious for reasons that appeared to range from intoxica-
tion to assault and battery. Two women were dressed in
high heels and short shorts and tube tops, shivering from
the assault of winter, offering their puffy bodies to any
man who tarried near their corner. Every second building had been abandoned by both owner and tenant, only
to be reclaimed by squatters doing and dealing dope and
transients looking for a roof for a night and willing to
trespass to get one. The bar in the middle of the block
looked like it specialized in absinthe; the shop on the
corner offered both pornography and ice cream. And at
the center of it all was the Tenderloin Children's Project,
proving that no part of a city is too abandoned for
parents to bring kids into it.

If a child is raised in such an environment, by the time
it reaches the age of twelve it knows that it has grown up
in a sewer: They don't have Tenderloins on *Sesame
Street*. With realization comes outrage—someone's going to pay and that someone is often an innocent party,
appearing in the wrong place at the wrong time and

behaving in a way that suggests a lack of respect, which is the only thing of value the kid has to protect. Institutions like the Tenderloin Children's Project exist to channel that outrage toward something productive, toward achievement, not destruction. It's an uphill battle, of course, which was the kind of fight Charley Sleet specialized in.

It was Saturday morning; I expected the place to be teeming with kids and it was. Most of them were Asian and most of them were gathered around a computer in the far corner of the main room, listening to a young Asian man talk about chat rooms and news groups and web pages. I smiled to myself. Conservatives have done away with affirmative action at the state's premier university on the assumption that too many slots were going to unqualified minorities. If they truly do go to a merit system at Cal, eighty percent of the school will be Asian and most of the unqualified applicants will have both white skins and irate parents.

Another group of children, older and more ethnically diverse than the computer kids, was lined up against a wall being shown movements of self-defense by a young man wearing black pajamas and displaying flashy martial moves. Still another cluster, numbering only six, sat in pairs on the floor playing chess on warped and tattered boards. In another corner, a sullen teenager in baggy pants and a hooded Raiders jacket was washing gang graffiti off the walls, probably as punishment for some similar transgression.

The discipline in the room was impressive—no one could be heard but the instructors and the faint thumps of rap music chugging through the sound system—but the facility itself was pathetic. There was barely enough space to accommodate effective instruction and the lack of rudimentary amenities was striking—except for the computer tables, there wasn't any furniture in sight. The paneled walls were warped and stained, the linoleum floor was curled and scabbed, the acoustical ceiling was soft and sagging, suggestive of a porous roof. Still, the majority of kids were smiling and more than a few seemed rapturous.

At first I saw no one resembling Hank Morrison, the guy Al Goldsberry had talked to at Charley's behest, but in the next minute a man emerged from a room in the back and stood in the center of the floor, arms crossed and eyes active, in the manner of an overseer. I went up to him and told him my name and said I was looking for a man named Morrison.

"I'm him," he said, with a perfect pitch of indifference. His eyes continued their inspection; his arms stayed crossed on his chest.

He was big and buff, dressed in Levi's and a faded Giants T-shirt, his pecs and biceps stretching the black cotton fabric to its limits, his black eyes and sharp jaw both fearless and friendly, essential attributes for anyone dealing effectively with kids. His bearing suggested that the only thing that would command a hundred percent of his attention was a knife fight.

"What can I do for you?" he asked after taking stock of me and maintaining his distance.

There were several paths to take and I chose the wrong one. "I'm here to see Tafoya Burris."

He raised a brow and looked at me. "You a cop?" He paused. "No, you're not a cop."

"Why does it matter?"

He shrugged and stayed silent.

"Tafoya might have some information I could use," I said.

"Information about what?"

I smiled. "That's between me and her at this point."

He made an elaborate search of the room. "Funny, but I don't see the 'her' part of that combination."

I opted not to fence with him. "She comes to the center, right?"

He shrugged. "She plays chess sometimes."

"With Charley Sleet sometimes?"

"Sometimes."

"So where can I find her?"

"She's not here."

"She doesn't come in on Saturdays?"

"Sometimes."

"So where can I find her?" I repeated.

Morrison unhooked his thick arms and looked at me with unbridled disdain. "Look. Most people who come looking for these kids don't want to do them good, they want to do them harm. Abuse them physically or sexually; exploit them economically; use them as weapons in a domestic dispute; get them to rat on their peers or their parents. I get real used to not saying much about them."

"I can understand that. But I'm a friend of Charley's."

"So you say."

"I'm friend enough to know he's in trouble."

He shrugged. "So I heard."

"I'm trying to do something about it."

"Like what?"

"Find out why he became a killer, for one thing."

"And you think that's going to make a difference?"

"It might."

"Might not, too. If reasons counted, wouldn't be a black man behind bars in this city."

I didn't have time to debate the theory and practice of punishment or the genesis and culture of crime. "Charley spent some time here lately," I said, before Morrison could wander off.

"A lot of time," he corrected.

"Working with kids."

He nodded. "Working with kids."

"The trial in the courtroom involved a kid. Or at least what happened to a woman when she *was* a kid."

"Did it?"

"The woman's name is Jillian Wints. Know her?"

Morrison looked down his nose at me. "She live down here in the 'Loin?"

I shook my head. "Jordan Park and the Marina."

He laughed. "Don't get many kids from those places."

I finally lost my cool. "Look, Morrison, was Charley doing good down here or not?"

"He was okay."

"Then why don't you cut me some slack and help get him out of trouble?"

"I got to make sure that don't mean someone else gets *in* trouble."

"Someone like Tafoya, you mean."

He shrugged. "Whoever." His gaze focused on someone across the room. "Hey, Juwanna. That better not be a box cutter in your pants. I find a cutter, you be barred for a month."

Juwanna shook her head but edged toward the door all the same, and finally disappeared in a rush.

"She's a good kid," Morrison said. "Too bad it takes more than that."

"What else does it take?"

He looked toward the sagging ceiling. "A miracle. We done now?"

It took some doing but I made my voice conciliatory. "Here's all I know. I know Charley was friends with Tafoya and I know he was concerned enough about her to ask his friend Dr. Goldsberry to take a look at her to see if she was being abused. Goldsberry told him it was a possibility. A few days later, Charley went off his rocker in a case that involved another victim of sexual abuse. I'm trying to find the connection. You got a problem with that?"

"Not so far."

"Okay, then tell me where Tafoya lives."

He shook his head. "We don't give out that kind of information. Project policy. They find out I talk, I lose my job."

Morrison seemed both adamant and sincere; I began to back off.

"Then tell me this. The psychologist in the courtroom the day Charley shot Leonard Wints seems to be the same psychologist who's been treating Tafoya Burris."

"Which means?"

"I don't know what it means. It's one of the things I'm trying to find out."

"Then why don't you talk to the psychologist?"

"I have. She won't tell me anything either."

"Well, you're wasting your time down here, because Tafoya isn't going to be——"

He looked past me toward the front door. "Speak of the devil," he said.

I turned to look. Danielle Derwinski was walking toward us at the pace of a drum majorette, wearing a blue twill jumpsuit with a zipper down the front and white sneakers that squeaked as she walked. She was so fiercely focused that she didn't recognize me.

"Hank, what's this about Tafoya?" she began, panting from the pace of her entrance. "I hear the police took her——"

When she'd finally absorbed who I was, she stopped. "You."

"And you."

"What are *you* doing here?"

"What are you?"

"I *work* here."

"Since when?"

"Since they opened the doors; I volunteer at the center every other Saturday. Since I've never seen *you* down here before, I assume you're here on business."

I matched her attitude as best I could. "That's right. And my business tells me you lied to me, Danielle. You lied about not knowing Charley, you lied about not knowing of a connection between him and the Wints case, you lied——"

She held up a hand to stop me. "Spare me the righteous whine." She shook her head in exasperation. "If I ever meet a truly grown-up male, I'll kiss his feet and buy him a magnum of champagne."

"And if I ever meet a shrink who doesn't need therapy more than her patients, I'll kiss her ass and buy her a bottle of scotch. Unblended."

Hank Morrison was laughing at our face-off. "I see you two have met. Love at first sight, it looks like."

Danielle dismissed me with a look of irritation. "We need to talk," she said to Morrison.

"They took her out of here this morning."

"Where to?"

"The station, I guess. Or maybe the morgue."

"Surely they wouldn't make her——"

"I hope not," he said. "But you never know. Cops'll do anything."

"Who's in the morgue?" I interjected.

Morrison looked at Derwinski, and Derwinski looked at me. "None of your business."

"If it has to do with Tafoya, I think it is my business."

She hesitated, then shrugged. "The guy in the morgue is Tafoya's stepfather."

"What happened to him?"

"The usual in this part of town," Morrison said.

"Murder? Or OD?"

"Murder."

"When?"

"Yesterday."

"Do they think Tafoya did it?"

Morrison laughed sardonically. "They *know* Tafoya didn't do it."

"Then why did they want her?"

"Just routine, they said. Jacking her around, is what it was. Like always."

I looked at Derwinski. "Was her stepfather the one who abused her?"

She started to say something, then stopped. "I can't get into that."

A lightbulb went on in my skull and I started to sweat. "Where did this murder happen? Why are they sure Tafoya didn't do it?"

Morrison looked at Derwinski, and Derwinski stayed silent.

"Come on. This could be important."

"It happened in jail," Morrison blurted finally. "That's how they know. Bastard used to work here. Got busted for stealing funds from the project and got himself killed in the slammer."

"His name isn't Burris, it's Lumpley, right?"

"Yeah. You know him?"

I shook my head. "He was killed at San Bruno, right?"

Morrison shrugged.

"Shit."

"Shit what?"

"I think Charley killed him."

"What?" The word came in a chorus of two.

"Charley got out of jail yesterday. After he was gone, they found a stiff in the shower. I'm betting it was Tafoya's stepfather."

Morrison shook his head. "He's in it for real now. One he might skate on, but two? They got him good this time."

I didn't say as much, but I was afraid I agreed with him.

CHAPTER

22

A MAN YELLING OUT OF A BACK ROOM CALLED MORRISON to the telephone. After he left, I turned to Danielle. "Can we go somewhere and talk?"

"Now?"

"Yes."

She shook her head. "I'm going to the station to find Tafoya."

"Why?"

Her nose wrinkled with irritation. "So I can keep her from ending up like Jillian Wints. Then I'm booked with kids down here till noon. Then I need to run errands." She furled a brow and spoke with reluctance. "We could meet this evening, I suppose. For a short time."

"Where and when?"

She named a bar on Fillmore Street and the hour of eight o'clock. She wasn't happy but I didn't care. Time was running out. Something important was coming to an end, something rare and irreplaceable was about to evaporate unless I put a stop to it and right now I had no stopper. If my company was distasteful to Danielle, so be it. She was still the best lead I had into the heart and mind of Charley Sleet.

I did some errands myself for a couple of hours—buying groceries, getting gas, carrying some clothes to the cleaner's—then went to the office and used the phone to track down Wally Briscoe.

Cops are notoriously tough to locate by anyone but another cop because most of the people who are trying to find them have an agenda: Criminals want to threaten or cajole them and the media wants to make them look bad. But I caught a break in the person of a bartender at the Bohemian Cigar Store who knew Wally from way back and gave me his home number when I told him how crucial it was.

Wally was about to leave for the ball game, a Saturday meeting between the Warriors and SuperSonics. The Warriors were out of it but the Sonics were not—another chance for the locals to play spoiler—and Wally was primed for the game.

"Can't it wait till Monday?" he asked when I told him I needed to see him.

"I want to show you something. It'll just take a minute."

"I go all the way down to your office, I'll miss the tip-off."

"I'll meet you somewhere else. What route do you take to the game?"

He thought about it. "Be at the Union 76 station at Geary and Park Presidio at noon sharp. I can give you five minutes."

"I'll be there," I said, and I was, after touching base with Tommy Milano and learning that none of Charley's old haunts had seen his burly person lately, certainly not since he'd broken out of jail. Tommy fired off a lot of questions that I couldn't answer, then asked what he should do next. "Pray" was all I could think of to tell him.

I'd been at the gas station ten minutes when Wally pulled up in his Jeep. There were three buddies in with him, presumably fellow officers, dressed for a game and primed for a good time. The two in back were normal-sized but the one in front was huge. All three wore Giants caps and two wore Warriors jackets as well. They probably had autographs from Barry and Thurmond and Mullin at home, on balls and cards and programs; I bet no more than one of them had a wife. I don't think I'd have enjoyed sitting near them at the game—one of the biggest mistakes you can make is to cross a cop on his day off when he's bound and determined to have fun, even if it means being crude and obnoxious.

Wally got out of the car and came over to mine. Before the door slammed behind him, his friends muttered something I didn't catch but the tone was snide and insulting. Wally waved for them to shut up, then got in my car and closed the door.

"I got only a minute."

"A minute's enough." I gestured. "Any of those guys know Charley?"

"Naw, they work the Sunset. Charley never went out there much. Said the salt air was bad for his lungs." Wally laughed. "Only thing bad for his lungs were those honking cigars he used to smoke. God, those things were foul."

We shared a memory of Charley and his toxic stogies.

"What's this stuff I need to see so bad?" Wally continued, a look of extravagant irritation on his face for the benefit of his traveling companions.

There were some preliminaries to take care of. "Have you got any more dope on the jailbreak?"

Wally shrugged. "Not much. They think a deputy named Curtis was the one who let him out. Seems Curtis's kid got caught in a meth raid out by City College last year but Charley recognized the name and let him skate on the beef. Friday morning, Curtis returned the favor. Now he's behind bars himself."

"And the dead guy's name is Lumpley, right?"

Wally blinked. "That's not public yet."

"I know."

Wally shook his head. "You got wires into everything, don't you?"

"I haven't got a wire to Charley. Have the manhunters come up with a lead?"

"Not that I heard," Wally said. "But I probably wouldn't."

"Gary Hilton came calling on me."

"Figured he would." Wally smiled. "A real jim-dandy, isn't he?"

I nodded. "He thought I was aiding and abetting."

"Gary assumes the worst about people. It's got him a long way up the ladder—youngest detective in the division."

"But not the smartest."

"Not far from it. Why? He give you some serious grief?"

"Not really, but he wanted to. He have anything personal against Charley?"

Wally's eyes wandered. "Probably; he isn't Charley's type of guy. But I don't know nothing specific."

I gestured toward the Jeep. "In case your buddies over there think otherwise, I don't know where Charley is either."

Wally wriggled uneasily. "You know cops. We think all civilians have something to hide."

When we glanced their way, the guys in the Jeep beckoned Wally to rejoin them. Wally waved to show he understood. "I got to get moving, Marsh. We got this tailgate thing lined up. Couple of chicks work dispatch for the Alameda sheriff. If they're primed ahead of time, they get real friendly when the Warriors are winners." His tone left no doubt what form the friendliness came in.

I reached for the photo I'd found in the watering can in Flora's garden, the one of Charley and another young cop fresh from the police academy. I passed it to Wally. "Who's this?"

He glanced at it. "Charley."

"I know. Who else?"

He looked at it again. "Don't know."

"Look more closely. And remember, it's from thirty years ago."

He studied the photo for a few seconds. "This looks like Sanchez."

"Who's that?"

"Charley's first partner. Yeah. That's Roberto Sanchez for sure."

"I thought rookies didn't partner each other. I thought they put rookies with more experienced men."

Wally nodded. "Usually they do, but Sanchez and Charley were partnered up because Ingleside was under-staffed when they came in. They worked together more than a year before Charley got assigned to a senior man."

"Where's Sanchez now?"

Wally hesitated. "He's dead."

"Since when?"

"Long time ago."

"He die on the job?"

Wally nodded. "He and Charley chased some suspected one-eight-seven into a warehouse down in Visita-cion Valley. Charley went around to the rear of the building, Sanchez waited out front for backup. When the backup got there, Charley went in the rear and made lots of noise and the perp came out the front, guns blazing. Sanchez went down from a round in the neck; DOA at General. Charley took it hard. Even when I hooked up with him, you still couldn't say Sanchez's name without sending him into a fit."

"Why didn't Sanchez stay behind cover?"

"Who knows? Rookie courage, probably."

"What did Charley have to say about it?"

Wally hesitated. "Don't ask me. I didn't know him back then."

"Come on, Wally."

"Hey. I can't remember what I ate for breakfast. What Sleet had a bone-on for thirty years back is the least of my worries."

"Was there a shooting inquiry of any kind?"

"I don't know, Marsh. Jesus. What's the problem here? That's ancient history."

"I have a feeling it's not so ancient."

"What's that supposed to mean?"

"I don't know," I admitted.

"So is that it?" Wally asked, his hand on the door handle. "I got a ball game to go to."

I put a hand on his arm to stop him. "The guy they found dead in the jail."

"Yeah? What about him?"

"He was in for embezzlement but the paper implied they were looking into other charges. I'd like to know what they were."

"I'll try to find out." Wally smiled wryly. "They're figuring Charley took Lumpley out, too, you know. Before they're through, they'll hang every open case in the city on him."

When I didn't do anything but shrug, Wally went back to the Jeep. What he said to his buddies made them laugh. I gave them a silent curse and a friendly wave and sent them on their way, then tagged along behind.

The two in the back kept their eyes on me as they headed down Geary. They weren't happy about being tailed by a civilian but they didn't know how to stop me without missing the game.

We crossed the bridge, then I took the exit to Highway 24. As the Jeep continued south toward the Nimitz and the Coliseum, one of the guys in back flipped me the bird. I gave him a round of applause.

CHAPTER
23

CONCORD USED TO BE A SMALL SUBURB AT THE HEAD OF THE
San Ramon Valley, just south of Suisun Bay in the early
morning shade of Mount Diablo. Now it's a major city
that sprawls across lands that were formerly orchards
and grasslands the way the tents of an occupying army
used to sprawl across a battlefield. Every time I go out
there, they've added a new lane to the freeway; every
time I go out there, the smog is more noxious; every time
I go out there, Mount Diablo seems more incongruous,
just another obstacle to further development. Someday I
expect them to grade it flat and pave it over.

I joined I-680 going north, then took the Treat Boule-
vard exit and drove east until I crossed Haynesworth
Avenue and found the address of Charley Sleet's sister-
in-law, Emily Hookley.

I'd phoned ahead to make certain she'd be home when
I got there but she was so vague and noncommittal I
wasn't sure how she'd react when I actually showed up.
Probably the way most people react, with surface friendliness and subdermal trepidation.

In winter, the temperature in the valley can be twenty

degrees colder than in the sea-warmed city and today was one of those days. It must have been close to freezing and the heater in my Buick wasn't up to the task. I was glad to get out of the car and leave it to fend for itself, with only a cottonwood for a windbreaker.

Emily Fulton Hookley's house was a fifties suburban box, beige siding with blue shutters, a fenced yard, a one-car garage, and a green composition roof. It was well tended, which gave it a leg up on most of its neighbors, but it was unimaginatively decorated, without flower or shrub or other adornment beyond the blue planks of the shutters and the red brick of the stoop. The drapes were drawn and the gate was closed. It was the house of someone who trusted neither the world nor themselves, who saw danger in the slightest affirmative action, disaster in the reckless lives beyond the fence. There are millions of people just like her in the world; they're taking over the country and in the name of a wrathful God they're trying to put a stop to the nascent flights of fancy on the part of everyone else.

I rang the bell. The door opened. The woman who peered out at me was small and thin and gray-haired, with wire-rimmed glasses and tiny pearl earrings atop a flower-print dress and thick black shoes and a handkerchief stuffed under her belt. She didn't smile and she didn't frown; she didn't do anything but look at me with a blank expectancy: I could be whatever I wanted to be.

"My name is Tanner, Mrs. Hookley," I began.

"Yes?"

"We spoke on the phone this morning. I told you I'd be dropping by to talk to you this afternoon."

"You did?"

"Yes. I want to talk about Flora."

She blinked. "Flora? Where is she?" She craned her neck to look beyond me. "Is that her out in the car? Why doesn't she come in? Surely she isn't still mad about the frosting. You must be Charley." She stuck out a tiny hand that was as gnarled as a knot. I had no choice but to grasp it. "You've certainly changed since I've seen you last."

"I'm not—"

She tugged on my hand. "Please come in out of the cold, Charley. Just leave Flora out in the car if that's how she wants to behave. She'll come to her senses soon enough. I'll bet she's got goose bumps already."

To the tune of her brief giggle, I stepped inside the house. It was at least three times as warm as outdoors and smelled of molasses and mint tea. "I'm not Charley Sleet, Mrs. Hookley," I said as I released her hand. "I'm just a *friend* of Charley's."

"She must still be mad about the Bundt cake," Emily Hookley said, her mind far away from mine, her eyes on the window that looked out on the street. "I told her it didn't matter to *me* what kind of frosting she put on it. I *like* white frosting but I certainly don't *demand* white frosting. The lemon was fine. A trifle tart, I thought, and the rind wasn't grated nearly fine enough, but it was perfectly fine if you like that sort of thing." She lowered her voice. "Not many do, of course. Ethel and Grace made *faces* when they took their first bite. They wouldn't tell Flora that, but they told me, don't think they didn't. But where's the harm? That's what I say. Where's the harm in a little lemon frosting? Are you still a policeman, Charley?"

I decided to play along and see where it got me. "Yes, I am."

"It must be interesting work."

"Sometimes. And sometimes it's very boring and sometimes it's pretty confusing."

"Flora worries about you, I know that much. She's afraid you'll come to some harm."

"I know she does, but I'll be fine. Speaking of Flora, I wonder if—"

"Would you like some hot tea, Charley?"

"No, thank you. I—"

"Maybe you should take some out to Flora. She'll be freezing in that car." She giggled once again. "I'll bet she's wishing she wasn't so stubborn about now, don't you? I hope the neighbor boy doesn't see her out there. He likes to tease old ladies. It makes him feel important, I guess. You'd think he'd be ashamed of himself but he isn't. Not many are these days."

I tugged her back toward the subject. "I think Flora's all right; she doesn't seem to mind the cold that much. And I'll keep an eye out for the neighbor boy. May I ask you a question, Miss Hookley?"

"Of course you can, Charley. And please call me Emily. I've told you that before, I'm sure."

I reached in my pocket for the photo of the infant I'd found in Charley's garden and held it out to her. "Do you know who this is, Emily?"

She adjusted her glasses on her nose. "It's a baby, isn't it?" She lifted the glasses and rubbed her eyes. "These cataracts make things fuzzy, but that looks to me like a little baby."

"Yes, it is. But whose baby is it? Do you have any idea?"

She frowned and shook her head. "They all look alike to me, don't they to you? Little dough lumps with a few black currants pressed in them. Like scones ready for the oven. Do you like scones, Charley? I think I made some for you once, but I can't remember for sure."

I told her I like scones, then waved the photograph to attract her attention. "Could this be Flora's baby, Emily?"

"Flora?" She looked out the window toward my car, which seemed to be shivering in the cold. "I don't see her out there. Do you suppose she's gone off somewhere? Maybe you should look for her—it's not safe for women to walk by themselves in this neighborhood. There have been several incidents."

"Flora will be fine. I'm wondering about the baby, Emily." I showed the picture to her once again.

She squinted at it, then looked up at me, her eyes flat and sorrowful. "Now I see why you made her stay in the car."

"Why?"

"Because we're not supposed to talk about it in front of her."

"The baby?"

She nodded. "They told me not to and I've tried my best to avoid the subject. Maybe a word or two to Ethel and Grace, but that's all. I swear."

"Why didn't she want you to talk about it?"

"Because she gets upset. Charley does, too. You probably already know that, since you're his friend. You probably have to watch what you say, too. But I imagine you've slipped a time or two."

I was relieved to be back in my own persona. "Charley never brings it up," I said.

"It's just as well. They used to bite my head off if I mentioned it, even just to say how sorry I was."

"I'm sure Charley's gotten over it now."

"Well, I'm glad of that. Bygones should be bygones, no matter how tragic the situation."

"What was so tragic about the situation?"

"Why, what happened to the baby, of course." Her lip trembled and her eyes wandered with perplexity. "Isn't that what we're talking about? Or am I confused again?"

I hurried to reassure her. "Yes, it is. We're talking about what happened to the baby. Did it die? Is that what happened that was so sad?"

She frowned at me sternly. "Of course it died. What else would have made Flora so upset?"

"I thought maybe she had given it up for adoption."

"Adoption? Now, why would she do a thing like that? Flora dreamed of a baby her whole life. She had more dolls than Grace and me combined. She tried to steal one of mine once but I caught her red-handed." Her voice dropped and her hands clasped. "I never trusted her after that. Not really." She looked out the window again, to see if the thief was roaming the neighborhood.

"So Flora didn't have a baby girl and give her up for adoption?"

"No, she did not. And it was a boy, not a girl. Harold

Horace Sleet. Horace was our father's name. He died when I was ten."

"How did he die?"

"He was thrown off a horse, out on Stone Valley Road. Hit his head on a stone and split it open. He was dead before they got him to Danville."

"I meant how did little Harold die? Flora's baby."

"Oh. Well, why didn't you say so? Harold died in the fire. Don't you remember, Charley? It was only a year or two ago. Surely you can't have forgotten already."

"I haven't forgotten, Emily. I just need some details. How old was Harold when he died, do you think?"

"Not even a year. I'd already gotten him a present for his first birthday. A little blue blanket. Luckily, the woman at Capwell's let me return it when I told her what had happened. Flora felt responsible, of course, but it wasn't her fault in any respect. Surely you don't accuse her of negligence, Charley. She risked her life as it was."

"Of course I don't accuse her. But whose fault do you think it was?"

"Why, that man who owned the place on the ground floor. He's the one that caused it all. They said he bribed the inspectors not to make him improve the wiring."

"What store was that? The Bluxome Bakery?"

"It wasn't a bakery, it was a *tavern*. Don't you remember? It started by the fuse box and then spread to the apartment above. Charley was on night shift and by the time Flora woke up and realized what had happened the entire nursery was consumed in flames. She tried to save him, of course, but the hallway was a wall of fire by that time. It singed most of her hair as it was; the tip of her nose was red for weeks. They all said little Harold never had a chance. There was barely anything left of him to bury."

Emily looked out the window again. "She was never the same, really. Neither was Charley. I think they still cry over it every night of their lives. A thing like that won't leave your mind. Not ever. Not if you live to be a thousand." She turned back toward me, her eyes bright with resolution. "I think I'll make Flora a spice cake. That's one thing we agree on. Spice cakes are the best, don't you think? Especially this time of year."

I told her I thought Flora would like a spice cake just fine. Then I asked her the date of the fire.

"Why, it wasn't that long ago—1960 something, I believe."

"Where did it happen?"

"On Post Street. Not far from the Opera House. It was a nice neighborhood back then."

"Who owned the tavern, do you know?"

"I forget. Some Armenian, I think. They never had relations after that, you know."

"Charley and the Armenian?"

"Charley and Flora. She was afraid that if she got in a family way again something bad would happen to the new one. She never let him enjoy her favors after little Harold died, not one single time. Isn't that the saddest thing you ever heard?"

As a matter of fact, it was.

CHAPTER
24

WHEN I GOT BACK TO THE CITY, I SET MY SIGHTS ON THE widow of Charley's former partner, Roberto Sanchez. I got her name—Maria—from Joyce Yates at the *Chronicle,* who punched up the article on the shooting and gave it to me, along with a few details I hadn't known before but nothing I thought was important. Since her computer didn't have a current address for Maria Sanchez, I went searching in the phone book.

Not surprisingly, there was no listing. Since my source at the phone company had been a victim of the plague of corporate downsizing, which left her without a job or a pension, I was on my own. I finally got lucky by calling the PBA—the Police Benevolent Association—and asking to speak to the widow Sanchez for reasons that had to do with an annuity policy. They gave out her number a little too easily and I used a reverse directory to look up her address.

I was surprised that she lived in the city—most cops don't, allegedly because they can't afford it but in truth because they don't want to raise a family in the place where they enforce the law, which isn't reassuring to the rest of us. I decided not to call first, since I wasn't sure what to say and it's too easy for people to duck you when they're hiding behind a phone line. Hoping to catch her before she sat down to dinner, I drove to her home on Alvarado Street in the Outer Mission.

The house was a handsome two-story box, with a brown stucco facade, a covered front stoop, and even a smidgen of yard. I climbed to the door and knocked, reluctant because I was going to be dredging up a horror that had doubtless been long buried. Since it's what I do more than anything, you'd think I'd be used to it.

The woman who answered was younger than I expected, plain but attractive, dressed in Levi's and sweatshirt and Reeboks. "Yes?" she said, with more than a little annoyance.

"My name is Tanner. I'd like to speak to you, if I may. About your husband."

Her lips wrinkled sourly. "Good luck."

"How do you mean?"

"I mean I don't have a husband."

"I'm sorry. I was referring to your *late* husband."

"Early, late, whenever. You must have the wrong place."

"Are you Maria Sanchez?"

She shook her head with burgeoning disgust. "Now you're half right."

My brain finally kicked in. "You're Maria's daughter."

"You finally hit a winner. Congratulations. You must be hell on the lotto."

It was tempting to work that sarcasm over a bit, but since that wasn't part of the job, I made do with apologizing for the confusion. "Is your mother at home?"

"Why?"

"I need some information from her."

"What kind of information?"

I smiled. "Maybe I should save that for her."

She stiffened and crossed her arms. "I don't know

what she could possibly have to say that you'd be interested in hearing."

"Why not?"

"Well, for one thing, she hasn't been out of the house in twenty-five years except to go to church." She looked at her watch. "Which she's going to be doing in about ten minutes, by the way. She goes to confession on Saturdays."

I repeated my earlier theme. "I'd like to talk to her about her husband."

"Her husband's been dead almost thirty years."

"I know he has."

She'd expected to surprise me and was jarred when she hadn't. "Then what could she possibly know of importance after all this—"

"Just tell her I'm a friend of Charley Sleet's," I interrupted. "And that he's in trouble and I'm trying to help him out. Please. It really is important."

"I don't think she—"

"Please tell her that much. If she won't see me, she probably doesn't have what I need anyway and I'll leave without any trouble."

"Wait here," she said glumly, after a moment of indecision. Cooperation wasn't something that came naturally to her.

When she returned, she was frowning with disapproval. "I guess you can come in, but please don't take long. Her strength isn't what it should be and she really does need to go out in a while."

"Is she ill?"

"She's in mourning."

"For whom?"

"Her husband."

"But he's been—"

"I know. I spent years trying to get her to move on with her life, but I've given up. She lives how she lives and there's nothing I can do about it. Funny thing is, when I look at my own life and the lives of most of the people I know, what I see is that even living like a nun, she's happier than the rest of us." She shrugged. "Go figure." She stuck out a hand. "I'm Carmen, by the way."

"Marsh. Nice to meet you."

"Yeah." She started to add something but decided not to. I had a quick sense that she had considered coming on to me. I get that sense a lot lately. I must be going nuts.

She led me through the living room and down a narrow hallway and into one of two small bedrooms in the back of the house. Along the way, I caught a glimpse of what amounted to a shrine to Maria's dead husband, complete with icons and artifacts and votive candles. I wondered if she conducted formal services and decided she probably did.

Maria Sanchez was sitting in a chair in her bedroom, her lap covered with an intricately knit afghan, her shoulders draped with a soft woolen shawl, her fingers knit into the lumpy lace of a rosary. The curtains were drawn and the lights were off. The only luminescence was a soft white light that came through a thin gauze drape, as though it was filtered through a cloud. A thick black Bible lay on the table beside her, along with an asthma inhaler, a half-full glass of water, and a small brown pill bottle. Woeful, maybe, but lots of lives are lived with less.

When I entered the room, she looked my way but her face remained expressionless. Her hair was gathered in a graying bun at the base of her skull. Her feet were shod in slim black slippers, her fingers were bare but for the beaded rosary and a single gold band. Her shoulders were slumped and her breaths were labored. Everything about her suggested advanced age and decrepitude except her face.

Her face could have belonged to a teenager. Seamless and blemish-free, her skin glowed as if it were the wrapper around a single source of illumination whose origin was somewhere near the soul. The shadows that played across her face added to the hint of mystery and indication of suffering. Her eyes, while neither sparkling nor warm nor welcoming, were alert and knowing and challenging, implying that nothing I was bringing with me could possibly dismay her.

Her teeth gleamed like pearl inlays in the mahogany mask of her complexion, but the fact that I could see them at all was encouraging. "Mrs. Sanchez? My name is Marsh Tanner. I'm a friend of Charley Sleet's."

She nodded once, then spoke in a reverential timbre. "I know who you are. Charles mentioned you many times. He used to say that if I needed anything and he wasn't available, I should feel free to call on you."

I'd never heard anyone call him Charles before. "That's still true, Mrs. Sanchez. You may call on me at any time."

She bowed her head, then raised it. "I would not presume to do so, but it is kind of you to make the offer."

I smiled. "It sounds like you know Charley pretty well."

"He and Roberto were like brothers; he is as close to me as my family. After Roberto died, Charles came to see me every day for many weeks. He still comes," she added softly. "Just not so often."

"When's the last time you saw him?"

"Two months, perhaps. Just after Christmas."

"Have you read the papers in the past few days?"

She nodded. "Carmen has told me about it. I think it must be a mistake. I'm sure they will see the truth soon enough."

"Not all of it's mistaken, I'm afraid."

She glanced toward the Bible. "I am sorry to hear it. But there must be a reason for what he has done. Charles is a good man. The only man I've ever known who was the equal of Roberto."

I let the eulogy resonate before I continued. "The last time you saw him, did he seem different to you at all, Mrs. Sanchez?"

"No. Not really. He was tired, but then he was always tired." She smiled. "He was still with the jokes. Still with the names of men he thought I should see. Still with the suggestions of where I should go to have fun."

"So he was the same old Charley?"

"Yes. Of course. Why wouldn't he be?"

It seemed cruel to tell her what I suspected about his health. "So you haven't heard from him recently?"

"No. But I have worried. Is he all right?"

"I don't know," I said truthfully.

"Perhaps you should go to the jail and see him."

"He got out of jail."

"That's good, isn't it?"

I shook my head.

"You mean he did it improperly?"

"Yes."

"I see."

After a moment's thought, she seemed more pleased than shocked by the development. The Ten Commandments must leave wiggle room.

"May I ask you about your husband, Mrs. Sanchez?"

"Roberto? What about him? All that was so long ago, I don't see how it could mean anything to anyone but me."

I thought of the shrine in the next room and saw that she was thinking of it, too. "Was there anything odd about his death, Mrs. Sanchez?"

"Odd? How do you mean odd?"

"Was it an unavoidable part of police business? Did he just make a rookie mistake? Or was there something else involved?"

Her lips stiffened and her back straightened. The rosary beads fell to her lap, untended for the first time since I'd entered the room. "Roberto did not make mistakes. Even as a rookie, he did the right thing, always. He had a commendation from the mayor and it was only his first year on the job. Charles put him in for it," she added, as if to confirm the strength of their bond.

"He and Charley must have been close."

"As close as brothers, as I told you. They would have

given their lives for each other. Whenever he was late getting home, I worried that Roberto had done just that and that Charles would come to call and tell me Roberto was gone." She closed her eyes. "And one day, he did."

I waited for the spasm of memory to subside. "Did Charley tell you what happened the day your husband died?"

"Of course."

"What did he say about it?"

"He was angry."

"At Roberto?"

"At the man who didn't do his job. At the one who didn't provide the . . . what do they call it? . . . the cover. He was mad at the one who knew the danger from the killer but ignored it."

"How do you mean he knew the danger?"

"The man they were after had committed much violence in his life. He was armed and dangerous and insane. The backup knew this because he had arrested the man previously but Charles and Roberto did not because they were rookies. Even though he knew his ways, the backup failed to provide a warning to Roberto when the man came out of the building. He started shooting before Roberto could protect himself."

"Do you know the name of the officer who didn't provide the cover?"

"His name was Walters."

"Clifton Walters?"

Her eyes hardened like black glaze. "Yes. The man who was murdered recently. That man is the reason Roberto is dead."

"And Charley told you this?"

"Many times. He seemed to need to talk about it, at least in the beginning. He seemed to need me to tell him that it was not his fault that Roberto was dead. I did so, of course, very often, but I'm not sure he believed me right away. In time he did, I think, but not at first."

"If I insult you with my next question, I apologize."

She shrugged. "I am Chicana; I am not easily insulted."

"Were you and Charley lovers, Mrs. Sanchez? I mean after your husband died?"

I expected her to take my head off, but she only smiled, then shook her head. "We talked about it once, joking in the way you do when you speak of things that should go unmentioned but must be mentioned all the same, but no. Charles was married to a woman he loved very much and I was Catholic, so it was not something we could . . . And by the time Flora died, I had decided that this was the life I wanted. To live with my daughter and my memories and the comfort of the word of God." She regripped the rosary and closed her eyes.

For some reason, the description of her life was chilling to me. "It seems a shame that you don't share your life with another man."

She opened her eyes and looked at me. "I tried it the other way, for a time. After a suitable period of mourning had passed, I received callers who wanted to sell me things, and went on dates with men looking for a whore or a mother, and attended parties where people were drinking and dancing and taking drugs to endure the sinful lives they led, and worked at jobs with bosses who wanted me to trade my dignity for a promotion and a decent wage. I saw all of that and I decided I preferred this."

She picked up her Bible and was gone, spiritually and emotionally, if not physically. I left her to her reading. When her daughter showed me out, she asked me not to return. I hoped I could honor her wish.

CHAPTER
25

"MY BEST FRIEND HAS GONE ON A KILLING RAMPAGE. AND I don't know why, and I don't know what to do about it."

I hadn't intended to state the problem so baldly or pathetically, but Danielle Derwinski wasn't in the mood for dalliance and I wasn't in a mood that let me project anything but helplessness.

Part of her problem was me. I'd arrived late for our meeting—traffic had snarled and it had taken me an hour to get home from Maria Sanchez's place. When I got there, there was a message from Clay Oerter to call him back at some number that wasn't familiar to me, in the 916 area code.

When he came on the line, he spoke in a rush. "I've been in Rio Vista all day. He's not here, I don't think."

"Are you sure?"

"If it was anyone but Charley, I would be. I went up to the cabin and peeked in the windows and walked around outside looking for traces of habitation and didn't find a thing. I'm not an experienced woodsman, but the dirt and dust looked pretty much undisturbed to me."

"Where are you?"

"A cafe in Rio Vista."

"Did you ask around town to see if anyone's seen him?"

"A few places. Gas station. Bait shop. Things like that."

"Well, do what you think's best. If you're sure he's not there, come on back to the city."

"I can't be sure, Marsh. Shit, you know Charley. He could set up shop at the corner of Powell and Market and no one would know he was there until he wanted them to."

I knew Charley, and Clay was right.

"Come on back," I concluded after thinking about it for several seconds. "We'll talk tomorrow. Maybe leave your business card around town so they can call you in case someone spots him."

"I already did that," he said. "I really don't think he's here, Marsh. I think he's right under our noses and we're too dumb to know it. He's probably laughing his ass off."

I'd told Clay I agreed with him. Thirty minutes later, I was in the Alta Plaza Bar on Fillmore Street, standing firm beneath the weight of Danielle Derwinski's ferocity.

A more active issue than my tardiness was that Danielle had had a bad day. I don't know what specific problems she'd unearthed down at the children's project—these days it seems that there's no boundary some people won't cross, whether they're cousins or clergymen or cops, when it comes to abusing kids—but whatever they were they had made her peevish and impatient and more than a little indignant. My strategy was to do and say as little as possible in the hope she would eventually calm down. So far it wasn't working.

The bar was aggressively yuppie and excessively crowded, the Pacific Heights swells warming up for a good time by flashing their egos and their finery within a neoclassic ambience, exactly the kind of place I abhor and avoid. But Danielle cut a fine figure in a black wool pinstriped pants suit over a yellow broadcloth blouse, so I cut the ambience some slack and tried to make myself relax.

For my part, I was pretty much a mess—as I'd hurried to change after talking with Clay, I discovered that nothing that looked decent was clean: I'd made do with Levi's and a plaid shirt that had been draped over a chair for a week. I don't think Danielle was charmed by my low-rent Ralph Lauren, maybe because our waiter was better dressed than I was, which he'd noted long before he got to the table and had adjusted his manner accordingly.

"What's this about a rampage?" Danielle asked when the waiter had gone off to get drinks. There was the slightest sag of boredom in her face, as though I were a backward child whose deficiencies needed to be indulged but not engaged.

"If I'm right, Charley Sleet has killed at least three men in the past three weeks, and for all I know there could be a dozen more."

My recital of the Book of the Dead finally got her full attention. "You're joking, I hope."

"I don't joke about cold-blooded murder served in boxed sets of three."

The waiter returned, paying lots of deference to Danielle and none at all to me. After she took a sip of Chardonnay, she smiled at him and nodded. He left without asking me how I felt about the scotch. I felt the way I always feel, that one wasn't going to be enough.

"Have you found out why he killed Leonard Wints?" she asked when the jerk was out of earshot.

I sipped deep before I answered. "Wints was killed by accident, it looks like."

"How could it have been an accident? He was shot in the back of the head."

"I think Charley was aiming at someone else."

"Who?"

"I'll let you know when I'm sure." I paused for effect. "It's not impossible it was you, you know."

"Nonsense."

"Are you Armenian by any chance?"

"Not a drop."

"Good."

She shook her head with exasperation—I was still the wayward child. "But what does Armenia have to do with anything?"

I shrugged. "Ethnic animosities, historic conflicts, simmering resentments," I mumbled, "just like in the Balkans." Maybe I wasn't going to need another scotch after all.

"You said there were three," Danielle murmured after a moment. "Who were the others?"

"There's a cop named Walters," I said. "He died because his dereliction of duty resulted in the death of Charley's first partner. That one happened thirty years ago. Then there's the guy in the jailhouse—the late Mr. Lumpley. Charley killed him because he'd been stealing from the children's project. And from what you said, I think he'd also been abusing his daughter, which gave Charley another reason to take him out."

"What did I say to make you think that?"

"That you're trying to keep Tafoya from becoming as screwed up as Jillian Wints."

She met my look but didn't say anything.

"One interesting aspect of this is that you're connected to two out of three of them," I chided. "Chapter nine in your memoirs, no doubt."

She shrugged absently. I got even madder. When the waiter came by again, I ordered a double. While I was waiting, I did what I usually do to fill time, I asked some questions.

"What did you do, approach Charley about using

some muscle on Lumpley once Tafoya told you about her problems with Stepdaddy?"

Danielle shook her head. "Quite the contrary. Mr. Sleet was the one who first determined that Tafoya was being abused, based on his contacts with her at the center." She smiled. "He has rather amazing powers of deduction, doesn't he?"

"You don't know the half of it."

"Anyway, he knew I'd been doing volunteer work down there for a couple of years, and that I knew Tafoya at least slightly, so he told me about what seemed to be going on in her home. I took Tafoya on as a formal patient after the initial interview, on a pro bono basis, of course. Mr. Sleet maintained his interest in her, needless to say, and I kept him apprised of her progress."

"Apparently his interest encompassed getting himself thrown in jail so he could murder Tafoya's abuser."

"You don't know that for certain, do you?"

"If you mean can I prove it, no. If you mean do I know it beyond a reasonable doubt, then yes. Why didn't you tell me about you and Charley the first time I came to your office?"

She lifted a brow. "What was there to tell?"

"That you knew him and worked with him and respected him. And would help get him out of trouble by giving me an explanation for his behavior."

She was shaking her head before I finished. "But that wasn't what you wanted from me. What you wanted was to know why on earth Charley killed Leonard Wints and I had no idea what the reason was. Because, apparently, there was none, since suddenly you're calling it an accident."

"But you pretended not to know him at all."

"I thought that was the best way to preserve my patients' confidentiality. Frankly, I was less worried about Jillian Wints than about Tafoya Burris. If word got around in her peer group that she was having sex with her stepfather, it would have been devastating. She is so young, and so lovely, and so vulnerable psychologically, it might have destroyed her entire personality structure if the fact of abuse became public."

"Charley knew all this about her, I presume. How vulnerable she was and everything."

She nodded. "To some extent. Not from me, necessarily—I don't think I told him much that he didn't already know."

"My take is that he killed Lumpley to stop the abuse but also to keep him from talking about it, so Tafoya wouldn't be shamed by the secret."

"That sounds plausible."

The waiter delivered a second round of drinks. He looked at Danielle like he wanted to take her home and show her off to Mom. He looked at me like he wanted to dip me in disinfectant.

When he was gone again, I met her gaze. "I need to know if there are any other Tafoyas out there."

"How do you mean?"

"I mean do you know any other people for whom Charley might become an avenging angel? Is there anyone else who's likely to be on his hit list?"

She closed her eyes and shook her head. "Not that I know of. My God. This all seems so—"

"Medieval?" I offered.

She sighed at the vernacular. "That's as good a term as any in this case."

"So there's no other child to whom Charley was as close as he was to Tafoya?"

She thought about it. "I don't think so. I mean there were others who needed help, of course, but their problems were more . . . diffuse than Tafoya's. He would have had to erase the entire socioeconomic structure of the city to eliminate *their* problems. I think that task is beyond even the redoubtable Mr. Sleet."

"Don't be too sure." I waited for her to meet my gaze. "I need some help with this, Ms. Derwinski."

She met my look and held it. "I believe our interests

are joint in this matter. Up to a point, at least. I liked him, too, you know."

"I'm glad to hear it," I said. "Next subject. Has he been in touch with you in the past few days?"

"No."

"Not even to ask how Tafoya's doing?"

"No. No messages. Not anything."

"Swear to God?"

She smiled.

"Which means I'm still stymied in terms of finding Charley. So I need to talk to Tafoya."

Danielle stopped swirling her wine. "Why?"

"To find out if she's seen him."

"I can't let you do that."

"Why not?"

"Because if you ask about Charley, she'll know you know about the abuse."

"No, she won't. She'll just know I know she and Charley were friends."

"And she'll assume Charley told you about her and her stepfather and she'll be mortified. I doubt very much that she can help you anyway."

"Charley wouldn't have killed Lumpley without being sure that Tafoya would be better off afterward."

"Even if he talked to her, it doesn't mean she knows where he is."

"No, but she's the only lead I've got."

She put her glass back on the table. "Then you'd better get another."

"I thought you said you liked him."

"I do. But I have other responsibilities."

"Shit."

I slumped in my chair, tired, depressed, and defeated. The ice in my scotch was minuscule and melted; the blood in my veins was watery and anemic; the cells in my brain were scorched and short-circuited. The waiter glided by without stopping. I looked at him, then I looked at the room. "Assholes," I muttered.

"What are you doing? Why are you acting this way?"

"Maybe because I'm pissed off."

"At me?"

I waved a hand. "At all of you."

"Why?"

"Because."

"Because why?"

Somehow I'd gotten drunk. Somehow I'd become the child Danielle had assessed me as. Somehow I didn't care enough about anything to refrain from answering her question.

"Because all of you have friends and I don't have one anymore. Because all of you have lovers and I don't have one of those anymore either. Because all of you have money and I *never* had any of *that*. And because I'm tired of the whole fucking thing."

"What thing?"

"Charley. You. Me. Mostly I'm tired of me. I'm sick to hell of *me.*"

Danielle nodded morosely. "I know how that feels. Believe me."

"Bullshit."

When she was certain my ugly outburst was spent, she reached out and patted me on the hand. "I know it's upsetting, but it's obviously something that he felt he had to do."

"But why? He's become a serial killer, for Christ's sake. What would make him do that?"

"How old is he?"

"Fifty-six."

"Maybe it's early-onset dementia. Maybe the past has laid claim to the present and is making him relive old horrors and react as if they just happened."

"Did you see any signs of dementia when you talked with him about Tafoya?"

"No, but I wasn't looking."

"Well, I didn't see any either. And I think I would have."

"Then maybe it's post-traumatic stress. Cops see so much evil they feel like they're drowning in it sometimes, that it's taking over their lives. Maybe he felt compelled to do something dramatic about the situation, to rid the city of monsters the system hadn't been able to eradicate."

I sighed and shook my head. "I'm sure that might be true of lots of guys and even lots of cops, but I don't think it's true of Charley."

"How do you know?"

"Because Charley's the least stressed person I know. He likes his job; he loves the streets; he gets high on helping people; and he doesn't fear or despise a single soul, not even the worst of the slime that he deals with. The only thing that would stress him out is if they told him he couldn't do it anymore."

"He resigned from the force, remember?"

I rubbed my face with my hand. It felt rough and prickly, like an old stump from an old tree, useless and maimed and discarded. "I don't know what to do," I said through my fingers. "It doesn't make sense. None of it."

"But it does in a way. His victims weren't random, they were people who had done horrible things to him or to someone he loved."

"But I've done wrong, and my friends have done wrong, hell, even you've probably made a mistake once or twice. Does that mean we ought to be taken out and shot?"

She grasped my hand. "But we haven't caused the deaths of innocent people."

My stomach knotted in defense against my memory. "Speak for yourself," I said. My hand retreated to my lap.

She drained her drink and stood up. "When's the last time you had a home-cooked meal?"

"Nineteen sixty-four, give or take."

She extended her hand. "Come on."

"Where?"

"My place. I'm going to fix you some dinner. We'll stop at the store on the way."

I looked at my watch. "I don't think I can—"

"Sure you can," she said. "I don't take no for an answer. Not about anything."

CHAPTER
26

I RARELY SHOP FOR FOOD WITH SOMEONE WHO KNOWS WHAT they're doing. My own needs are pretty much taken care of at the frozen-food case, the bread shelf, and the cookie aisle. The rest of the store is essentially a mystery; I've always assumed they throw most of it away or give it to charity before it rots.

But Danielle knew what she was doing. After we agreed on Italian as the governing ethnicity and pasta as an acceptable entree, she went to work. Garlic and basil, olives and olive oil—what does that "extra virgin" business mean anyway? A baguette of bread and three kinds of cheese, only one of which I'd ever heard of. A bag of uncooked pasta out of a bin, in the shape of stars and bow ties, that cost three times as much as the rotelle I buy in a box. Lettuce that was called radicchio and arugula, bread crumbs that were called croutons, and little red and green things whose names I didn't catch but which looked slightly slimy. And two bottles of Chianti Classico to the tune of forty bucks. The total came to almost a C note and she wouldn't let me pay for any of it.

Her house was on Baker Street, a small but perfectly rendered Victorian a couple of blocks west of the Alta Plaza, its colors on loan from the Mexican flag. One of my first clients had lived near there once; I'd ended up shooting her husband in a vain effort to keep him from shooting her. She did lots of damage in the world before she was through, but lots of damage had been done to her before that.

Danielle waited till I found parking up the street, then unlocked the door and led me to the front parlor. The furnishings were more modern than period, with woods and fabrics that matched the stains of the floors and the wainscoting. The art was glossy geometry and shiny Cibachrome, to neither my taste nor my bank balance. The mantel was masked in colorful tiles and ceramics, the floor was bleached fir with lots of throw rugs to protect it, the windows were draped in folds of beige and white checks. The atmosphere was more cordial than cozy—I was invited to stay, but not for too long.

"Nice place," I said.

"Thank you. It was my ex-husband's before we married. He traded it for my share of his pension plan."

"Good deal for you."

"Not really. His stocks have done far better than the real estate market."

"You can't live in a stock certificate."

"No, but you can trade it for something that's suitable. But I've grown to like the place, actually. Needless to say, I've removed all of Mark's traces except for his Jacuzzi. Why don't you make yourself comfortable while I throw this together? There's liquor in the cabinet in the corner."

"Can I help?"

She blinked. "Do you cook?"

"Instant pudding and Minute rice."

"Then how could you help?"

"Sharpen the knives, open the cans, chop up the carrots. On second thought, maybe not the carrots."

"Why not?"

"I have a tendency to cut myself."

She laughed. "Come on. All you have to do is open the wine and keep me company."

We repaired to the kitchen. It was huge and airy and expensively remodeled, with a refrigerator the size of a barn, a butcher block the size of a hay bale, a stove the size of a truck bed, and pans the color of old coins. I opened the Chianti and poured it into stemware with heads as thin as paper.

Our toast was silent and oddly serious; for a fleeting instant, it felt like a requiem for Charley Sleet. But then she got to work. Boiling, chopping, pressing, stirring, slicing, grating—she let me help with the last part and my hands smelled of cheese for three days. It took an hour to get it ready and twenty minutes to devour. The disparity between effort and effect is one of the reasons I don't cook.

Along the way, I asked some questions about the preparation process, but Danielle clearly wasn't in the mood for cook chat. The stand-off continued through the main course—she only relented over decaf espresso and some store-bought tiramisu.

"Full?" she asked ten minutes after I'd achieved that very state of grace.

"Quite. It was great."

"So you're in a better mood?"

"Much."

"Good."

"Thank you for making the effort."

"I enjoyed it, as a matter of fact. I never go to that much trouble just for myself."

"Me neither." I smiled to show I was joking—I couldn't have come up with a meal like that if Bill and Hillary had showed up, hats in hand, begging for sustenance.

"You probably don't *have* to cook," she said. "You look like the kind of guy women make hot dishes for."

"On occasion. But this was a cut above tuna casserole." I sipped some Chianti. "I appreciate being included. I don't imagine you spend many evenings alone."

"Almost all of them, actually."

"I'm surprised."

"Why?"

"You're attractive, smart, successful—everything a man's supposed to want in a woman."

"That's what they say they want. What they seem to end up with is a woman with round heels and big breasts whom they can coerce and intimidate and enslave."

"Who says?"

"My patients."

"Maybe their experience isn't the norm."

"I think it is, as a matter of fact. But on the personal level, it doesn't really matter."

"Why not?"

"I'm not looking for a man at the moment."

"Why not?"

She threw my words back at me, along with an impish grin. "I'm attractive, smart, and successful. And content to leave things just the way they are."

"I don't believe you."

"And I don't care."

I laughed. "What if someone special came along?"

"They haven't for a long time."

"But what if?"

"I'm not sure special would even show up on my radar anymore. I think maybe I'm too old for an important relationship."

"How old are you?"

I expected a dodge but didn't get one. "Forty-four."

"That's not too old for anything."

She looked at me and smiled. "Are we talking about me or are we talking about you?"

I matched her grin. "Both, I hope."

"Okay, if someone special showed up, I'd probably pursue it. Despite all the horror stories I hear at the office, I'd still rather be in love than out of it."

"And what if they weren't all that special? What if they were just okay?"

"A mediocre relationship. Is that what you're asking? Would I settle for one of those just for the sake of . . . what?"

"Companionship. Engaging repartee. Sexual satisfaction. More than one but less than all of the above."

"But it's never that simple, is it? For one thing, if you're not in love with the person, it becomes very hard to forgive them."

"Forgive them for what?"

"For everything they do that irritates us." She walked to the liquor cabinet and opened it. "Brandy?"

"Sure."

She poured a healthy dose of VSOP into two snifters and we went into the parlor to sip them. She flipped a switch and filled the air with Mozart and Bartoli, then turned a knob and filled the fireplace with flames. Soon there was the pop and snap of a real wood fire, courtesy of the logs on the grate.

Danielle sat on the chair and I took the sofa. She flipped on a small table lamp that bathed her in a soft light that turned her into something luxurious, a gently sculpted marble bust, something out of reach of men like me. I knew there was nothing in it for me long-term, and I didn't think I cared, but the short term was beginning to look promising provided I didn't blow it.

She kicked off her shoes for comfort; I made do with rolling up my sleeves. Then I lifted my snifter. "To the charm and skill of my hostess."

She aped the gesture. "To the silent strength of my guest."

We drank deeply, then looked at each other over the puddles of brandy. The firelight made a collage of her features, highlighting one and then another in random and exotic sequence. A small smile was the only hint she gave of what was on her mind, but the rise and fall of her chest was more rapid than normal and the flesh on her face was flushed. My own symptoms were at least as obvious.

"I don't do this very often," I said.

"Do what?"

"Enjoy an elegant dinner with an elegant woman."

"Well, I don't do this often either."

"I hope you're not accusing me of being elegant."

"What I meant was, I'm not often around people who are comfortable with silence. It was a pleasure not to be babbling all evening."

"I doubt that you've babbled since you were fifteen."

"You must not have been listening to Mr. Allison at the CMI. Psychobabble is my stock-in-trade."

"If it was, Charley Sleet would never have let you near Tafoya."

She closed her eyes and sighed. "Can we not talk about that anymore tonight?"

"Fine."

"So if not evenings like this," she inquired dreamily, "what *do* you do on Saturday nights?"

"Watch TV. Go to a ball game. Drink too much scotch at Guido's."

"Where's that?"

"North Beach." I named the restaurant.

"I've been there. I didn't know it had a bar."

"It's in back. Admission is sort of by invitation only. I'll take you some night if you want."

She shrugged off the offer. "You don't date?"

"Not regularly. I've had a girlfriend on occasion, though not on this one as it happens."

"When was the last time?"

"Betty. Schoolteacher. We broke it off a couple of years ago."

"Why?"

"She wanted kids and I didn't. Which turned out to be rather ironic."

"How so?"

I didn't want to get into Eleanor and how she came to

occupy my life. "It's not important. What about you? Why isn't there a line of men outside your door? Or are they down at the deli taking a number?"

She laughed. "Hardly. For one thing, I don't have a context—I don't meet many men in my work, I'm not a joiner, and I don't hang out in taverns, so opportunities rarely present themselves. My last serious relationship was five years ago. He was a psychiatrist."

"Too bad."

She laughed. "That's putting it mildly."

"Aren't you lonely?" I asked, more candidly than I intended.

"Sure I am. Aren't you?"

"Yep."

"What do you do about it?"

"Less and less. I seem to be deciding that dating is too much trouble even though I don't like the idea of living the rest of my life this way."

"Why not?"

"What if I get sick? What if I end up a shut-in? What if I—"

She bristled. "You want a nurse, is that it? Well, guess what? You can rent them by the hour. You don't have to marry them."

My face was red and my chuckle was uneasy. "What about you? I find it hard to believe that you're content to live out your life as a spinster."

"I don't think about it much and I certainly don't use that word to describe my status. When I do think about it, I decide it wouldn't be so bad, all things considered. I mean every man I've ever been with has tried to change me in some way. I've worked hard to become who I am—I'm not about to give it up."

"Not even for love?"

"Not even for that. Whatever that is."

"How can you call yourself a therapist and not know what love is?"

Now she was the one who blushed. "You can be a bit of a bastard, you know that?"

"Being a bit of a bastard is *my* stock-in-trade."

We sipped in silence for several minutes. The fire burned down, leaving the room deeper in shadow and its occupants deeper in a stew of memory and speculation.

"What?" she asked after she switched the CD from Bartoli to Sarah Vaughan and refilled the snifters with brandy.

"What what?"

"What are you thinking?"

"Just the usual."

"What's the usual?"

"You don't want to know."

"Try me."

"I was just thinking how attractive you are. And wondering what you'd look like without clothes. And how you like men to make love to you." I paused. "I know. Just another sex-crazed male. More grist for the mill at the office."

"Feminists aren't against sex, you know."

"That's good to hear."

"And most women enjoy it when men consider them attractive. They just don't often enjoy what comes next."

"Understandable."

"Is it?"

"Sure. On the other hand, if nothing ever came next, where would we be?"

She grinned. "For one thing, I'd be out of business."

"Me, too."

We toasted our brief confederation.

"What do you think should come next with us?" she asked, swirling the brandy, sniffing the bouquet, curling her legs underneath her, and looking at me with daunting directness.

"What *should* happen? Or what I *wish* would happen?"

"Either."

"Should is probably I thank you for a wonderful evening, offer to wash the dishes, then clear out when you tell me you'll handle it."

"And the wish part?"

"I imagine you can guess."

"What if I wanted that to happen, too?"

"You'd have to give me a sign."

"Why?"

"Because I don't take rejection well and because I'd guess you're a pro at it."

"What kind of sign would you need?"

"Whatever. I'm a pretty good interpreter."

"Would you be able to tell that the sign was only good for one night? That it expired at midnight and wasn't renewable?"

"I think I've seen that one already."

"Good."

She pursed her lips in a sexy pout, then ran her tongue along their thick red rims. "Is that too blatant?"

"There's no such a thing as too blatant."

She laughed and drained her snifter. By the time she was done, I was standing over her. "Do you have a preference where this happens?"

"How about right here?"

"Here is fine. But don't you want to put down a towel or something? In case there's some runoff?"

"If you do it right, there won't be." She was naked in twenty seconds. "Do you want me front or back?"

"Your choice."

"I think like this."

She slid to the floor, then crouched on her knees, her rear end presented to me, her breasts pressed flat by the seat of the chair. "It works best if your thighs are between mine."

"I take it we don't bother with preliminaries."

"The only preliminary you need is a condom."

I laughed. "Do I get to do anything but follow instructions?"

"Not this time," she said.

CHAPTER

27

IT WAS AFTER TWO WHEN I GOT HOME AND THEY WERE waiting for me. Three of them, piling out of a green Pathfinder as I drove up my street, surrounding my car while my mind was on the delights I shared with Danielle, looking as though they did this kind of thing on a regular basis. By the time I appreciated what they were up to, the car door was open and there was a gun in my neck and a hand on my shoulder: Never drive around town with your door unlocked.

"Out," the big one ordered, his Glock a hot thumb taking the pulse of my carotid artery.

I looked into the murky confines of the garage. "Let me park it first. It's in the way as it is."

"So are you, asshole," he growled, then dragged me out of the car as easily as he would have removed a six-pack. With another curse, he shoved me against the front fender. When he patted me down for weapons, he didn't bother to be delicate—an ounce more effort behind the slap at my groin would have put me on the floor in a fetal curl, which was probably what he had in mind.

There were three of them all told, small, medium, and large in size, dressed the way I was, in Levi's and flannel shirts with the additional accessories of black ski masks and brown boots. They were assassins out of Eddie Bauer, thugs out of L.L. Bean, generic and competent and scary.

Despite the masks and the mufti, I was certain I knew who they were—the big guy had worn the same shirt when he'd joined Wally Briscoe at the ball game. Which meant they were cops, at ease outside the law, rogues out to do damage and save their skins, as casually corrupt as lifelong mafiosi. They were trained to kill and probably had done so both lawfully and not—the only issue at the moment was what they wanted and how far would they go to get it.

I opted to stay dumb for as long as I could. "Take it easy, pal. My wallet's in my pants. There's only a few bucks but you can have it all. I don't have a cash card, so there's no use—"

The big one was still boss. "Shut up. When we want something, we'll tell you what it is."

"If this is a kidnap, I have to tell you that no one I know can afford a ransom of more than three figures. And most of them wouldn't pay that."

"Figure this, asshole." He slammed his pistol against my left temple. I spun around, then embraced the fender to keep from falling to the concrete floor. Welcome to law enforcement—they've been doing it that way since the Romans were roughing up the Christians. It's counterproductive in the long run—just ask Marcia Clark—but that never seems a sufficient deterrent.

I indulged my instincts. "You fucking oaf. What do you think you're doing, mugging me in my own home? The landlady's a light sleeper; there'll be cops here in two minutes."

He couldn't resist deserting his cover. "Sooner than that, asshole."

Since he had stopped playing, I could stop, too.

"Plainclothes or uniform?" I asked. "And how was the game, by the way?"

"Fuck you. I said keep quiet."

With one hand once again pressing the Glock to my neck, he herded me out of the garage and in the direction of the Pathfinder. When we got there, he opened a door and shoved me in the rear seat. Along the way, there was time to confirm that Wally Briscoe wasn't one of them— none of the three came close to duplicating his pudgy features. I wasn't comforted by his absence.

The other two got in on either side of me in back and the big man sat behind the wheel. The smaller of my seatmates was armed, with a sleek little Colt Double Eagle. The worst weapon wielded by the other guy was a case of halitosis.

The Pathfinder surged to life and wound down Telegraph Hill, then swung left on Broadway and right on the Embarcadero and whizzed along the eastern edge of the city and the western edge of the bay. No one said anything, even in response to my quips.

Twenty minutes later, we were deep into fantasyland, a semi-resurgent but still mostly industrial area composed of bright new condos on one side of the road and the hulks of abandoned shipping terminals on the other. By the time we passed the Delancey Street Restaurant, crossed the Lefty O'Doul Bridge, and the Embarcadero became Third Street, I decided they were taking me someplace to kill me.

We drove along the tattered fringe of the city, a strip along the bay shore that had not yet been revitalized. In appearance, the area was like a drain that was clogged with the flotsam and jetsam that had washed ashore in a storm. A community of transients ensconced in dilapidated buses and campers shared space with several dry docks and piers that were rotting from disuse. A few businesses had held on, though, mostly marine shops and small cafes that had survived the closure of the shipyards. It was all rather nostalgic and anthropologic, but then we took a left on Twentieth Street and entered the world of the Road Warrior.

Abandoned vehicles stretched as far as the eye could see, rusting hulks secured behind an inadequate cyclone fence and bearing little plastic numbers propped on their tops that implied someone somewhere would want them for something. Despite the dark of night, the vehicles seemed alive somehow, a nest of wasps gathering strength for flight in the morning, a cave of bears lumbering out of hibernation, a gang of thieves coming awake in their secret lair. But even though the Potrero police station was less than three blocks away, and even though the worthless vehicles were officially lodged in the police impoundment lot, rescue was not going to happen. They had brought me there precisely because it was their turf.

They got out of the car and dragged me with them. The only light leaked from a distant lamppost; the only smells were of decay and putrefaction and spilled fuels. The traffic up on Illinois Street looked to be on missions as lethal as our own. I ran through a list of options— flight, resistance, bluff, and bluster—but didn't find any I liked. These guys were pros, and pros don't spook with words unless they come backed by some heavy hardware.

The biggest one stuck a hand on my collar and yanked me down an asphalt path that led through a hole in the fence and deep into the cluster of vehicles, to a point that put us out of sight of the road. They all seemed familiar with the place—I wondered how many men they'd dragooned the same way and if any had survived the experience. Given the amount of rusty metal in the vicinity, it seemed as possible as anything else that I'd eventually die of lockjaw.

The big guy tugged me to a stop in front of a VW minibus that seemed a relic from some futile uprising, and a suitable backdrop to a firing squad. By the time I regained my balance and surveyed the situation, all three of them had weapons in their hands and the weapons were trained on me. No gun control plan in existence takes the guns away from cops.

The big guy still took the lead. "We need to know one thing. You tell us without a fuss, we all go home happy."

I borrowed a line from *Rockford:* "Does your mother know you do this kind of thing for a living?"

He slugged me in the stomach. I lurched forward, grasping my guts to keep them sufficiently aligned to allow them to function. My breath whistled in my ears; my eyes watered in sympathy with my pain. By the time I straightened up, we all knew it wasn't the end of things, we knew it was just the beginning.

"A smart mouth won't get you anything but grief, motherfucker," the big one said, then spit a gob the size of a golf ball onto my left shoe.

By the time I was breathing normally, the big guy had a rope in his hands. Not a thick rope but more like twine, or maybe baling wire, each end wound around a piece of wood, leaving an effective length of three feet. Two seconds later, the rope was draped around my neck and the pieces of wood were allowing him to tighten it without losing his purchase.

"Talk," he instructed.

"About what?"

"Sleet."

"Well, he's about five-ten, two-thirty, with a neck like a chimney and arms the size of—"

"Fuck that shit. Where is he?"

"Who?"

"Sleet, asshole."

The rope became as snug as a necktie. "I don't know," I said.

"The fuck you don't. You're his asshole buddy. He don't fart you don't light him a match."

"I don't know where he is," I repeated. "I've been looking for him myself. Ask Wally Briscoe if you don't believe me."

"Leave Wally out of it," the middle-sized one said. I wondered what Wally had done to earn his largess. I guessed all cops are in debt to all other cops, which is why it's so easy to corrupt them.

"Why?" the big one demanded.

"Why what?"

"Why you looking for him?"

"So I can talk him into giving himself up before someone like you hunts him down and kills him."

"Asshole."

The necktie became a garrote. I fought for breath, my lungs laboring to expel my exhaust, then inhale fresh fuel for my brain. My throat surged to expand its dimensions but was held fast by the insistence of the rope. It was hard to see how I was going to get out of this mess if I couldn't talk to them.

"What's he up to?" the little one asked. It was the first time I'd heard his voice. It was thin and cutting and familiar, like the bay breezes that swirled around us. He didn't sound nearly as frightened as I felt.

The rope slacked. "What's Charley up to, you mean?" I asked.

"Yeah. Charley."

"I guess he's off his rocker," I said.

"Why? What the hell happened to him?" The whir of wonder in his voice was surprising—I'd figured the cops were the ones who had the answer to that one.

"I don't know," I said. "I'm trying to find that out, too."

"We won't hurt him," the middle one chimed in, with a surprisingly sincere timbre. "We just want to talk to him."

The big guy and I both laughed.

"I'm not sure about you," I said to the middle one, "but the guy with the rope wants to kill him." A tug at my throat made the final words a croak.

"What's he got on you guys?" I asked when I finally felt some slack. "What makes you so afraid of him?"

"He's got shit," the big man growled. "He's a punk."

I was certain it was the first time that term or anything like it had been applied to Charley Sleet. From the abashed aspect in his eyes, even the big guy knew it was absurd.

"He never understood," the middle one piped up earnestly, his voice a distant whistle in the heavy night. "He's blind or something—he doesn't see what we see; he doesn't know what we know."

"And what might that be?"

"That they're animals. Every one of them. All we deal with is animals, day after day after mother-loving day. All we see is a fucking zoo."

"Hey," the big guy said. "That's an insult to my dog, calling them animals. They'd have to be trained with a fucking choke chain to get as smart as animals."

The little one laughed with quiet strength, the way Goebbels might have laughed on a tour of the crematorium. I was beginning to think that he, not the big one, was in charge of the operation.

The middle one wasn't done with the subject. "They *value* nothing, they *respect* nothing, and they *know* nothing. You should see how they live. The filth is unbelievable. It's disgusting, it's repulsive, it's inhuman. Bob's right. His *dog* wouldn't live like that."

"Like I said," the big one concurred. "I mean he might lick his dick once in a while, but he don't sleep in his own shit, he don't lie in his own puke, he don't let rats gnaw on his kids, and he don't peddle his lady's ass to stoke a crack habit."

And suddenly we had a contrapuntal chorus of police prejudice, big Bob and his buddy tossing stereotypes back and forth like shuttlecocks.

"Problem is, you can't frighten them and you can't reason with them either."

"Yeah. The only thing you can do is hammer them."

"Even then they're too stupid to be frightened."

"What it comes down to, they're too stupid to live."

"All they can do is fuck and take drugs. A fucking *hamster* can fuck and take drugs."

"And gun each other down in the street. They're real good at that part. Hell, if we weren't trying to stop them, they'd all be dead."

"Which wouldn't be so bad, but they expect the decent folks to pay for the damage. Problem is, the liberals been buying into that since Franklin fucking Rosenfield. But no more. Newt and the boys going to make the street scum fish or cut bait for a change."

"Shit. Only thing they can cut is each other."

The big guy had had enough sociology. "Where the fuck is Sleet?" he demanded of me again.

The twine clutched tighter at my throat; a line of blood dripped along my trachea toward my chest. I saw stars, my lungs heaved in panic, my head seemed to swell to the point of explosion. "Tell me, asshole," he ordered, and tugged the twine tighter.

Consciousness became elusive. My eyesight dimmed, my sense of who and where I was began to fade. I was dizzy and nauseous and insensate, afloat on a deficit of awareness. My knees began to buckle and my stomach began to heave. When I raised my hands to loosen the rope, he knocked them away with ease.

The next thing I knew he released me—I fell to the ground in a heap, eating a mouthful of dirt. I think I was unconscious for a moment—it seemed to frustrate them or worry them that too much time was passing.

"Where is he?" the big one demanded again.

I could only shake my head and spit out dirt.

"Enough," the small said suddenly. "Rough him up, break something nonessential, and come on. It's getting light." He strode toward the Pathfinder in a huff.

The big one looked down at where I lay. "Which one?" he asked.

"One what?"

"Finger."

I held up the one I had to spare—third finger, left hand. He broke it with a single twist. I don't think I screamed, but I might have.

CHAPTER

28

I GOT BACK TO MY APARTMENT BY 5 A.M., COURTESY OF A courageous BART employee who gave me a lift to the Montgomery Street station and a cabbie who took me on faith after I told him I didn't have enough money to pay the full fare up to Telegraph Hill.

It hurt to breathe, it hurt to move, it hurt to think. My finger was swelled triple size and my guts felt as if they had been torn and shredded and wadded into a something resembling a hamburger patty. My thought processes had been knocked out of kilter—I dashed up the stairs to my apartment but by the time I got there I'd forgotten why I'd been in such a rush. Only when the cabbie leaned on his horn did I remember I was supposed to be finding the money to pay him. Going down the stairs hurt even more than coming up.

After the cab had rolled off down the hill, I moved my car into its assigned space in the garage, then trudged back up to my digs. After six aspirin and two slugs of scotch, I was still as achy as a flu patient, but my senses seemed to be more in control of themselves. I needed some sleep, but it occurred to me that it might not be a good idea, given my probable concussion. So I tried to read the paper, I tried to watch TV, I tried to eat some soup and some cereal, but all I could really do was hurt.

My mind roamed to and fro, without anchor or vector or achievement. One question that lingered in the vicinity was what I should do about the beating I'd just suffered. Since the guys who had banged me around were cops, the usual avenue of protest was foreclosed. On the few occasions when I'd run afoul of rogue cops in the past, Charley Sleet had intervened on my behalf, at least if I'd asked him to. But Charley was on the run himself and as far as I could tell the rogues were in charge of the store, sort of the way it is in Congress these days. I decided not to do anything vis-à-vis the police department until I'd talked with Wally Briscoe.

Another question was what the cops who banged me around were up to. Did they want Charley out of the way out of principle, or to avenge some long-simmering slight, or was he a more specific threat to them, an obstacle to some sort of scheme? I had no idea, and no inclination to find out any time soon unless the answer would lead me to Charley. Since my assailants seemed more ignorant on that score than I was, my instinct was to leave it alone.

Another question was what to do about my physical condition. I probably should have gone to the hospital to make sure I'd suffered no serious injury, but that would take hours and even days if they found something suspect and I didn't have that kind of time. Maybe Al Goldsberry could check me out; I wondered how early in the day I could ask him to make a house call.

He gave me the answer himself, less than an hour after I'd posed the rhetorical question. "Is it too early, Marsh?" he asked after I picked up the phone that rang at the decibel level of jet engines. "If you're not up, I can call back later."

I waited for a splash of pain to subside in the reaches of my head near the left temple. "It's fine. What's up?"

"I found it," he said simply.

"Found what?"

"The hospital that treated Charley."

"So I was right."

"Yep."

"Where'd he go?"

"UC Med Center."

"Really?"

"Really."

"Sounds serious."

"Is serious."

"So what's wrong with him that took the best hospital in the state to diagnose?"

"I . . . you sound funny, Marsh."

"I'm fine. Just tell me what—" My guts took a sudden lurch to the left, tumbling over and under themselves, then knotting and cramping and making a fist. "Maybe you should come over," I said after I caught my breath, in as close to my natural voice as I could manage, which wasn't all that close.

"Now?"

"Yeah. If you can."

"Okay. No problem. I'll be there in twenty minutes."

"Good. And, Al?"

"Yeah?"

"Bring your black bag."

"For what?"

"Broken finger; possible concussion; possible internal injuries."

"Jesus, Marsh. If any of those are real possibilities, you should be in a hospital."

"I don't have the insurance," I said, and put down the phone before Al could give me a lecture on preventive medicine.

The phone rang again ten minutes later. I looked at the clock: six-thirty. I hadn't had so many calls at this time of day since my friend Betty Fontaine had given birth to her baby and couldn't wait to tell me about it, ad nauseam.

I picked up. "Marsh? It's Clay."

"Hey. Where are you?"

"Back in the city."

"I don't suppose Charley's there with you."

"No such luck. Why don't we meet for breakfast and I'll tell you about it."

"Can't. Al's on his way over. Why don't you pick up some rolls and come, too. We'll compare notes."

"Danish or bear claw?"

"Bear claw."

"Or sticky bun?"

"Bear claw."

"Or croissant?"

"Bear claw."

"What's Al going to want?"

"Nothing, probably. You can't stay that thin and eat pastry."

"It's just rampant metabolism. I'll get him a bismarck. See you in thirty minutes."

I took a hot bath and two more aspirin but it took three times longer than normal to get dressed and I never did manage to fold enough of myself so I could tie my shoes. By the time Al rang the bell, I could stand up straight and breathe fairly normally but I couldn't bend or twist or make a fist with my left hand. But what the hell? I wasn't a bartender, for Christ's sake.

"Who did it?" Al said the instant he saw me.

"Fell down the stairs."

"Bullshit. This is a beating. I've seen plenty, most of them laid out on an autopsy table. I'd say at least two of them had at you."

I shrugged. "Guilty as charged."

"Who were they?"

"Masks."

"What did they want? Money?"

When I shook my head, it felt like I'd driven a nail in my temple. "Information."

"Did it have anything to do with Charley?"

I nodded. "Apparently most people believe I've hidden him in the attic."

He started to ask more questions, but when I winced at a blade of pain slicing through my right side he decided not to. "Let me look at you," he said instead, and gave me a rapid exam, with stethoscope and flashlight and fingertips.

My head and gut seemed fine, he told me when he was through, but I should take some tests to be sure. I told him I would when I had some spare time. He smiled and shook his head and said with some kinds of injuries time isn't available and his professional medical advice was to check myself into a hospital as soon as possible. I told him I'd take it under advisement.

When I didn't say anything else, he set my finger and bandaged it with a plastic splint that looked like an ossified condom. When he asked if I wanted a scrip for some painkiller, I told him I thought aspirin could handle it. Then I asked him how much aspirin was too much. When he told me, I hoped he was joking.

He was finishing the finger when Clay Oerter showed up. I went through the "what happened to you?" routine once more, then we divvied up the rolls and poured the coffee. Finally we got down to business.

"So no trace of our boy up at Rio Vista?" I began.

Clay shook his head. "As far as I could tell, the last time he was there was more than a month ago. I talked to everyone I could find and checked out the cabin from outside. Nothing but mud and spiderwebs." He rubbed his nose and sniffed. "My sinuses are going berserk. It's Molds 'R' Us up there."

"Which doesn't mean he won't show up at the cabin tomorrow," Al pointed out.

"If he does, I'll be notified," Clay said smugly. "I've got some people on the lookout."

"What if they call the cops on him instead?" I asked. "The papers are full of his picture. There's even some kind of reward. How do you know you can trust them?"

"I spoke their language," Clay said, and rubbed his

fingers together in the universal sign for the exchange of currency sub rosa.

I turned to Al. "What did you find at the Med Center?"

He didn't meet my eye. "You're not going to like it."

"I don't suppose I will."

It took him a while to begin. When he did, his voice wavered and his eyes watered. I knew it was awful long before he got there.

"Charley was admitted to the center three months ago," he said. "Complaining of vision problems, balance problems, orientation problems, insomnia problems. The initial findings were inconclusive; it took them a week to convince him to submit to a CAT scan."

"And?"

Al shook his head and rubbed his eyes. "Tumor the size of a walnut down near the brain stem. Inoperable. Malignant. Metastatic."

"Shit," Clay and I said simultaneously.

"I suppose there's no question," I asked, just to be asking something.

Al shook his head. "The best men in the city were called in on consult; if there was a way to get rid of it surgically they'd do it, but there isn't. The guy who looked at the chart said Charley hadn't seen a doctor for ten years. The tumor had been around for a long time."

"There's other things besides surgery," I said.

"They were considering a chemo series, but Charlie wouldn't hear of it. Left and never came back. That was six weeks ago."

I took a deep breath. "How long does he have?"

"Couple of months. At most."

"Sometimes there's spontaneous remission, isn't there?"

"Most times there isn't."

"The good die young," Clay whispered.

I completed his thought: "Which means he hasn't got a chance."

Suddenly the weight I'd carried around since I first

learned of the shooting in the courtroom magically and perversely lifted. Uncertainty produces dread and apprehension, but now there were no doubts. Now there were no mysteries. Now the world was inalterably reduced, its contours all too clear and fixed and featureless. In two short months, my friend Charley Sleet would be dead and my future would never be the equal to my past.

"Could the tumor explain the behavior?" I asked after a while, just to tidy things up. "The homicidal mania and all that?"

Al shrugged. "Sure. Possibly. Everything changes with a tumor—chemistry, physiology, psychology. Everything."

Clay looked at me. "Could it be a defense to a murder charge, Marsh? Temporary insanity or something?"

"Maybe. If it deprived him of the ability to distinguish right from wrong. A guy like Jake Hattie could probably make a jury believe it did."

"Did it?" Clay asked Al.

"I don't know," Al said, then showed why he was a good doctor—disease and death made him both logical and furious. "But if he's going to be dead in two months, it doesn't matter much, does it?"

That reduced us all to silence, funereal and absolute and terrifying. "Did *you* find anything helpful, Marsh?" Clay asked in due time.

"Not really, except it seems possible that he's killed at least two men in addition to the guy in the courtroom."

"Who?"

"Why?"

I went through the names and the explanations. "Are there any other people you know of that he has a grudge against?" I asked sourly.

"Why?" Clay asked.

"That might be a way of finding him."

They looked at each other and shrugged. "I can't think of any," Al said.

"We didn't know him as well as you did," Clay pointed out.

I didn't know whether it was a compliment or a criticism; all I knew was that it was a fact.

"If we don't find him, he could die without us ever seeing him again," Clay murmured with something close to wonder. "Do you have any leads at all?"

"Only one," I said. "And she's twelve years old and I have no idea where the hell she is."

CHAPTER

29

SINCE IT WAS SUNDAY, I ONLY KNEW TWO PLACES WHERE I might find Tafoya Burris—the children's project or the church.

Running a stakeout in the Tenderloin is like spending a day as a meat inspector—there are more cheerful ways to occupy your time. I parked illegally in a loading zone on Ellis near Leavenworth on the theory that the only loading to be done in the building at my flank would feature packets of white powder most commonly delivered by foot, not truck. I settled in with a book—the new Russell Banks—and a thermos of coffee, a bag of Oreos, and a bad attitude. There are lots of things to be afraid of in the Tenderloin, but what I was afraid of this time was that a stakeout wasn't going to provide enough activity to keep my mind off Charley.

But I was wrong. In the space of the next two hours, I was witness to a cornucopia of felonies—five drug deals and one drug bust, one simple assault, one attempted mugging, one larceny by trick, and six disturbances of the peace involving booze or braggadocio. One guy knocked on the car window and accused me of being a narc; another assumed I was a crack customer. A third offered to suck my cock. I hadn't seen that much criminal activity in one place since the day I visited the stock exchange.

There was so much going on, in fact, that I almost missed her. I would have missed her if I hadn't been glancing in my rearview mirror periodically, mostly for self-preservation, because the building she came out of wasn't the children's project, it was Glide Memorial, the major social institution in the Tenderloin. Glide is a haven for hundreds of people who have no other source of sustenance, whether physical, nutritional, or spiritual. Its leader, the Reverend Cecil Williams, is as close as real people come to sainthood.

Tafoya was walking with another girl her age, wearing the same tan slacks and pink shirt she'd had on the day I saw her at Danielle's, obviously her best outfit. She was laughing with her friend and strolling easily through the fractious streets, but her senses were hyperalert all the same, as aware of who and what was around her as a point man for the airborne in the highlands, properly cognizant of the potential for disaster in the neighborhood in which she lived.

She was like a daisy in a ditch, irrepressible and incandescent, a survivor of the undeclared war in the city streets. But there was a smudge of sadness in her eyes as well, an air of melancholy and resignation incongruous in one so young, a sadder-but-wiser aspect that might have been grief over her stepfather's demise or might have been the residue of his misconduct.

I waited until she turned at the corner, then got out of the car and followed her. The contrast between the girl and the environment was breathtaking. Tafoya was fresh and young and eager and alive; the neighborhood was derelict and decrepit and abandoned and forlorn. As if to accentuate the difference, she picked a thistle that was blooming out of a crack near the curb and carried it at her breast like a scepter; an archangel couldn't have looked more beatific.

The men along her route teetered on the brink of unconsciousness, undone by coke or booze. Women sat on the sidewalk and begged for change. Small children were herded and hurried along by parents terrified of letting them run loose. A dog ran free, a hunk of something brown and bloody dangling from its mouth— I hoped it was a slice of calf's liver.

After the dog disappeared, I shuddered and looked at Tafoya again; predictably, she seemed unfazed. Places like the Tenderloin seemed to have a chance at revival a few years back, but now no one wants them to thrive, they want them to become zoos that display the lower forms of human life within unbreachable boundaries, as cautionary lessons to us all. Americans are not a pretty people any longer; perhaps we never were.

Her friend stopped at a bus stop and leaned against the pole to wait for her ride. The bus was two blocks away. It might get there in a minute, it might get there in an hour, it might not move for days. After one last whispered confidence, Tafoya waved good-bye to her friend and continued down the street. I meandered after her, prepared to buy drugs or beg change if that's what it took to remain undetected, but before I had to do any business, she vanished in the middle of the next block.

When I hurried to the spot where I'd last seen her, I found myself at the entrance to the Turk Towers, a misnomer if there ever was one. The towers were only three stories tall, a portion of which housed a defunct laundromat from which everything but a skin of lint had long been removed. The Turk part came from the street address but the only thing the street or the building had in common with the Ottoman Empire was that they were all three past their prime.

Three names were printed next to the eight numbers on the security system by the door, but the device that let you speak to them had been ripped off. One of the names was Lumpley, the guy found dead in the jail. The apartment was 2-C, so that's where I headed, with more than a little reluctance. I'd been ambushed in a Tenderloin walk-up once and had no desire to relive the experience.

When no one answered in 2-C, I pressed all the other buzzers in the hope that someone would be expecting someone, but no one responded to my plea. Visitors weren't likely to be good news in that part of town. I was afraid the lock might thwart me, but a moderate shove got me inside the building. I doubt I was the first to gain entry that way.

The smell wasn't as bad as I feared—no feces, no urine, no vomit—but the musk of mildew and rug rot was bad enough. The walls were smeared with green paint and gang graffiti, the floor was linoleum with an inadequate grip on its base. The brass chandelier was missing all bulbs but one, the potted plant had been potted too long. Someone had taped a poster of Whitney Houston to the opposite wall and someone had laid a blooming weed on the table by the stairway. The someone in both cases must surely have been Tafoya.

As I climbed the stairs, they told me to lose weight; when I knocked on the door to 2-C, no one answered.

I banged again. "Tafoya?"

Still nothing.

"Tafoya. My name is Tanner. I'm a friend of Charley Sleet's."

There was a rustle and a thump and the sound of a voice being muffled. Sweat broke cold on my brow; my nerves vibrated like harp strings.

I turned the knob. Locked. I pressed against the door. Some give, but only slightly. Inside, someone called out. I pressed my ear against the door.

"Don't. Please. I don't *want* to."

"I give the asshole six rocks for some fly pussy, baby. What's wrong? He *told* me how much you liked it. Said you and he did the bang-bang all the time, front, back, and sideway. So don't do this to me, baby. Just lie back and let me do my thing."

"He's dead."

"Who dead?"

"Devon."

"Yeah? Well, he die with my soup in his pocket, so the deal still on. Let me show you what I got for you, baby. You going to like it fine."

I banged on the door with my fist. "If the door isn't open in six seconds, I'm breaking it down. The cops are on their way. You better quit while you're ahead."

"Mr. Sleet?" a high voice called out, desperate and eager, then relieved. "Is that you, Mr. Sleet?"

The second voice was raw and ravenous. "Get in *line,* motherfucker. I already got it up. You get second helpings."

"Leave her alone, buddy. Rape's a bad rap."

I listened but heard nothing but thumps and bumps and groans.

"Here I come, asshole." I threw myself against the door and succeeded only in bruising my shoulder.

"Help me, Mr. Sleet. Please help me."

"Keep your ass *out,* motherfucker. This don't concern you—the bitch is bought and paid for. When we done, I let you know."

"Let her alone. She's just a child. You'll do time for life if you rape her."

"Shit, man, I doing life already. Folsom bound to be an improvement over Turk Street."

I lunged at the door again and this time the jamb started to splinter.

"I'm a private detective," I yelled. "I'm an officer of the court and I'm licensed to carry firearms. You don't come out, I come in shooting."

The first part was true—I was licensed—but the last part wasn't—I didn't have my gun with me.

Lucky for me, a siren sounded somewhere nearby. It didn't have anything to do with me or Tafoya, but the guy in the apartment didn't know that.

A chain rattled beyond the door. An instant later, it flew open and a small black man scampered out of the apartment. His arm was crossed over his face, his shirt was ripped open to show a narrow pigeon breast, his fly was undone and his belt was flapping at his waist like a gill. I threw a punch at him as he ran by, but I was off the mark. I wanted to go after him, but thought better of it when I saw the door start to swing shut.

The face beyond the narrow gap between the door and jamb was so exquisite it made the entire building seem palatial. My heart did a reflexive bump and grind that put me in league with the guy who'd just left.

Her eyes were wide with hope and fear—there's lots of things to be afraid of in the Tenderloin and she'd just experienced one of them. Another was that the guy who came to the rescue was often worse than the one who caused the problem in the first place.

"Are you Mr. Tanner?" she asked me, her voice stiff and coltish and stalwart.

"Yep. Are you all right, Tafoya?"

She lowered her eyes. "I'm fine. Is Mr. Sleet with you?"

"No. How did that guy get in?"

"Devon gave him a key, he said."

"Are you sure he didn't hurt you? Maybe you should go to the hospital."

She shook her head. "Did Mr. Sleet send you to see me?" The hope in her voice was palpable.

"Sort of," I said, and sensed immediately that my little white lie was detected.

"I'm not supposed to open the door to anyone," she said coldly, and started to close it in my face.

"You can call Mr. Morrison at the Children's Project to vouch for me. I talked to him yesterday. He knows what I'm trying to do."

"They took our phone out," she said simply, laying waste to my character reference.

"What time does your mom get home?"

She shrugged. "When she feels like it."

"Is there someone else who could come here while we talk for a while? It's about Charley," I added when she didn't respond. "He's in a lot of trouble. I'm trying to get him out of it."

I'd given up hope by the time the door opened fully once again. She stood in the entryway serene and alert, looking at me and then beyond me at the stairway where her attacker had retreated. When she saw it was clear, she stepped back. "I guess it's all right. You did sort of save me, I guess. Do you want some tea or anything?"

"No, thanks. But help yourself."

"I hate tea. I like Sunny D."

She led me into the studio. It was as neat as a pin and clean as a whistle, with cheap but sturdy furniture and minimal but complete accessories. The windows were painted black, the Pullman kitchen was tiny but sufficient, the rollaway bed was shoved tactfully behind a curtain, the walls were decorated with pictures of Jesus and Martin Luther King and Salt-n-Pepa and a tiny drawing with trees and flowers that looked to be Japanese. I'll bet Tafoya had cleaned and straightened every inch of it.

The only chairs in the room were part of an ancient dinette set. I sat in one, Tafoya sat in the other; I was afraid mine might buckle beneath me. Tafoya looked at me with a bright expectancy, as though I might be some sort of personal savior. I see that look a lot and so did Charley, probably because most of the people we deal with are so badly in need of one.

"Have you spoken to Charley recently?" I asked.

She hesitated, then shook her head. One thing young people don't do very well is lie to strangers.

I decided to detour rather than travel straight on. "Do you know what Charley's been up to, Tafoya?"

"I know what they say at the center."

"What do they say?"

"That he killed some people."

"Do they say who?"

"My stepdaddy, for one."

"Do you think he did it?"

He eyelids fluttered. "I . . . yes."

"Why would he do something like that?"

"Because of what happened."

"What did happen, Tafoya?"

She paused. "Nothing."

"I don't mean to pry, but it must have been real bad. For Charley to do what he did, I mean."

"It was bad but he still shouldn't have done what he did to Devon. I could have handled it myself. Last time he did it I hurt him. He stayed away from me for a month."

I closed my eyes and plunged ahead, as usual in search of information I didn't want to possess. "How long had it been happening, Tafoya?"

"Since I was nine."

"How long has Charley known about it?"

"Since he saw Devon slap me at the center one day."

"Have you talked about it with anyone but Charley?"

"I talked with a caseworker once; welfare or children's service or some such. But she didn't do nothing. And Mr. Sleet made me talk to a woman who comes to the project on Saturdays. I been to her office a few times."

"Do you like her?"

She smiled. "She's okay."

"Anyone else?"

She shook her head. "The police came, but Mama wouldn't let them in."

"Were the police asking about your stepfather?"

"I think so. I'm not sure."

"Did your mother know what her husband was doing to you?" I asked softly.

Tafoya's eyes flashed. "She says it *didn't* happen. Not the way I say it did. She says if it did, I must have asked for it."

"You don't believe her, do you?"

Her lip puffed. "I know what happened, I know it was wrong, and I know Mr. Sleet did what he did to stop it."

"He's been here today, hasn't he?"

"Who?"

"Charley."

She shook her head.

"I think he has, Tafoya. If not today, then yesterday."

Her back arched. "What if he was? What would it matter?"

"It wouldn't matter but it would help if you told me where he went."

"I don't know."

"He didn't tell you?"

She shook her head.

"What did he talk about?"

She hesitated, then looked toward the rear of the apartment, toward what must have been her bedroom. "My stepdaddy."

"Anything else?"

"Miss Derwinski."

"What did he say about her?"

"That I should let her help me."

"With what?"

She shrugged. "With life and stuff."

"Well, I'm trying to help Charley, Tafoya. Some men are out to get him and if you could tell me where he is I could go warn him that they—"

"I don't *know* where he is. Honest, I don't."

She started to cry, deeply and convulsively, with obvious pain and anguish that had to do with more than Charley.

"It's all right. Don't cry. I'll find him some other way." I gave her time to compose herself, then asked, "What did he talk about when he saw you down at the children's project?"

"We didn't talk about much, really. I didn't, at least. Mr. Sleet talked about sports a lot."

"Why didn't you talk?"

She grinned through a spray of tears. "For a while, I wasn't saying much."

"Why not?"

"I don't know, I just didn't feel like it. Then Mr. Sleet talked to me and had that woman talk to me, too, and things got better. I talk all the time now." Her smile bloomed as fresh as the weed in the foyer.

"Do you have any idea where he went after he left here, Tafoya?"

She shrugged. "Home, probably."

"Were you ever at his home?"

"No."

"Did he ever take you places?"

"He took me places to eat sometimes. He liked Chinese."

"Chan's."

"Yeah. Chan's."

"Anyplace else he took you?"

"To eat?"

"To anything."

"He took me to a graveyard once. He said his wife was buried there. He talked about her a lot. He said he went there every week to take her fresh flowers."

"What day was that?"

"Sunday, I think. Yeah. We went there twice. Both times on Sunday. Like right about now."

I took Tafoya to the Children's Project, told Hank Morrison what had been happening when I arrived at her apartment, and asked if he could take care of it. He told me he could. I hated to add to his burden, but there was a place I had to be.

CHAPTER

30

IF YOU DROP DEAD IN SAN FRANCISCO, CHANCES ARE YOU won't be buried in the city, chances are you'll be buried in Colma. Colma is five miles south of town and most of its landmass is cemetery. There are all kinds of cemeteries in Colma—Greek, Catholic, Irish, Jewish, Italian— legions of headstones ascending the hills and cascading down the vales, depositories of the dead arranged in ethnic and spiritual clusters as far as the eye can see. Wyatt Earp is buried there, and so is Levi Strauss. For some people it's depressing to see so much evidence of mortality gathered in one place, but for me it's a cheery sight, a reminder that so many have gone before. If it were really all that awful on the other side, I think we'd have heard about it by now.

I'd been there when they buried her, of course—it was a May day that was raining and cold and gloomy, climatologically suited to the occasion. The mourners had numbered more than a hundred, many of them cops but many not, among them several homeless alcoholics and junkies that Charley and Flora had given a boost to along the way. What amazed me was how they managed

to get all the way to Colma, since planning and promptness weren't big parts of their lives anymore.

It goes without saying that Charley had borne up well,
stoic through the hymns, stalwart through the benedic-
tion. He'd invited all of us back to his place afterward,
and although we didn't really think he wanted us there,
we didn't see how we could refuse. He'd made a pot of
chili and some green salad for the occasion, and thawed
a batch of Flora's famous brownies that she seemed to
have prepared by the gross, and we'd all gotten drunk
except Charley—I'd spent the night on his couch, too
bent out of shape to drive home. When I came to the
next morning, I was the sole remaining person on the
premises—Charley had gone to work on schedule, leaving a thank-you note and a piece of cold toast in his
wake. I never was sure what he was thanking me for,
maybe that I hadn't thrown up.

As far as I know, he never did break down except in
the tiny increments that were spread over the next dozen
years, withdrawing little by little into a mechanistic,
ritualistic existence that did a lot of good for others but
not a lot for Charley. We'd worried about him in the
beginning, to the extent of indulging in a frenzied spate
of fruitless matchmaking some years back, but predictably it was all for naught. And as usual, Charley took care
of the problem himself, a big hunk of the cure in the
person of Marjie Finnerty. I hoped they'd had time to
get somewhere close to happiness, because it was beginning to look like their time was running out.

I had only a vague recollection of where Flora's grave
was. After cruising the main drag, I narrowed it down to
Cypress Lawn, the Hills of Eternity, and Woodlawn. I
finally chose the latter—its contours seemed familiar, as
did the turreted stone facade. I drove through the arched
entrance, then parked on a hillock from which I could
scrutinize most of the likely grave sites as I waited for
Charley to show up.

Sitting on the damp grass with my back against an
obelisk in the military section of the cemetery took me

back to my high school days. I'd been a trumpet player then, and from time to time I would be taken out of school and driven to the local cemetery, then secreted in the distance till it came time to play taps for a deceased veteran after he received a rifle salute from his fellows in the American Legion. I hadn't thought much about death back then but I'd sure thought a lot about it lately. I'm not certain what conclusions I've drawn, except to hope that when it comes it comes quickly and painlessly and that whoever does the final calculus gives credit for not doing harm in the world as well as for doing good.

A siren sounded off to the east, suggesting another tenant for the town. An erratic procession of cars came and went on missions of mourning similar to what I hoped would soon be Charley's. I spent the next several minutes thinking about Flora.

She hadn't liked me much, I don't think, probably because I'd taken her husband away from her so often. But she was a good woman who never voiced objection to my face and seldom denied me Charley's companionship even though she had the right to. She would be in heaven if there was one, but I was inclined to think she was feeding a family of worms somewhere within thirty yards of me, no more and no less a fate than that, common to us all.

I've never bought into the angels and afterlife mythology, but as I creep toward fifty I speculate about it more than I used to. The problem is, I'm not sure what I would want an afterlife to be even if I had a choice. Things that most people find rapturous—from Disney World to Fisherman's Wharf to *Forrest Gump*—tend to leave me cold. Maybe that means I've already been consigned to hell.

To wrest my mind off the hereafter, I conjured up Danielle. I'm an old-fashioned guy. Whenever I sleep with a woman, I always wonder if she could be the one, a lifelong mate, the girl of my dreams, someone to take home to Mom if I still had one. I think of such things even when the woman makes it clear, as Danielle certainly had, that she has nothing of the sort in mind, that she only has room for a romp.

We were misfit, which we knew going in, which was probably why the sex was so good. Because we knew there would be no carryover, we didn't bother to be dainty, or solicitous, or demure, we just took what we wanted for as long as it lasted and it had lasted for quite a long time. I'd seldom enjoyed myself more, and Danielle professed pleasure as well, but there was no invitation to spend the night.

Which was probably just as well. She made her living blaming men for women's problems, and even though I didn't doubt much of the blame was justified, I didn't think it was fair for her to tar me with that broad brush, at least not without knowing me better. As far as I knew, I hadn't been a major trauma for any woman ever except to the extent that a mutual breakup is bothersome to both parties. If I have any talent at all, it's in convincing women that leaving me is in their own best interest, that they will be better off without me.

Charley drove his Dodge through the gates at four-fifteen. He was driving slowly, doubtless alert for oddities, doubtless advancing indirectly on his target rather than taking dead aim. Like me, he parked some distance removed from his objective. Like me, he waited in place for several minutes to see if anything out of the ordinary made an appearance. If he was like me in another respect, what he was mostly afraid of was cops.

When ten minutes went by and he hadn't seen any, he headed for the grave. He was dressed in Levi's and a chambray work shirt and carrying a bouquet of daisies in one hand and a pistol in the other, hidden in the folds of his hunting jacket. What was more shocking than the artillery was what the tumor had done to his gait. He was hunched over and off plumb, a parody of Quasimodo who walked with a simian limp—if I came on such a man on the street I would have been tempted to call an ambulance.

I didn't figure he'd stay long, so when he knelt at

Flora's grave site I took off at a trot, crouching to keep as many stone sentries between us as possible. I set my course for a point equidistant between Charley and his car, so if he retraced his steps before I got in position I would have a shot at cutting him off. Not for the first time that day, I wished I was carrying my gun.

An Asian family was gathered in tears around a gravestone at the exact spot where the vectors should cross. When they saw me coming, they gave me looks of sympathy and condolence but my expression must have told them I wasn't in that sort of mood. As I set up shop nearby, removing my coat and crouching for cover, they hurried to convey their respects, then scurried to a nearby van after leaving behind a bouquet of lilies. The name on the headstone read WONG.

Crouching and wary, I heard him before I saw him. I was pretty sure that if I'd been armed and wanted to, I could have shot him from behind my cover, which was the only way I could have overpowered him, crippled or no. But I was even wrong about that. Before I could step in his path and confront him, he said, "Taken up grave robbing, Tanner?"

I laughed and stood up. "Can I interest you in some burial insurance, sir? We're featuring a two-for-one special this month—you and the victim of your choice."

He didn't respond or slow down, so I had to hurry to keep up. "Long time no see," I babbled at his back.

"I've been busy."

"I'll say you have. There were rifle platoons in Nam that didn't have that kind of body count."

His shoulders hunched against my joke. "It's not funny."

"Really? I thought it was some kind of farce. But in farce they come back to life, don't they? Any chance of that happening here? . . . You have no comment, I take it."

"My comment is, shut the fuck up. What happened to your finger?"

"I threw a punch at a brick wall. When do you plan to tell me what's happening?"

"It's a long story."

"I've got a long time."

"I don't."

"Are you speaking temporally or actuarily?"

"What the fuck does that mean?"

"It means I need to talk about all this."

He shook his head but didn't slow down. "Not now."

"Then when?"

"I'll let you know."

"In that case, why don't I just tag along?"

"What for?"

"For one thing, some pretty tough guys are out hunting for you and most of them carry guns and badges, which makes it hard to head them off."

"They're not so tough," he muttered.

"Everyone's tough with a Glock in his hand. Even Gary Hilton."

That one put a hitch in his shuffle. "That prissy little bastard couldn't take me on the best day he ever had."

Since I was in that category myself, I wasn't moved to dispute him.

When he reached the car, Charley stopped and turned toward me. The lines in his face were deep with fatigue; the red in his eyes was pathetic. I had to stop myself from touching him the way I would touch an injured child.

"You need to let me alone for a little while," he said levelly. The words were so slurred and sloppy, I barely understood them. "I've got things to do."

"More killing?"

"If there's more killing, it won't be my doing."

"Good. So when can we talk?"

"Not now."

"When?"

"Tomorrow."

"Where?"

"I'll let you know."

"How?"

"Phone."

"When?"

"Six. Tomorrow night. Your apartment."

"How do I know you'll do it?"

"Because I say so."

"I suppose it's charming that you still think that's enough."

We locked up for a while, our eyes entwined in a Greco-Roman grapple. When no one yielded, not even symbolically, he opened the door and got in the car and rolled down the window. "Spend much time down this way, Marsh?"

"Hardly any."

"Then you know you won't have a chance in hell trying to tail me. I could put you in places you'd need a helicopter to get out of."

I shrugged elaborately. "Maybe I'll just go to Marjie's and wait."

He turned the ignition key so hard I thought he would break it off in the slot. "That wouldn't be a good idea."

"Why not?"

"Because if you did that, all bets would be off."

I waited till he met my look. "Most of them are off already, aren't they, Charley? Isn't that what it's all been about?"

After muttering his favorite curse, Charley tugged the Dodge in gear and drove off. As he rounded a corner and disappeared, I surveyed the surroundings. The dead were everywhere, pummeling me with proof of impermanence. I was overcome with foreboding, a chilly certainty that something dire and apocalyptic lay dead ahead, that I needed to be extra careful of what I said and did, that I needed to beware of everything. On the way back to the car, I tried to shrug my premonition off as nothing, but I didn't even come close.

CHAPTER
31

WHEN I GOT BACK TO MY APARTMENT, I CALLED MARJIE Finnerty. She wasn't home. In as precatory a tone as I could muster, I left a message on her machine urging her to call me. Then I fixed a drink and drank it. Then I fixed another drink and drank that, too. And then I stopped. If Charley called earlier than expected, I needed to be able to play the hand he dealt me. More than that, I needed to be able to prevail.

For an hour or so, I bobbed on recollection, my tethers loosened by booze, my mind flitting like a moth till it came upon something worth settling on. What it had trouble settling on was Charley. The killings had taken me deeper into his past than I had ever been and because of what I'd learned—the dead child, the marital celibacy, the whore on Turk Street—my memories were suddenly suspect. I was like a cuckolded spouse—the knowledge of the infidelity makes every aspect of the conjoined past seem fraudulent and subversive and makes the husband feel like a fool. I was starting to feel that way about Charley and I didn't like it. But maybe that wasn't it at all. Maybe I was just steeling myself against the time when he would no longer be here.

When my thoughts flew from Charley to Jillian Wints, I picked up the phone and called Danielle at her home.

"I need to talk to your patient," I said when she came on the line.

"Tafoya?"

"Jillian."

"I thought you said it wasn't about her."

"It isn't."

"Then why do you—"

"I need to tell her that."

She paused. "Why don't I take care of it in our next session?"

"I'd rather do it myself."

"Why?"

"Because of the way she looked at me, I guess. She was as terrified as if I'd tried to molest her. Plus, she called Charley an assassin. I need for her to know it's not so."

"I understand what you're trying to do, but I still can't—"

"Five minutes," I insisted. "Then I'm out of her life for good."

"I'm sorry; I can't."

"You have to."

Something in my voice made her shift into a gear more flexible than automatic. "If I talk with her at our next session and prep her, maybe the week after next you can—"

"I can't wait that long."

"Why not? If she's not involved, I don't see why time is of the essence for her."

"Not for her. For me."

"But why? What's the hurry?"

"I'm not sure. But I'm asking you to indulge me."

When she spoke again, her voice was modulated in the manner of a practicing therapist, distant, uninvolved, and exasperating. "You talk like you've had a glimpse of the future."

"I think maybe I have."

"You sound as if it wasn't a very nice picture."

"It wasn't."

"What brought it on?"

"I'm not sure."

"It was him, wasn't it?"

"Charley?"

"Yes. You found him, didn't you?"

"Yes."

"What did he say?"

"Not much. We're supposed to meet later on."

"When?"

"When he calls."

"What does he want you to do?"

"I don't know yet."

"But it's something, isn't it?"

"I think so."

"And it frightens you."

"Maybe a little."

And then the therapist became a friend, gentle and reassuring and supportive. "You don't have to do it, you know."

"Yes, I do."

"No, you don't, and the reason you don't is that he's not the man you used to know. Because of all that's happened he's someone else now. You don't owe that someone anything."

I laughed. "Nice try, Doctor."

She sighed. "You're a grown man, and we have no professional relationship, so what you do with Charley is up to you, I suppose. But leave Jillian out of it. Please. She's in no shape to—"

"She has a paranoid fantasy in her head. A part of it's based on the assumption that Charley Sleet intentionally murdered her father, and that's not—"

"I can *tell* her that. I *will* tell her that."

"If she doesn't hear it from me, she might not believe it."

"Why wouldn't she?"

"Because no one knows the truth except me and Charley and I think Jillian is real good at rooting out truth."

"She is that. Unquestionably. You're a good judge of character." She paused long enough to reconsider, but she wasn't quite there yet. "I don't know, Marsh. I'd like to help, both you and Jillian, but—"

"Please. It's something I need to do. I'll get out of your life, too, if that's what you want. Just tell me where I can find her."

The war between her person and profession reduced her voice to a whisper. "Okay," she relented. "Five minutes. Say your piece and be done with it."

"Promise."

"She's subletting a place in the Haight. Against my better judgment, I might add. Although it does seem to help her to be around people even more attenuated than she." She gave me the address, then laughed. "She's more together in the early evening, for some reason. So if you have to do it, do it now."

"Thanks. And by the way. Those phone threats you were getting? If you haven't had any more in the last three weeks, my guess is they were from Devon Lumpley. He was probably afraid you were going to tell the cops what he'd been doing to Tafoya. So Charley did you a favor, too. Just thought I'd mention it."

I was strolling Haight Street within the hour. As usual, it took me back a quarter century—people still laced their brains with drugs; people still wore velvet and tie-dye; people still slept in damp doorways; people still worshiped bad music; people still frequented the Black Rose Cafe and saw movies at the Red Vic. I felt thirty years younger until I stumbled over a crack in the sidewalk and a young kid grabbed my arm to keep me from falling and said, "Easy, old dude."

The place Jillian Wints was subletting was on the corner of Ashbury and Page, not far from St. Agnes Church. The house itself was a sixties survivor, its psychedelic hues barely clinging to strips of weathered siding and the rotting ornamentation on the cornices and pilasters. There was a motorcycle recumbent on the walk out front and a pit bull recumbent by the door, chained to a rusty ship's anchor. The collar around his neck read SPIKE. When I asked Spike if he minded if I went inside, he seemed as neutral on the issue as a pit bull can seem.

I climbed to the second floor and knocked on the door to apartment 4. Jillian answered immediately, as though she were expecting me, but she opened the door only slightly, using a flimsy chain to protect herself from whatever she had decided I was.

"I'm Marsh Tanner," I began cheerfully. "We talked on the Green the other day."

Her fingers probed her throat, as though she worked her words like clay. Her blouse was rustic and rumpled; her skirt fell clear to the floor; her eyes still danced and darted like dervishes. "Danielle told me you'd come."

"Did she tell you why?"

The question made her even more skittish. "She's my therapist. I don't have to tell you what she said. I don't have to tell anyone."

That wasn't quite true and was less true all the time, but it was no time to debate the Supreme Court's assault on legal privileges.

"You don't have to tell me anything, Jillian. In fact, this time *I'm* going to do all the talking."

She gnawed on a knuckle. "Good. I guess."

"May I come in? It might be more private."

"You'd better not."

"Why not?"

"Because I don't have to let you."

She treated her civil rights like coupons—if she didn't use them, they'd expire.

"Okay. I'll stay out here and keep my voice down." She frowned. "Why?"

"So your neighbors can't hear."

"They wouldn't care if they did. They only care about dogs and drugs."

I shuddered at the image of the pit bull on crack. "Do you remember what we talked about before, Jillian?"

"The man who killed my father. Rain something."

"Sleet. His name is Charley Sleet. And there's no question he's the one who shot your father."

Her eyes glazed as she lapsed into rote behavior. "To silence me. To reclaim the forum. To debunk my memories and repel my—"

I shook my head. "No. That's what I came here to tell you, Jillian—it didn't have anything to do with you *or* your father. Charley wasn't an assassin, Jillian; he wasn't trying to keep you from speaking out about what happened when you were young. It was all a big mistake."

Her irises spread like wine stains on a linen tablecloth. "A mistake? What kind of mistake?"

"Mr. Sleet shot the wrong man. He wasn't aiming at you; he wasn't even aiming at your father. He killed the wrong person, Jillian. That's all there was to it."

"But he was—"

"A cop. I know. They're supposed to know how to shoot straight. Only this cop is sick and his sickness made him miss."

"Sick how?"

"Brain tumor. He's not moving very well anymore. He shakes too much to hit what he aims at. And he's dying," I added, mostly to voice a fear of my own.

She thought about what I'd said, perhaps comparing the dysfunction within Charley's head to what was happening inside her own. "But I don't . . . what if you're lying to me?"

"I'm not."

"How do I know?"

"Danielle will tell you."

She frowned with uncertainty. "She already did, I guess."

"Good. You should pay attention to her."

"I do when I can," she said. "But what if she's an assassin, too? The CMI has women, too, you know. There are traitors even in—"

"I think you know better than that," I interrupted. "Danielle's on *your* side. And she always will be."

As I said it, I realized it was true—therapists have become like lawyers, advocates and adversaries, stubbornly defending their clients regardless of truth or consequence. I don't think it's a good sign. *E pluribus unum.*

When I got home, the only message on my machine was to call Marjie Finnerty at home no matter how late I got in.

"Tanner," I said when she came on the line.

"What's happening?" she asked. "You sounded so . . . distressed."

"I imagine you know more about it than I do by now."

"I don't know *anything.*"

"You mean you haven't seen him?"

Her throat tightened and the words were squeaks. "No. Have you?"

"This afternoon."

"Where?"

"Colma."

"What's in . . . oh. The cemetery."

"Right."

She sighed dispiritedly, as if Charley's continued devotion to Flora was a cross she had borne for a long time. "How is he?"

"Not good."

"The shakes?"

"And a limp. And partial paralysis. And some tremors."

"God."

"You really haven't seen him?"

"No. He obviously wants to protect me from what it's done to him. Apparently he's a monster in every sense of the word now." She choked back a sob, then apologized. "I'm sorry. I don't mean it that way. It's just . . ."

"I know."

"Is there anything I can do?"

"One thing."

"What is it?"

"How much do you know about your boss?" I asked.

"What?"

"The judge. Are you close to him?"

"As close as I care to be. Why?"

"He's Armenian, right?"

"Very much so. He revels in it."

"Are his parents alive?"

"Yes. They live on Diamond Heights."

"Retired?"

"Yes."

"From what?"

"You mean what did they do for a living?"

"Yes."

"They had a bar. A tavern."

"Down on Post Street?"

"Somewhere like that. Why?"

"What time does the judge come to work?"

"Eight-fifteen."

"On the dot?"

"Yes."

"Are you on duty already?"

"Usually."

"Can I get in to see him then?"

"When?"

"Tomorrow morning."

"If I leave word at the north entrance, you can."

"Will you?"

She paused. "Not till I know why."

"The why is that Charley wasn't shooting at Leonard Wints; Charley was shooting at Judge Meltonian."

Her gasp was as sharp as a broken seashell. She had presumed a catastrophe but had gotten something more.

"You must be joking," she said.

"Sorry."

"But why? Because of me? Because he was jealous or something? My God. I shudder every time the man puts a hand on me."

"Charley?"

"The judge. I'd never in a million years let him—"

"It wasn't jealousy," I interrupted. "It was revenge."

It took her a while to absorb the concept. "Revenge for what?"

"Something bad enough to make Flora and Charley abstain from sex for the last thirty years of their marriage."

"My God. So *that's* why he was so . . ."

"What?"

"Grateful," she said.

CHAPTER

32

IT TOOK ME A WHILE, BUT I FINALLY GOT THROUGH TO MINDY Cartson. "One question," I said when she came on the line.

"What?"

"Jillian said you told her the deck was stacked against her lawsuit."

"So?"

"What did you mean by that?"

"That's a privileged communication."

"No, it's not. That's not legal advice, it's legal whining. What did it mean?"

"I don't—"

"Don't you mean Meltonian was predisposed against you? Based on his ruling in other cases?"

"I . . . yes. That's it exactly. Why is it of interest to you?"

"Just business," I said.

I spent the rest of the evening watching the only VCR movie I own—*The Fabulous Baker Boys*. I've seen it ten times but it still does the job.

The first thing Monday morning I was on the steps of

the temporary courthouse. Five minutes later, Marjie Finnerty opened the door and let me into the building. She was carrying keys and wearing a blue pants suit. She looked scared and abashed and impatient. I was a little scared and abashed myself.

"Hi," she said.

"Hi."

Her eyes were querulous and unfriendly. "What's this all about? What does Judge Meltonian have to do with Charley's rampage?"

I shook my head. "Sorry. The judge can tell you or Charley can tell you, but I don't think I can."

"Why not?"

"Because it's not about you, it's about them."

She crossed her arms and looked at me with a mix of irritation and skepticism. "Are you sure you're right about this? I don't think Charley even knew the judge."

"I'm not sure he did."

"Then what—?"

"History," I said. "Past imperfect. Memory ascendant." When I didn't say anything more pertinent, she shook her head and shrugged her shoulders and we rode the elevator up to her office.

"I'll see if he can see you," she said when we got there, then ducked inside Meltonian's chambers. She reappeared a moment later. "He can give you five minutes." She sat down at her desk and turned on her computer. She wasn't happy but she didn't know what to do about it. I wasn't happy either, but I was doing all I could.

The chambers were dark and dusky, lined with heavy drapes and musty law books that created a hushed and forbidding antechamber, as though interrogations and inquisitions were conducted in there outside the normal purview of justice. The judge was in shirt sleeves, sipping creamy coffee from a Starbucks mug, flipping idly through a deposition transcript. He was svelte and handsome and magisterial, the Prince Charming of the civil courts. What I was about to say wouldn't faze him, at least not outwardly.

He knew I was there but he made me wait. "What can I do for you, Mr. Tanner?" he asked after he figured I knew my place, genially enough, but without notable interest in the answer.

"You can pay attention while I tell you what happened in your courtroom last Tuesday."

He raised a brow. "You mean when Detective Sleet shot Mr. Wints?"

"That's part of the story but not the whole story."

"You're telling me you know why he did it?"

"I am."

He put down the transcript and leaned back in his chair. "Please proceed."

He didn't ask me to sit down but I did anyway. When he didn't offer me coffee, it pissed me off. I opened fire with both barrels.

"The main thing you need to know is that Charley wasn't shooting at Leonard Wints that morning, Charley was shooting at you."

That brought him up straight. "At me?"

"At you."

He looked toward the door and then back, as if trying to recall who I was. "What on earth for? Some ruling I made? I didn't even know the man. And I never compromised Ms. Finnerty, no matter what she may—"

"It didn't have to do with sex," I interrupted, "and it didn't have to do with jurisprudence. And not all that much to do with you, actually."

"Then what—?"

"Are you close to your parents, Judge?"

He blinked at the shift in focus. "I . . . yes, I am. Quite."

"They must be proud of your accomplishments."

"Of course they are. Not that I've done all that much compared to some, but still. I don't understand what an eighty-year-old Armenian couple has to do with what happened in my court Tuesday morning, however."

I decided to stay slippery. "Your parents used to own a bar on Post Street, am I right?"

"Yes, they did."

"They had a big fire in the bar back in the sixties."

"Did they? I don't know anything about it."

"You never heard them talk about the fire that destroyed their bar overnight?"

"No. I don't think they ever mentioned it. They must have thought it would be upsetting to me. They said little about the tavern business in general. I think they were embarrassed by their trade."

"How old were you back then?"

"In 1960, I was four years old."

"Do you have any burn scars?"

"No. I told you I know nothing about any fire. But even if there was one, I wouldn't have been injured. We didn't live over the bar, we lived in Parkside out near the zoo. If it happened at night, it's doubtful my parents even knew about it until after the fire was put out."

The judge wanted to dismiss me but couldn't bring himself to do so without knowing the rest of the story.

"Back in the sixties, Charley Sleet and his wife, Flora, lived over your parents' bar," I said.

"You're kidding."

I shook my head. "The fire was caused by faulty wiring. Your parents paid a bribe so they wouldn't have to fix it. Charley's son was devoured in the flames. Flora never got over it. I'm not sure Charley did either."

Meltonian's eyes watered and his hand trembled. He glanced at the law books beyond him, as if taking refuge in their prohibitions and their principles. "I didn't know. I'm sorry. That's very tragic."

"The tragedy hasn't ended yet. Charley's been a great cop for more than thirty years but now he's got a tumor at the base of his brain. It seems to have made him a vigilante. He's killed at least three people in the process of righting old wrongs."

Meltonian squirmed, then coughed nervously, then frowned. "Are you saying he wanted to punish my parents by murdering me? For a fire that happened thirty years ago?"

"That seems to be it. That and your tendency to let off child molesters."

He reddened and recovered his old self. "I haven't let off any child molesters."

"That's not how I hear it, but it doesn't matter. What matters is that Charley would like you to die."

"My God. Are you sure about this?"

"Reasonably."

"What do the police say?"

"I don't know. I haven't talked with them."

"You mean they haven't *captured* him yet?"

"Not that I know of."

"My God." He stood up and began to pace. "I should take precautions."

"I think so. Your parents should, too."

He grabbed his suit coat and put it on. "This is unbelievable. Like something out of the Old Testament. My parents are almost eighty years old. This could . . . What's your role in all this, Mr. Tanner?"

"I'm Charley's friend. I'm doing a little damage control."

His lip curled meanly. "It's a little late for that, isn't it?"

I smiled. "I said control, not prevention."

He closed his eyes and groaned audibly. When he opened them, the fear had been laced with calculation. "Does Marjie know about this? She was romantically involved with the man, I believe."

I shook my head. "I thought you or Charley should be the one to tell her."

"How do you think she'll take it?"

"I think she'll be relieved to know he wasn't entirely deranged."

I waved good-bye to the judge and his clerk, then went back to the office to wait for a call. I didn't get it for another eight hours. It was the longest eight hours I ever spent.

When the phone finally rang, my heart hopped like a bullfrog. "Marsh?"

"Charley?"

"Free tonight?"

"I can be."

"Good. Know where Twentieth Street crosses Illinois?"

"Sure do." It was two blocks from where the cops had broken my finger.

"There's a bar there called the Main Mast. Be there at midnight. I'll be in a gray Ford pickup. You'll want to bring your Walther."

I laughed because it was sounding so absurd. "Where'd you get the truck?"

"I found it about an hour ago."

"Glad your days in grand theft auto aren't going to waste. What's going down on Illinois Street, Charley?"

"A little crime prevention activity."

"Isn't that a job for the cops?"

"I am a cop."

"No, you're not."

"Yeah. Well, let's consider ourselves deputized. We'll call it a citizens' militia. No use letting those right-wing thugs have all the fun. If you're still willing to help me, that is."

"I'm willing to help you, Charley. I'm just not sure this is the way to do it. You want me there, you have to promise to do the right thing once we've done whatever we have to do."

"What's the right thing?"

"Turn yourself in and let Jake defend you."

His laugh was harsh. "By morning, you can do whatever the hell you want with me." He broke the connection before I could get more details or make his pledge to be sensible more binding.

The more I thought about it, the worse it sounded. Charley needed help in the form of a gun. Charley had sacrificed everything he stood for and believed in to bring justice to an unjust world, which meant he would cheerfully sacrifice me to that very same goal. Of course I had the option of not showing up on Illinois Street or of alerting the authorities to the rendezvous or both. But I wouldn't do any of those things because it was Charley who was asking and because Charley had never in his life failed to come when I called. I got out the Walther and oiled it.

Midnight. Six hours from now. The more I thought about it, the more I sensed there were things I needed to do.

Usually I call ahead, but for some reason I didn't this time. I guess I wanted to measure the welcome I'd receive if I wasn't announced and prepped for, if I appeared out of nowhere to press my subversive claim to my child, if I acted more overtly like Dad.

"Marsh!" Millicent Colbert exclaimed when she saw me. "How wonderful. What happened to your finger?"

"I broke it."

"How?"

"I got it caught in something."

"How awful."

She was wearing robin's egg Levi's and a white broadcloth shirt beneath a mildly harried look. Only her face showed wear and tear, but it was the kind of wear and tear that's a by-product of high energy and intense pleasure.

"Sorry I didn't call," I said, "but I was in the neighborhood, so . . ."

"You don't have to call. Not ever. Not if you don't mind a mess."

"Hey. I can do mess. My *roommate* is a mess."

"I didn't know you had . . . oh." She blushed. "You're talking about yourself."

"Yes, I am."

"Come on in. She just finished dinner. We're going on a stroll in the neighborhood in a little while. You're welcome to come with us, but maybe you'd rather see her here, where she'd be more . . . focused."

"Let's see how it goes."

We went back to the nursery. Eleanor was in her

playpen, wearing a pink jumper and tiny white Nikes and playing with a big rag doll. I was glad to see they still made rag dolls, though this one probably cried and wet and pledged her allegiance and came with a computer chip and a condom.

"Eleanor, look who's here. It's Mr. . . . I mean it's our good friend Marsh."

"Hi, Eleanor."

She looked at me but didn't smile. On the other hand, she didn't cry or throw anything either. I opted to be flattered.

"Let's come out and play, why don't we." Millicent reached into the playpen for our child. As Eleanor came out of her cage, she seemed to reach out for me. I took her in my arms, cradling her awkwardly above my injured digit, and lumbered to a love seat and sat down to play with her.

We did horsy and bumblebee and itsy-bitsy spider and that was half my repertory. We did peekaboo and piggy goes to market and soooo big and that was the other half. As I was casting about for further entertainments, Millicent looked at her watch. "I like to take her out while she's still alert enough to notice things. You'll come with us, won't you, Marsh?"

"Sorry. I don't have time."

She didn't take her eyes off Eleanor. "Then maybe we'll just stay in today. Since we have a special guest."

"No, you go ahead and take your walk. I just wanted to stop and say hello."

"Well, we're very glad you did. Aren't we, Ellie-pooh?" She tickled our child under her chin. I stood up and handed her back to her mom.

"Have I told you how impressed I am with the way you're raising her, Millicent?"

"Yes, but it's always nice to hear it."

"Well, you're doing a good job. You're a great mother."

She smiled and patted Eleanor on the shoulder.

"Thank you. She's an easy child to mother. And you're a great godfather. I still see you as that, you know, even though you said you didn't want to be one."

"Thank you."

"She knows you, you know. I can tell."

"So can I. I hope."

"Well, she does. And it's obvious how much you care for her."

"That's good. I mean, I wanted to be sure you both knew that. How much I care."

Millicent frowned. "Are you going away, Marsh?"

"Not that I know of."

"You sound like you're planning a trip or something. What I'm saying is, we'll miss you if you go away. We'll miss you very much. Both of us."

Our eyes met long enough to convey deeply felt and complex messages. "I'm glad," I said, and kissed both of them on the cheek, then hurried to my car and drove off before they could see that I was crying.

When I got back to the office, I phoned Clay Oerter. "You can call off the dogs," I said when he came on the line.

"Why?"

"I found him."

"Where?"

"The cemetery."

"You mean he's—"

"Not his. Flora's."

"Oh. How's he doing?"

"Not good. His body's a mess from the tumor. He can't stand up straight; his speech is slurred; he can't walk very well."

"He should be in the hospital, not running around . . ."

"Shooting people," I said to complete the thought. "Anyway, I'm going to see him later tonight. He's got some project in mind. After that, I'm going to try to make him come in from the cold. I'll let you know how it comes out."

"Good luck."

"I'll need it. You might put Jake Hattie on alert."

"Will do." Clay paused. "You sound frightened, Marsh. It's the first time I've ever heard you sound frightened, I think."

"I guess maybe I am."

"Frightened of what?"

"I seem to be afraid that I'm going to have to kill him."

CHAPTER

33

CHARLEY WAS WHERE HE SAID HE'D BE, AT THE CORNER OF
Illinois and Twentieth, fifty yards from the impoundment lot where I'd been beaten and broken by the big
guy. He was slumping in his truck, looking more like an
inebriate than an avenger, obviously on stakeout. I
parked a ways away, then walked to the truck and tapped
on the window.

"I hear there's a fugitive from justice around here
somewhere. Seen anyone that fills the bill?"

He opened the door and let me in. The air was cold
and the seat was colder—he must have been waiting a
long time.

I canted against the door and looked him over. He was
still wearing his hunting coat and boots, a chambray
work shirt and a Norm Thompson rain hat. All three
seemed too large for him, making him look slightly
comical. It was the first time I'd had that reaction to
Charley and it depressed me.

"You've seen better days," I said, just to start things
off.

"Who hasn't?"

"When I saw you at the cemetery, it looked like you were in pain."

He shook his head. "It's not pain."

"Then what is it?"

"Neuritis."

I laughed. "They haven't called it that since Anacin ads in the fifties. Why aren't you letting them treat you?"

"For what?"

"The tumor in your fat head."

"Who says I have a tumor?"

"Your doctor."

Charley swore, emitting a puff of white mist in the frigid truck. "He's not supposed to gossip about his patients."

"He didn't."

Charley smiled weakly. "Then you must be a detective or something."

"And you must be one pissed-off cop. Is the number still three, or are there some I don't know about?"

"It's three."

"Are there going to be more?"

"Probably."

"How many?"

"Three or four."

"Minimum or max?"

"Max."

"Are you expecting me to kill some of them for you or are you going to handle it yourself?"

"I'll handle it."

"Then why am I here?"

"You're the second front."

"As I recall, the second front didn't fare too well in the big number two."

"It turned the tide, is all."

"A lot of dead Russians probably didn't give much of a shit about tides." I gestured toward the bar. "Who's inside?"

"Cops."

"The same ones who took me here and beat me up?"

"Probably."

"What are they doing in there?"

"Getting ready to divide the spoils."

"What kind of spoils are we talking about?"

"Money, drugs, contraband—whatever they've managed to filch this month."

"Cops?" I repeated.

"They call themselves the Triad." He gestured. "The old power station down Twentieth is sort of their clubhouse."

"Triad?"

"It's some medieval crap. Three levels of honor, or something. Funny how racists always look for some sort of myth to support their habit."

"Funny how often they're able to find one."

Charley grunted, then grimaced in pain.

"You all right?" I asked.

"Not really."

"Anything I can do?"

"Not really."

"What is their habit?" I asked after a while.

"Preying on innocent people."

"Extortion?"

"That's the least of it."

"What's the most?"

"Drugs. Whores. Whatever turns a profit."

"How long has this been going on?"

"Years," he said. "Most of the guys in there now are second generation. Including Hilton."

"Gary Hilton's in there?"

"Yep."

"How many all told?"

"In the Triad? About thirty. Some are more active than others. Only four showed tonight."

"How active is Wally Briscoe?"

Charley chuckled drily. "Not very, since he got married."

"But some of his buddies are."

"Yeah. Wally has a tough time saying no."

It started to rain. The windows steamed up, the traffic thinned to a sputter, the truck became a vinyl igloo, hermetically sealed, impervious to its environment. "Can I ask a question?" I said.

"Sure."

"What's going on in your head, Charley?"

"What do you mean?"

"You know what I mean. You used to worship the system. For all of its faults, you used to believe it was the best we could do and close to infallible. Now you're thumbing your nose at it."

"Only where it failed."

"Over time."

"Right. Over time."

"And you're taking action yourself because you've got nothing to lose."

"Something like that."

"How about your reputation? How about your integrity? How about your friends?"

His laugh was mocking and dismissive. "Clay and Al pretty pissed at me?"

"Not pissed. Mystified and perplexed and worried. But not pissed."

"Good."

"The one who's pissed is me."

He laughed. "Why so?"

"Because you didn't tell me a fucking thing. Not about the woman; not about the cancer; not about the cop; not about the child; not about anything. You didn't let me help; you didn't let me talk you out of it; you didn't let me stop you."

"Which is exactly why I didn't tell you."

"Hell, on the best day I ever had I couldn't stop you from snapping your fingers."

"You could now," he said wistfully. The words wafted toward me from a weary, tired man, weak and getting weaker, terrified of his deterioration. This was clearly his last stand: I was going to try for as long as I could to regard it as noble.

"The cancer's a tough break, Charley. But it may not be all bad. It may be your way out."

"In court, you mean? Some sort of insanity nonsense?"

"Jake thinks it might fly."

"That's not the kind of out I'm looking for," he said, then watched as a black Explorer pulled up in front of the bar. The driver went inside, then emerged a minute later with four of his buddies in tow. They strolled down Twentieth toward the bay, swearing and swaggering in their civvies, but cops all the same. One of them was huge and especially vulgar. It was nice to have a face to match the body that had mauled me.

Charley looked at his watch. "I think they've got a quorum," he said.

He opened the door and got out. I followed suit and joined him by the roadside. "You going to tell me the plan or do I just follow your lead?"

"You don't need to know the plan, you just need to know your part."

"Which is?"

"The powerhouse is the white building with the curved windows and tile roof. I've already paved the way for you. Give me ten minutes, then slip in the front door and get behind cover and make a nuisance of yourself."

"What kind of nuisance?"

"Say you're from customs, or DEA, or the feebs—the ineffective bureaucracy of choice. Tell them to freeze. Use pompous lingo. I'll take care of things when they totally ignore you and start running out the back."

"Sounds like the way you and Roberto Sanchez tried to take care of things thirty years ago."

"You know about that?"

"I know about a lot of stuff."

"Well, this time there's backup."

I looked around. "Where?"

He opened his coat. Beneath its drape was a sawed-off riot gun, a Tech-9 assault pistol, and the Ruger that used to be in his nightstand.

"Jesus, Charley," I said. "Is even one of them street-legal?"

"Nope."

"You could wipe out the Chinese army with that stuff."

"They deserve it, Marsh. They deserve as bad as I can give them."

"We must not read the same Bible."

"If the Bible had anything to do with anything, I'd have a wife and a son. Ten minutes," he repeated, then walked toward the powerhouse, the shotgun a terrible stunted tool in the crook of his arm.

I could have left, of course, got in my car and disappeared, and spent the rest of the evening in bed. But that would mean Charley would die. I could have called the cops and hoped enough good ones were still around to break it up, but that would mean Charley would be humiliated. So I tagged along, silently, reluctantly, nervously, not knowing whether I wanted the operation to succeed or fail, which in most cases is a recipe for disaster.

When we reached the building, Charley pointed to a car parked across from the entrance. I interpreted it as my staging area. When I was in position, he pointed at his watch, flashed five fingers two times, and continued around toward the rear of the powerhouse.

I looked at my watch—12:32. Unless I exerted myself, ten minutes from now someone would die. Unless I became a counter-terrorist, in ten minutes there would be a miniature holocaust. Unless I improvised brilliantly, I was going to become an accessory to mass murder. Armed with that knowledge, I sat where I was and waited.

Maybe it was because Charley was my friend and I owed him one last favor. Or maybe it was because the guys inside had beaten me up and enjoyed it. Or maybe it was because I was frustrated with the system, too, and had been for a long time. Or maybe I was just a coward. Whatever the reason, the next time I looked at my watch

I counted to twenty, then drew my gun and eased through the door and hid behind what looked to be a big brown turbine, made of cast iron or something similar. When my heart quit throwing punches at me, I started yelling.

"Customs! Freeze where you are. The building's surrounded and we have a warrant to search for contraband. Place your weapons on the floor and your hands on your heads. Move! You have no chance of—"

The shooting started with a burst from inside the building, directed aimlessly at my perch. The sound was immense and painful but none of the rounds came close enough to do damage. I crouched as low as I could go and waited. In the next second, answering shots came from out back, and after that the firefight was on. Luckily, it was elsewhere.

There were only four more exchanges, the last a single shot from a handgun. Then came the predictable cries and screams and threats of further harm. Then came silence.

When it had been quiet for two minutes, Charley called my name.

"What?"

"Come on back."

"You all right?"

"Fine. You got any ammunition left?"

"Yeah."

"Good," he said. "Make sure there's a round in the chamber."

CHAPTER

34

WHEN I GOT TO THE REAR OF THE POWERHOUSE, THERE WERE five men facedown on the ground, the spokes of a rough-hewn wheel with Charley Sleet at its hub. They were all spread-eagled, with handguns lying somewhere near their person but not near enough to do damage. Charley was looming over them, cradling the riot gun negligently in his arms, the Tech-9 sticking out of his pocket like a loaf of brown bread.

All but one of the men on the ground were begging for mercy in various forms of entreaty. The exception was the smallest of them, Gary Hilton, the one, I was now sure, who had directed the assault on me two nights before. The rest of the men looked terrified, but Hilton seemed vaguely amused, as though Charley were about to try clog dancing for the first time.

Charley was mumbling something to himself as he worked, applying those plastic strap handcuffs they use these days, one to a customer, stringing the men up like so many butterballs. When he was finished, he looked at me with a glint of triumph.

"The bald guy's still got it," I said, giving him his due.

"So it seems," he agreed affably. "I understand you have a previous relationship with some of these gentlemen."

I looked them over till I came to the guy who'd broken my finger. In other circumstances, I'd have been inclined to rough him up a bit, but this time I made do with a quip: "You're going to have to be lucky if all you get out of this is a broken bone."

"Bone, shit. He's going to kill us."

"No, he's not."

"Fuck he isn't," the big guy grumbled.

"No, he's going to call Ingleside and get a paddy wagon out here and charge you with whatever crimes you've been committing in that powerhouse back there. Then you're going to jail and Charley and I are going to Guido's for a stiff drink."

"Bullshit," the big guy repeated. "He's going to waste us. Try to stop him, he'll kill you, too."

I looked left. "Maybe you should disabuse him."

Charley's smile had become as stiff as one of his victims. "Sorry. No can do."

"Sure you can. I'll call it in myself. I've got a cell phone in the car."

"Don't leave us, man," the big one pleaded with me.

"Yeah," another one piped in. "The bastard's psycho. He wants to pop us all."

"Just like he did Walters," a third one offered.

Hilton stayed silent and self-possessed. Even his clothes were still crisp.

I gave them what solace I could. "I'm sure justice will prevail, gentlemen. In contrast to your normal practice."

Charley's cackle was like hard wood split by a maul. "Now you've really got 'em scared."

"Why?"

"That's what they're afraid of most of all," he bellowed. "That now I'm just like them."

When he'd finished snugging ten hands behind five backs, Charley issued an order. "On your knees, assholes."

When no one moved, he grabbed the guy nearest to him by the biceps and tugged him to his knees as easily as if he were made of papier-mâché. Apparently Charley wasn't as frail as I thought.

"It'll hurt less if you do it yourself," he said to the others as the guy who'd been jerked to his knees started whimpering about a separated shoulder.

One by one, four men struggled to a kneeling position. One by one, four men looked to me for help. One by one, they began to cry, all but Hilton, who still hadn't said a word.

"Okay, Charley," I said as my brow began to leak cold sweat. "I think they're suitably terrified—they'll tell you what you want to know. Ask your questions so we can get out of here."

Charley laid the riot gun on the ground and took his Ruger out of a belt holster and screwed a silencer onto the muzzle. It seemed to take him an hour; it seemed to make time a spectator that would wait for him to finish; it seemed to make my blood stop flowing through my veins.

"I know all I need to," he murmured as he worked in what seemed like slow motion. "I've known it for thirty years, which is how long some of these assholes have been feasting off the folk."

"Feasting how?"

"In every definition of the term. Including murder."

"Who got murdered?"

The litany was as nonchalant as a motto. "Guy named Chavez in the Mission. Guy named Jefferson in the Fillmore. Guy named Pearlstine in Lake Merced. They're equal opportunity assassins—hire out to whoever has the bread to make it worth their while. I hear the current rate is ten grand."

"What'd the dead guys do to get themselves killed by some cops?"

"Made someone mad, then kept their wallets in their pockets."

Without further ado, Charley walked behind the big

guy and put the Ruger at the base of his neck. I put my hand on the butt of my Walther but kept it where it was. The rest of me started to shiver.

"You'll be doing him a favor, won't you?" I said quietly, the scrim of sweat that bathed my body acting like a swamp cooler in the night breeze off the bay, making my voice quiver. When I stopped talking, my teeth started chattering.

"What kind of favor?" Charley asked.

"He goes to Folsom, there's a good chance the prison gangs will make his life miserable."

His grin was broad and lascivious. "You mean let *them* have all the fun?"

"Sure. Why not?"

Charley shook his head. "They got a balance of power working there now. He joins the Aryan Brotherhood, they protect him from the Mexican Mafia and the Black Guerrillas, and everything stays cool. Too much chance he hangs on that way."

"Give him up, Charley. Why waste your time?"

"He's the one who broke your finger, right?"

"I don't remember."

"Oh, he's the one. He was bragging about it in there."

"So?"

"So this."

Charley pulled the trigger. Thanks to the silencer, the report was no louder than a fish flopping out in the bay.

The big guy fell on his face like a fir. Blood gushed, then streamed, then seeped. One of the others started yelling until Charley set the gun on the back of his neck and the scream became a stifled wail.

"Jesus, Charley," I said with as much sanity as I could muster. "This is beyond the pale."

"The guy was a fucking sadist. What was beyond the pale was the way he spent his career beating the shit out of innocent civilians. Seventeen brutality charges brought against him; not one resulted in suspension."

Charley took his gun off the neck of the whiner and

strolled over to Gary Hilton and placed the muzzle in its familiar spot. Neither of them said anything and I stayed silent, too. I was afraid of a lot of things, but mostly of making it worse.

"I can trade," Hilton said with impressive calm. "I can give you stuff you never heard about. I can take down two dozen patrol and a dozen detectives. I can give you an assistant chief."

"Shut up," Charley instructed, then turned to me. "You can put a stop to it right here," he said easily, as though we were discussing trump in a bridge hand.

"Me?"

"Yeah, you."

"How would I do that?"

"You know how."

"No, I don't."

"Sure you do. All you have to do is kill me."

Although I'd sensed it was coming, it still hit me like a cannonball. In the aftermath of their impact, I barely found the wind to speak. "Shit, Charley."

"What we have here is a simple situation," Charley went on laconically, in what seemed to border on a state of euphoria. "It stops if you kill me; it doesn't if you don't."

"Why the fuck are you doing this to me?"

"I imagine you've figured it out."

"Tell me."

Charley shrugged. "I can't do much on my own these days, but at least I can decide how I die."

"But what does that—?"

"Come on, Marsh. You know what I want. I don't want these assholes to take me down. I don't want to rot in jail or in some fucking hospital with tubes up everything from my nose to my cock. I want to die by a hand I respect. A hand that was there when I needed it. A hand that hits what it aims at and only aims at what needs to be killed."

"You want me to be your Kevorkian."

"That's right."

"Put you out of your misery."

"Correct."

"And go to jail for my trouble."

"No chance. Justifiable homicide, open and shut. Defense of another; PC one-twelve."

"Who am I defending?"

He pointed to his right. "Those three."

I gestured toward Hilton. "What about him?"

"It's too late for him," Charley said, and pulled the trigger a second time. Same sound; same special effects—Gary Hilton was suddenly a well-dressed rag doll. The sight was so astounding I had to lean against the wall at my back to keep myself upright.

Now I was the one who started to plead. "Charley, Jesus. Don't do this. For God's sake. I know you're sick. I know you want to end it before the pain gets so bad you can't stand it. I understand that, and I'll help you find a way to die with some dignity. But don't do it this way. Let them remember all the good you've done, not this shit."

"The only memory I care about is yours."

"If I have to shoot my best friend, what kind of memory is that going to be?"

"You'll sort it through. Sooner or later, you'll see that this is the only way out. Hell, Marsh. I'd do the same for you and you know it."

I lifted my gun from my belt and let it dangle at my side. "No."

Charley seemed taken aback. "What?"

"I won't do it."

He gestured. "Then they're dead meat." He took his place behind the third man and placed the pistol in its deadly slot. When he was ready, he looked at me. "Still time to save them."

I shook my head. "Sorry."

"You stubborn bastard." With a flick of his wrist, Charley reversed his aim and stuck the muzzle of his gun in his mouth. "If you won't shoot me to save *him*," he mumbled around the metal tube, "maybe you'll shoot me to save *me*."

Somehow, I found myself laughing. "That tactic didn't fly in Vietnam. I don't think it'll fare any better down here."

His face flushed; his free hand made a fist. A model of cool until now, suddenly Charley was outraged, at his illness, at my recalcitrance, at the surviving members of the Triad, at something only he was privy to, who knew?

"You son of a bitch." I'd heard less frightening growls from tigers.

The muzzle of the Ruger slid out of his mouth and panned toward me. "I guess this is the way it goes down—you shoot me to save your ass. Self-defense, complete with witnesses. You don't even get booked."

I shook my head. "Not even close."

"I guess you want your precious Eleanor to grow old without a papa."

His knuckles whitened around the grip; his finger seemed to squeeze the trigger, his hand seemed to tremble. I raised my Walther and aimed at what I hoped was his shoulder. "This is insane," I said, but I don't think he heard me.

His finger tightened further and mine did, too, as though they were wired in parallel. Wars had started this way; widows had been made this way. But I didn't know what to do.

"Charley. Please, I—"

"Your call, Tanner."

"I'm not going to kill you, Charley. So just put that out—"

Something moved. Not Charley, but—

The sounds were simultaneous and stupendous. I was thrown back against the wall so hard I bit the tip of my tongue off.

The tongue hurt like hell, but for an instant I thought that was the only damage I'd suffered. But as I watched a stain spread across Charley's massive chest and an expression close to rapture cross his face, a pain that was so much more than pain that it became a narcotic, a tingly numbness in the nature of a toxic shock, spread up and over me from somewhere below the chest.

I became sightless and unfeeling, weak and tired and helpless. I tried to stand, but couldn't move my legs. I tried to speak, but it came out in burbles and bubbles indecipherable even to me. I tugged free my shirt and tried to feel for my wound but felt only flesh over bone, then something warm and wet that should have been my belly but didn't feel like any substance I'd ever felt before, didn't feel like me.

Then some inner hallucinogen kicked in. I saw things I had never seen and things I had last seen long ago, things that were dead and things that were merely distant, things that were comforting and things that sent slivers of terror darting through me that would surely be fatal if they passed through me a second time.

I called to Charley but he didn't answer. I called for my mother but she didn't answer either. I called for Peggy and then I called for . . . Eleanor.

And there she was, with her elfin smile, reaching a pudgy hand toward me, eager to be in my arms, happy to see her father. I called her name once more and she said something. It might have been Daddy, or might have been my name, or it might have been

. . .

might have been something so faint that I couldn't . . . but something that was surely

. . .

something that . . .
was definitely . . .

. . .

crucial

ENJOY SOME OF THE MYSTERY POCKET BOOKS HAS TO OFFER!

PETE HAUTMAN
SHORT MONEY 00303-8/$5.99
DRAWING DEAD 00302-X/$5.99

STEPHEN GREENLEAF
FALSE CONCEPTION 00794-7/$5.99
FLESH WOUNDS 00795-5/$5.99
PAST TENSE 01947-3/$6.50

DALLAS MURPHY
DON'T EXPLAIN 86688-5/$5.99
LUSH LIFE 68556-2/$4.99

JANE HOLLEMAN
KILLER GORGEOUS 00105-1/$5.99

WILLIAM S. SLUSHER
BUTCHER OF THE NOBLE 89545-1/$5.99
SHEPHERD OF THE WOLVES 89546-X/$5.99

ELIZABETH QUINN
LAMB TO THE SLAUGHTER 52765-7/$5.99
KILLER WHALE 52770-3/$5.99
MURDER MOST GRIZZLY 74990-0/$4.99

MICHELLE SPRING
RUNNING FOR SHELTER 87094-7/$5.99

JOHN DUNNING
THE BOOKMAN'S WAKE 56782-9/$5.99

Simon & Schuster Mail Order
200 Old Tappan Rd., Old Tappan, N.J. 07675
Please send me the books I have checked above. I am enclosing $_____(please add $0.75 to cover the postage and handling for each order. Please add appropriate sales tax). Send check or money order–no cash or C.O.D.'s please. Allow up to six weeks for delivery. For purchase over $10.00 you may use VISA: card number, expiration date and customer signature must be included.

POCKET
BOOKS

Name _____

Address _____

City _____ State/Zip _____

VISA Card # _____ Exp.Date _____

Signature _____ 958-12